THE DIRTY ONES
NEW YORK TIMES
BESTSELLING AUTHOR
JA HUSS

ISBN: 978-1-944475-70-3

Edited by RJ Locksley
Cover Design by JA Huss

CHAPTER ONE

I used to read to her.

That's the most prominent memory I have of Kiera Bonnaire. At the time it was anything available. Cereal boxes, magazines, instruction manuals, the dictionary. Ordinary, mundane things. She wasn't particular. She didn't need much. She just wanted to forget and the sound of my voice did that.

It was enough back then.

The stars aligned that night we all met up in the woods. That's how someone explained it to me once. Things just… happened and then there was momentum. It became a living, breathing thing with a life of its own and there was no way to stop it.

Me and Hayes. Sofia, Kiera, and Camille. Emily and Bennett. Louise and… no, she was alone, I think.

People often assume that good things happen when the stars align, but that's not always the case. Impossible events don't always lead to positive outcomes.

I think about this weird combination of aligned stars and reading to Kiera with a strange sense of invested detachment the entire drive down to Charlotte, Vermont from the Montreal airport. I used to think that Kiera and I had something special once. That it meant something more. That the stars lining up were a sign of what we could become. That if we just believed in our dreams our future together would materialize and the magic would take over.

Didn't quite work out that way.

I used to wonder if it was my fault, or her fault, or their fault.

But maybe it's nobody's fault?

Maybe no matter what you do or how hard you try, your dream and your future have nothing in common?

Maybe that's just the way it is?

I don't know. All I do know is that my trip down to Kiera's cottage today has nothing to do with the dream and everything to do with the nightmare that brought us together.

I'd let go of that nightmare years back. Thought I was over it. Thought I'd moved on. But a wave of apprehension grows inside me as the GPS on my rental ticks off the miles until we meet again. Like a nervous lover, though lovers is not a word I'd have used to describe who and what we were to each other. We weren't really friends either.

We were something else. Something in between. Possibly more like partners in crime, though we didn't do any crime, so that can't be it either.

I don't think there's a name for what Kiera and I were, but nonetheless, and for obvious reasons, she needs to be the first one I confront.

I glance down at the book in the seat next to me. I can't see it since it's in a plain white paper bag from the airport bookstore I bought it from. But I don't need to see it. I lived it.

I just went in to buy gum, that's all. Just some gum to chew on my flight back to New York. The snack store was crowded so I walked a few feet further to the bookstore, got my gum, stood in line, and then I made the mistake of looking to my left where two women were arguing over a book.

I glanced at the guy standing just behind me and we rolled our eyes like men united.

"Please," one of the women said in French. "It's the last copy. If you're not going to buy it, just let me—"

"I'm still deciding," the other one replied.

"I have to go. My flight is boarding right now. Please—"

"Will you just back off? Jesus. I had it first and it's--"

But that's when I stopped listening. Because that's when I saw the cover. It wasn't the image. The picture is some couple kissing or maybe just moaning in each other's general direction.

It wasn't the picture. It was the font. It was the title. It was—

—me, saying, "Excuse me," in French, as I opened up my wallet, pulled out cash, fanning it so I could calculate how much I had. "I'll give you three hundred and seventy-four dollars if you hand that book over to me."

"What the hell?" the begging girl snapped. "I want that book!"

I ignored her and concentrated on the one with possession. She squinted her eyes at me. They were small eyes. Not attractive in any way. Kinda beady and forgettable—except that's the only thing I remember about her now. "Why?" she asked.

"Because my girlfriend wrote it," I said. Smooth, like whiskey. Confident, like my father.

"What?" they both asked. In English.

"You're fucking with us."

"Are you serious?"

"I'm serious. Please, I'm on my way to visit her and I didn't buy a copy. I don't have time to stop and—"

"It's written anonymously, dumbass," begging girl said.

I ignored her. Kept my attention on the one still holding the book. "What's her name?" she asked.

"I can't tell you," I said.

"Then I can't sell it to you," she said.

"Look, if you give me your address"—I glanced at the snappy one too—"I'll have her send you both signed copies. But if I don't have this book in my possession when I see her in a few hours, she's gonna think I'm not supportive and break up with me. But—"

"He's lying," Begging said, switching back to French.

"Maybe," I said, still eyeing the one who actually had the book. "But you're not out anything if you give me the book. You're getting three hundred and seventy-four dollars for doing nothing."

Begging girl looked like she might blow, so I quickly got out my business card and pen, then held it out for her. "Write down your address."

She inhaled deeply. Eyed me. Then took the pen and card, wrote down her address, and dropped the pen in her purse. "She gets money, I get the pen."

"Fine," I said, leaning into the forgettable one. "You gonna take this deal or not?"

She snatched the cash from my hand, shoved the book into my chest, and then walked out of the bookstore without a second thought about that signed copy.

The begging one left too so I just paid for the book, walked out of the terminal, forgetting about my return flight to New York, got a rental car, and started driving south towards Vermont.

Now the GPS on my phone tells me to turn left in one mile and I begin to get nervous.

I read the inside cover of the book while I was waiting to cross the border into the US and felt an urge to vomit. But it's not a good idea to look sick while you wait to cross the US border, so I swallowed down the past that was trying to come up, and just put the book back in the bag.

How could she fucking do this to us?

We made a pact. We promised to never speak of it again. So how could she do this?

That's the question I ask myself over and over again during the two-hour drive down to Charlotte.

What the fuck was she thinking?

Does she need money? Is she sending us a message?

The roads are perilously icy after I pass through Burlington and by the time I arrive in Charlotte it's clear there was a major snowstorm recently. Maybe as recently as this morning. Glancing up at the late afternoon sky, I wonder if it's gonna snow again.

Snow plows are out in force, but when I finally find her house it's clear no one has plowed her long, winding driveway. Not after this most recent storm and probably not the last one either. There's no way my rental is gonna make it down to her cottage, so I just pull over as far as I can, hoping that the rental doesn't get hit by a plow while I'm gone, and step out in the slushy street.

Only a small corner of the quaint white cottage is visible through the forest of bare trees from where I stand and the thought of trudging through two and a half feet of snow to get there just makes me want to get back in that rental, drive to Burlington, and take the next flight back to New York.

But that book.

I stare at the white paper bag in my hand and sigh, moving forward on the exhale. By the time I reach her porch I'm freezing, soaking wet all the way up to my knees, and wondering if she still lives here. Because she hasn't shoveled her walk or the porch stairs either.

But that's so typical of her, right, Connor? Kiera was the outsider back in college. The one who didn't want to follow the rules. The kind of girl who never plows her driveway or shovels her walk. That's why you liked her.

I like her a lot less now. And it's not just the snow or the trek down the driveway.

If she wrote this book I'll…

I'll what? What can I possibly do?

I don't know. Something to make her stop, I guess. Except I don't have a clue what that might be. I hardly knew her back then and don't know her at all right now.

Why didn't I keep in touch with her?

I sorta kept track of everyone else after graduation. Kinda. I saw most of them occasionally and Bennett I see or talk to pretty much every day.

But last spring marked our tenth year out of undergrad. I figured it was over after graduation and Kiera was never really one of us, anyway. So I let Kiera go her own way.

Big mistake.

Because this book… this book is *unconscionable.*

I stand there looking up at the frosted windows of her cottage for a moment as the wind does its best to steal my breath away, wondering if she'll be happy to see me or just tell me to get the fuck off her property and never come back.

That's something Kiera would do and I have a moment of regret that I didn't come better prepared with flowers, or candy, or jewelry… or an apology.

"Jesus Christ. Get a hold of yourself, Connor," I mutter under my breath. But it's not a secret mutter because the words come out in a small blast of steam.

I high-step my way towards the cottage and with each step more and more snow packs down into the crevice between my foot and my shoe. I carefully climb her porch steps, gripping the railing to pull myself through the snow, and stand in front of the door.

Music comes from within. Opera. Something I recognize, but can't name. Something that takes me back to those days and confirms what I already knew the moment I saw that book.

She is stuck in the past.

I should've kept better track of her.

I raise my fist to bang on the door, but it opens a crack before I can do that.

And there she is. Kiera Bonnaire in the flesh. Long, unruly blonde hair still one of the most striking things about her. Eyes a color that cannot be described. Are they the lightest green? Or the lightest blue? Or the lightest yellow?

No one is sure.

No one is sure about anything when it comes to Kiera, except that they can be sure of nothing.

She is one of us, but not *one of us.*

She squints her eyes in recognition. Draws in a deep breath. Then says, "Connor Arlington. What brings you to my front door on this cold winter afternoon?"

The music is still playing. The title of the song comes to me now. Because I'm back. One look at her and I've been thrown back in the past. I am up in that tower. Playing those games. Watching her as she scribbles things down as fast as she can.

"*Barbiere Di Siviglia*," I say, the name of the song coming to me now.

She huffs out what could be a laugh or could be contempt, then says, "That's all we ever had between us, Con. Memories," as she opens the door wider. "You must really have something to say to me if you walked all the way up here from the street."

Oh, fuck, yeah, I have shit to say to you, Miss Bonnaire.

CHAPTER TWO

I don't normally look out the window. I'm not one of those writers who require inspiration. It's a fucking job, OK? And besides, there are more words inside me begging to get out than I could ever hope to write down. I don't need any prodding to put them down on paper. They flow out of me like water down a mountainside.

But I do have a nice forest view in the front of the house and a lake view out back, so every once in a while I'll just enjoy it a little as I do my thing.

Tonight I was looking outside, wondering how bad this next storm is gonna get, when I saw a man doing his best to trudge through the almost impassable barrier of snow to reach my house.

I even heard him cursing a few times. *Goddamn this. Goddamn her. Who the fuck lives in a forest and doesn't plow their driveway? Why the hell am I doing this?*

Never in a million years did I think the dumbass outside my cottage would be Connor Arlington.

He looks good though. His suit pants are covered in snow from the trek up to my door, but it's not enough to mar the memory or the image he creates for me now. His hair isn't as blond as it used to be back in college and his eyes looked dark when he was standing in the shadows under my porch, but now, under the soft light of my front room, they're the same brown-green as always.

Even though our campus was tiny compared to state universities, and small even for a private liberal arts college, we didn't travel in the same circles. Not until the night we both ended up in the tower, anyway.

Not that we didn't have things in common. Obviously we did. But I came on scholarship and he didn't. His great-grandfather's name was on a plaque outside the theatre. His father went there. Hell, I'm pretty sure everyone who went to Essex College was a legacy.

Including me.

At least… everyone in our little group was like that. Sofia's grandmother donated the eating hall. Camille's great-grandmother donated the land surrounding the college. Bennett's whole family took pre-law at Essex, so they regularly add to the library. Hayes' family donated the health center, and Connor's great-great-grandfather was the fucking founder. Some self-righteous pastor who owned the church next door and had a dream of elite education for a select few.

I got in because my grandmother applied for a scholarship the day I was born. She went there on scholarship, as did my mother. I don't really understand that, and was never curious enough to ask, but I'm pretty sure it's got something to do with sex.

My grandmother probably had an affair with someone important and this legacy of free college education was just the hush money.

Or not.

My mind works in mysterious ways, so I'm never sure if my intuition is true or just a byproduct of being a writer and constantly making up stories about fake people.

But sex is almost always the reason weird things happen, I do believe that much. That's been my experience, anyway. So I'm pretty sure that's why I got into Essex.

Because we are not poor. We're not Arlington rich—not even close—but we were certainly not needy enough to qualify for financial aid at any other school and so, hey, if sixty-thousand-dollar-a-year Essex College wants to pay my way for free, why not, right?

Of course, I now know what the catch was. There's a reason super-rich people keep to themselves. Create their own worlds. Live a different reality than the rest of us. And if I ever have a kid there's no way in hell they're gonna go to Essex because that world is pretty ugly once you get inside.

Connor brought the cold and the wind with him as he passed through the door. Snowflakes swirl around in my small living room like a whirling winter dervish, then settle at his feet as he stomps on my front mat.

"What the hell are you doing here?" I ask. The music is still playing, but the song ends and there's that brief interlude of static just before the next one begins. I step over to the ancient-looking Victrola and lift the arm up off the record and place it on the holder.

Connor sighs. "What is this?" he asks, rattling the paper of a white bag as he pulls out a book.

I look at it, squinting my eyes, wondering if it's one of mine. "I dunno," I say, taking the book from his hands and turning it over so I can see the cover.

The instant I read the title I know why he's here. "What is this?" I ask, echoing his question.

"That's what I'm asking you, Kiera. What the fuck did you do?"

"I didn't write this. Who told you I wrote this?"

"You're the… *writer*, who else would it be?"

I glare at him. Because I know what he almost said. *You're the* dirty *writer, Kiera. The one who writes filth like this.*

Fuck you, Connor Arlington. Just fuck you.

I open the cover and read the inside flap out loud. "'They said write what you know so that's what I did. I wrote dirty. I wrote'—what the fuck is this?"

"It's exactly what it looks like. And do you know where I fucking found it?"

"No clue," I say, walking into the kitchen and placing it on the counter.

"The Montreal airport bookstore sitting in the number three position on the goddamned *New York Times* bestseller list."

I'm filling my teapot with hot water when he finishes that sentence, my mind whirling around like the snowflakes did when they stole their way into my house. "It wasn't me."

"Then who the fuck was it?" His voice is loud. Commanding and very much like the voice I remember. He's not so different now. Still wearing the same expensive watch. Still well-groomed and on his way to conquering American politics. Still one of those arrogant, privileged assholes I used to know.

I already know the answer to my next question, but I ask it anyway. "Did you barge in on Sofia? Or Camille? And ask them if they wrote the stupid book?"

Silence behind me as I fit the top back on my tea pot, then turn around and place it on the stove. I glare at him as I turn the gas on high without looking and the *whoosh* of ignition brings a purple-blue flame to life.

He stares at it for a long moment, then tracks back to me. "They don't write *this shit.*"

This shit? Oh, hell, no. He did not just say that.

I lift one eyebrow high on my forehead and make a decision not to engage. "Is there anything else I can do for you, Connor? Because I'm real busy here."

He looks around. My little cottage isn't messy but it's not tidy, either. I'm wearing taupe yoga pants and an oversized tan sweater. I have knee-high shearling boots on my feet because my feet are always cold and they help me feel like I'm wearing clothes I could leave the house in, when I'm actually not. I don't remember if I brushed my hair yesterday or the day before. But fuck it. I don't owe him an explanation. I don't owe him anything. I paid my debt a long time ago.

"When's the last time you left the house?" he asks, taking off his coat.

"None of your business," I reply. "And why are you taking off your coat? You're not staying. In fact, I think you should probably leave right now."

"No," he says, draping his coat over one of my antique-white dining table chairs. "We need to read this book."

"I'm not reading that book. Take it with you because I have absolutely no interest in that book."

"Do you not understand what this means, Kiera?"

"I didn't write the fucking book, Connor."

"Then who the fuck did?"

"How do you even know it's about us?" I say, picking the book up from the counter and flipping it over to scan the back cover.

Connor snatches it out of my hand. "'I'm gonna warn you,'" he says, reading the back copy out loud. "'Our story isn't for everyone. It's not even for us. So if you're looking for the fairytale and the stupid fucking prince on his dumb white horse, you've got a hold of the wrong book. Move along. This is not your story, this is not your life, and this is not your opportunity to dip your frightened little toe into the dark pool of water and "try new things" and then pull it out and decide… *#NotForMe*. When you go in with us you go all in. So make a decision before you turn this page. Because I'm making one promise with this book. Just one. It's the truth. We are the dirty ones and this is our story.'" He slams the book back down on the counter and stares at me. "'We are the dirty ones and this is our story?' Are you fucking kidding me right now?"

I take a step back because his rage is very clear.

"*We*, Kiera, are the fucking dirty ones. That is *literally* the name we gave ourselves."

Our eyes meet. Hold there, suspending time. I pick up the book and thrust it at him. "I didn't write it. And if you think Sofia and Camille don't 'write this shit,' as you put it, then I guess you don't know them as well as you think."

"What the fuck does that mean?"

"It means they write this shit, Connor. The only difference between me and them is that they hide behind pen names and I don't. So maybe next time you find your deepest, darkest secrets splashed all over the *New York Times* bestseller list by an anonymous source, you should hold your fucking preconceived notions in check and wait to hurl those accusations until after you ask *all* your dirty writer friends if they're the author. OK?"

He's holding his breath. I only know that because there's silence as I finish and then he lets it out in a long rush of air. "Well… *fuck*!"

He shouts the curse word.

"Who cares, anyway. It's a stupid story." I pick the book back up and start thumbing through it.

"It's a true fucking story, Kiera. You know what we did. You know what's in there. And if you didn't write it then who did? Because when I find out—"

"There are no names in here," I say.

Connor is doing a two-fisted grab of his hair, staring down at his feet like there's some magic answer on his soaking wet shoes, when this comes out. "What?" he says, releasing his grip and taking two steps towards me to grab the book from my outstretched hand.

"Look," I say, grabbing the book back and opening it up again. Does he really have to be such an asshole? Now I have to find the page again.

"Give it to me."

I ignore him and thumb through until I see them again. "Look. It uses initials. CA. KB. SA. HF. BW. Right there." I stab the page and hold it out for him.

"Holy shit," he says, doing that hair-grab thing again. "Thank God. You know I'm in the preliminary stages of running for US senator, right?"

"No," I deadpan. "In case you haven't noticed, I don't own a television."

He looks around, taking in my home. And I find his scrutinizing stare to be uncomfortable. "You don't own a TV," he parrots back. "Do you even have internet here?"

"Nope. I get cell coverage if I walk down to the end of the driveway. But here in the house it's hopeless."

"What the fuck is wrong with you, Kiera?"

"What do you mean?"

"You can't just... live somewhere without phone coverage."

I make that little noise you make when someone is being stupid and you just can't take another moment of it. You know it when you hear it. Calling it a laugh is far too generous. And a huff isn't enough. Something between a snort and a sneer, I think. "This cottage is a hundred and twenty years old, Connor. And as far as I know, none of its occupants have ever died from lack of cell phone. Besides. The landline mostly works."

He glances over to an old-fashioned rotary wall phone in my tiny kitchen and makes that huff-snort again. Only it comes out like relief instead of sarcasm. Then he looks down at the book in his hands and says, in a very quiet voice, "What do you think it says? Everything?" But I can hear hope in his voice. Hope he's wrong.

"Obviously I have no idea, since five minutes ago I didn't know the book existed."

"Well, we need to find out. Pack a bag, we're going to New York."

"*We* are not going anywhere. You can go wherever the hell you want, but I'm staying right here."

"You can't just pretend this won't have consequences, Kiera. Did you forget what happened when we didn't do what we were told?"

"Yeah," I say, my voice now dripping with sarcasm. "I forgot."

"You know what I'm talking about. We need to figure this out."

"Again," I say, "I didn't write that book and I have no interest in knowing more. There is no way this book tracks back to me. And I'm not beholden to anyone like you are. So I'm just gonna pretend I never saw it."

He stares at me for a second. I can practically see his mind working as he untangles my words and fits them back together in some new Connor Arlington way. Then he moves forward, towards my hallway.

"What are you doing?"

He ignores me. Just throws open a closet door and looks inside. He looks the contents over, then closes the door and walks into my bedroom.

"What the fuck are you doing?"

He finds the light switch and by the time I catch up to him, he's already pulling open my closet door.

"Connor," I say. "What the hell?"

"Where do you keep your luggage?"

"I'm not going to New York with you."

"You are, Kiera. And you've got five minutes to pack or I'll just take you out of here with no clothes."

I cross my arms and lean against the doorjamb. "I'd like to see you try."

"How do you not understand what happens next? Huh? You know what happens next, Kiera."

"You don't even know that book is about us, OK? So just calm down."

He's found my suitcases and he's pulling one down off a shelf. "It is. Now pack."

"No. I'm not going. Did you even look at the weather today? We're in the middle of the biggest snowstorm in five years."

"It's barely snowing," he says, bouncing the suitcase on the bed. He starts to unzip it.

"That's because the storm took a break. But we're supposed to get a lot more tonight."

"How would you even know that? You don't even have a weather app."

"I have a weather radio. I might be simple but I'm not stupid."

He looks at the window. It's just about dark now even though it's only late afternoon. Then he walks over to it, pulling his phone out of his coat and holding it up as he looks for a signal.

It's snowing a lot harder than it was when he arrived. "I'm not lying. We're gonna get dumped on tonight. It's a five-and-a-half-hour drive to New York and there's no way Burlington hasn't cancelled all flights out. Like it or not, we're not going anywhere."

He places both hands on the windowsill, arching his back a little as he drops his head to stare at his feet.

"Just… calm down, OK? It's fine."

"It's not fine," he snaps, whirling around to face me. "It's not fucking fine. Why are you lying to yourself? Whoever did this…" He sighs, shaking his head. "Whoever did this knew what would happen."

"It's been ten years," I say. "It's over."

He laughs. "It's not over. It never ended, Kiera. Not for me. Not for Hayes. Not for Bennett."

"What do you mean? It ended back in school."

"It. Never. Ended," he growls.

I just stare at him. Blink a couple times.

"It never ended," he says again. "It was a trap, don't you see?"

"No," I say. "I don't see. I never got another message. I dropped the book off in the tower that night and walked away. You must know I didn't stay for graduation. I just packed up my car after finals and drove away that same night."

"Well, that's not how it ended for us."

"Explain," I say. And I hate to admit it, but my voice is shaky. The fear I remember creeps over me like a thick, dark mist. It starts at the small of my back and climbs up my spine until all those tiny hairs on the back of my neck are tingling.

"What do you mean?" I ask, crossing the room and placing a hand on his arm. "What's that mean?"

"I mean… it means whoever wrote this book knew what would happened if we ever told that story. It means…" He runs his fingers through his hair. Swallows hard. "I'm not going to get elected to the Senate. And if that was the worst thing that could happen I'd have written and published this book myself a long time ago. But we both know that's not all that can happen."

Emily.

Her name is on the tip of my tongue. So many years since I spoke it out loud. And I don't say it now. I catch myself just in time.

"You don't think—"

"I know, Kiera. Whoever made us write that book back in college did it for one reason only. To control us in the future. And now—"

"Listen," I say, shaking his arm. "We didn't do this. It was them, OK? Not us. Whoever published that book had permission."

"Don't be naive," he says, shaking off my grip. "I can take a lot of shit from people, Kiera. I can listen to a lot of lies. But not from you. Not when you know the truth."

CHAPTER THREE

And the truth is... the truth is that we did do all those things in that book. I feel time rewinding as I stand in Kiera's bedroom. I feel it like a person feels a haunting. Like bad luck following in your footsteps or a mistake catching up to you.

We did this.

"Just... calm down and stay here tonight, OK?"

The fear she didn't have when I arrived flows out now like a rushing stream of snowmelt in the spring.

It wasn't Kiera, I know that for sure. She has no idea what's been happening all these years. So that only leaves two other possibilities. Sofia or Camille. And I had no idea they were writing... *trash*. None.

Why would they do that?

"Where were you coming from?" Kiera asks.

"Montreal," I remind her. "I had a business meeting this morning and was flying home this afternoon. But I saw two women fighting over the last copy of the book just before I boarded and then I rented a car and came straight here."

"So you have clothes?" she asks. "Out in your car?"

I nod. "An overnight bag."

"Let's go get it before the storm gets worse. You can't go anywhere tonight. It's just not possible. You're stuck here. And you can make a call," she adds. Like I need some kind of motivation to snap out of the sudden despair I feel.

"Who will I call?"

"I dunno. One of them. All of them? I don't know. Do you have a wife?"

I shoot her a look that makes her put up her hands, palms out. Like she's backing off.

"Look, I just don't know you anymore, OK? I have no clue what you've been up to. I've just been living out here writing books since I left school. That's all I do. So I don't know who you'd call, but someone has to have noticed you didn't make it back to New York, right?"

I sigh, glancing down at my watch. "Believe me, everyone has noticed by now."

"So call them. Tell them you're staying with an old friend and you're caught in the storm. You'll be back as soon as you can."

"That driveway," I say. "Why the fuck don't you plow your damn driveway?"

"Sorry," she says. "I'll go get your bag. Give me the keys."

"No," I say. "Don't be dumb. I'm not sending you out into a storm to get my fucking carry-on."

She smiles at me and I realize I've missed that smile. And now I just feel bad for so many things. For not following up with her. For not making sure she was OK. For not saying goodbye.

But mostly for not saying thank you.

She didn't have to help us. They had nothing on her before she met us.

But she did help. She played her part and did what she was told.

Just like us.

"We'll go together then. Buddy system, right?" She smiles again, but it's not the same.

Or it is the same, I'm not sure. Because this smile is sad and a little bit afraid. And I hate that. I fucking hate it so much. Why did I come here? Why did I drag her back in? Why did I suspect her right away?

Because they planned it that way, Connor. They knew she was always the outsider and if anything went wrong, she'd always be there to get blamed.

"I'm sorry," I say.

"You didn't do this."

"I did. I came here. I blamed you, just like I was supposed to. I fell into the trap and now you're caught in it with me. I'm sorry."

"Forget it," she whispers. "If they wanted me back, they knew where to find me. My freedom was always an illusion. I knew that."

"Yeah, but I should've known better. I should've trusted you. I should've thought clearly and worked shit out. I mean, goddamn it. I had two hours in the car to get my shit together and work out the puzzle and I didn't. I just reacted the way…"

"The way they knew you would," she finishes for me. "You're just being you, Con. That's all."

"Yeah," I say. "Guess I didn't change much over the last ten years."

She smiles again. And again, it's that old smile. The one filled with sadness and fear. "Let me get my coat and we'll walk to the car together."

"Buddy system," I say, remembering how much we relied on it back in school.

She nods. "Buddy system."

It takes a good fifteen minutes to retrace my path from her house back to my car. And even using my footsteps as guides, it's not easy. The snow is falling hard. It covers the night sky like a sheet of white.

Kiera brings a small bag with her and checks her mail while I get in the car and turn it on, taking advantage of the fact that the engine is still warm, and turn the heat on while I decide who to call.

Kiera gets in, bag of mail in hand, and then slams the door. "Jesus. Every winter I ask myself why I stay in Vermont. If I was half as smart as I was talented, I'd be writing books on a beach in St. Thomas."

I smile at her, then look down at my phone. I only have two bars, but it should be enough to make calls.

"Did you make your call?"

"No," I say.

"Oh. Well, I'm not complaining," she says, taking off her gloves and waving her hands in front of the heater vents. "You're right. I'm an idiot for not plowing the driveway. I just figured I'd wait until after the storm was over."

I'm still staring down at my phone.

"What are you doing?"

"Deciding people's fates," I say.

"Don't be dramatic, Con. We all decided our fates long ago."

"I mean, if I call my committee manager, will he get dragged into this too?"

I think she shrugs. "I dunno. But going on past experiences, no. Because it was just us seven back then and I'm pretty sure it's just us seven now."

"Eight, you mean."

She pauses. Then, "Yeah. Right. Eight."

There's an uncomfortable silence after that. And once again, I fucked up. "Sorry," I say.

"No. You're right. There were eight of us."

"It's just… easy to forget that Emily was there."

"Yeah," Kiera says. "And then she wasn't."

"Right."

"Well, I think the consequences of telling no one where you're at outweigh the possibility that we might inadvertently drag them into our… problem."

Normally I'd disagree, but I can't just go missing. Not at this stage in my career. People are looking for me right now. People have noticed I didn't return to New York. I've missed meetings. Hell, I'll miss more meetings tomorrow morning. But none of that can be helped.

I tap my committee manager Steven's contact on my phone. Listen to the ring. Then, "For fuck's sake, where the hell are you?"

"I'm in Vermont," I say. "Stuck in a snowstorm."

"Vermont?" Steve bellows. "What the hell? You do realize—"

"I do realize," I say, cutting him off. I had an important fundraising event tonight. "But I had to go see an old friend in Vermont on my way home from Montreal and there's this massive blizzard going on, and—"

"Couldn't this little trip wait until… some other time?"

But there is no other time. Not in my future. My future is running for the Senate. I'm supposed to announce my candidacy any day now and once that happens, the public owns me. "Steven," I say, entirely out of patience. "I'm stuck in Vermont. That's all I have to say. Just… let people know I'm sorry and I'll be back as soon as I can."

"Tomorrow?" he asks.

"Doubtful," I say. "It looks like this storm is gonna last through tomorrow. Probably Thursday. So can you just… call my father and handle shit?"

He must hear the frustration in my voice because he says, "Uh… sure, Con. Sure. You got it. Call me tomorrow and let me know you're OK."

"I will," I say, then end the call.

"That went OK," Kiera says.

"It's his job," I say. "He's paid to be like that." Then I stare at my phone again.

"Should we call anyone else?"

"Yes," I say. "We should call Bennett."

We sit in silence for a few moments.

"OK. Are you gonna do that? I mean, I'm in no hurry to walk back to the house. I'll hang in the warm car for a while. But we can't stay here forever."

"I know," I say. "I'm just trying to think how I should say this."

"Oh," she says. And when I look over at her, she's biting her lip. She shrugs. "Um… well, tell him to go to the closest bookstore and look at the current *New York*

Times bestseller list. Frankly, I'm surprised you guys didn't notice it before this. If it's on the list it's been out at least two weeks now. The new list won't be announced until tomorrow afternoon."

"Right."

"That kinda makes me sick," she mutters.

"Which part?"

"The two weeks we didn't know. Like… whoever wrote it has to have been expecting our reaction. Fourteen whole days they knew what was coming and we didn't."

"Same old shit," I say.

"Yeah."

I tap Bennett's contact and he picks up on the first ring. "Vermont, huh?"

"How'd you know?"

"Steven just called me losing his mind."

"Yeah. I'm with… Kiera."

"Oh?" Bennett says.

"It's starting again."

Silence on the other end of the call. "Ben?"

"I'm here. Can you explain that?"

I look at Kiera and say, "Walk down to the closest bookstore and buy the number three book on the *New York Times* bestseller list."

"Why?"

"Because it's called *The Dirty Ones.*"

Silence.

"Bennett?"

"What the fuck do you mean?"

"That's all I know. I came to Kiera's to… I was gonna blame her, but it wasn't her. Can you just go buy the book and then call Sofia and—"

"Fuck that. You're coming home. We need to—"

"I'm stuck in a blizzard. I can't get home until Thursday at the earliest. Can you just… get everyone on the same page? And start asking questions, Ben. Because we need to figure out what's coming next."

Silence.

"Bennett?"

"Yeah. I'm here. I'll do that and call you back."

"I don't have cell service at Kiera's house."

"You're staying with her?" he says. "What the fuck, Connor? Go get a hotel."

I glance over at Kiera, find her turned away from me, staring out the window. "No. I'm not leaving her alone through this. I'm staying here. I'll call again tomorrow and check in. Thanks."

I end the call before he can say anything else.

"You don't have to stay with me," Kiera says.

"Yes, I do," I say. "Buddy system, remember?"

She huffs out a small laugh. "Yeah. Well, thanks. Any more calls to make?"

"Nah. Two is plenty. I'm fucking wet. I need to get out of these clothes." Our eyes meet for a second. Just a quick meet. Then we both look away.

I wonder if she's picturing me the way I'm picturing her. The way she always sat in the far left corner of that couch, scribbling away in the notebook. Eyes never quite able to meet mine back then either.

"OK," she says, opening up her door. "Then let's go."

I turn the car off, get out, and we spend the better part of fifteen minutes dragging our asses back up her driveway.

We stomp the snow off, crashing our feet on the door mat inside the front door, but it's hopeless. Ice balls cling to our pants like shimmering silver pearls.

She sits down on a small bench and begins taking off her boots, while I toe out of my shoes, then yank off my soaking wet socks.

The next thing I know she's peeling off her pants. Exposing her legs in a way that is both familiar and altogether alien at the same time. Her thighs are bright pink from the cold and she rubs her hands up and down her legs, trying to make them warm.

My pants are soaking wet too, but I hesitate. I don't know why. Kiera has seen my body more times than anyone else I know. More than Sofia. More than anyone.

She stands up, sensing my hesitation. "I'm gonna jump in the shower, but I'll save you some hot water and you can take one after."

"OK," I say, watching her walk away from me. Watching the way her hips move back and forth and the long line of her legs. "Kiera," I say.

"Hmm?" She stops at the door to the bathroom, leans on the doorjamb so her face is pressed up to it, body turned sideways. I wonder if she knows what she looks like when she poses like that?

"Leave the door open," I say. "Just in case."

She presses her lips together and nods. "OK." Then disappears inside.

I'm still standing there, watching the open doorway, when the water comes on. Still standing there when the coils of steam begin wafting their way out into the hallway. Wishing I could see inside. Watch her in the shower.

I wait, still and quiet, as that feeling fades. And then I strip down to my boxer briefs, hold my wet clothes in a heap in my arms, and find an excuse to stand in the bathroom doorway.

"Looking for your laundry room," I call, staring at the billowing shower curtain. There's a soft fuzzy silhouette of her shape as she stands under the water. Teasing me, I think. But not on purpose.

"It's at the end of the hall," she says back, water sputtering out with her words. "Just hang everything up over the radiator and let it drip dry."

"Thanks," I say, forcing myself to move on.

Her laundry room is a proper room. Bigger than her bathroom. And it has a back door.

There's a rod and hangers over the radiator. Like hanging up wet clothes is just part of her normal routine. I picture Kiera living out here alone. Lost in her ways. Just… being herself.

I have a moment of envy for that. It's so opposite to my life back in New York where every moment has been managed since I graduated from Essex College just across Lake Champlain.

And it is, literally, just a forty-five-minute ferry ride across the lake.

I bet if I look out this window tomorrow morning I'll see the fucking college. I guess I never realized how close she was all these years. I guess I never realized how she never really got away.

How does she stand it?

I mean, I get it. She's not rich like the rest of us. Though I don't doubt she makes a very nice living off her writing. She's been on the *New York Times* list before, I'm sure of it. I'm sure someone told me that a long time ago. Maybe Bennett. But for as long as I've known her, this cottage has been her home base. We used to come here back in school when we all needed to get away. It didn't look like this, not at all. It was a dump back then. Definitely didn't have a laundry room. Hell, the plumbing didn't even work. Kiera lived in the main house, just down the shoreline, with her mother. This cottage was built for a caretaker, back when the family had real money.

But we didn't even care. To us—meaning us, not Kiera—it was like the cabins we'd stay in for summer camp. This place always felt like summer camp.

The water turns off in the bathroom and I realize I've been standing here looking out the window for several minutes.

There's that well-known rattle of shower curtain rings as she pulls it back and I have an inexplicable urge to walk down the hallway and catch her naked. Catch her pull the towel around herself.

But there's a squeak of a hand rubbing steam off a mirror, then a faucet.

She's brushing her teeth.

I turn from the window, sighing, and step back into the hallway. When I reach the bathroom I stop and allow myself to stare.

She smiles at the mirror, like she's getting some secret glimpse of me I'll never see myself, then spits out her toothpaste, cupping water into her mouth with her hand to rinse.

That's when I see the exit hole the size of a bullet in her left shoulder.

I step into the hot steam left over from her shower and my fingers are pressing against the scar before either of us realize what I'm doing.

"God, Kiera," I say, mesmerized by the small jagged edges of pink skin.

"I'm fine," she says.

Which was the exact same thing she said right after it happened.

And she was not fucking fine. "You were not fucking fine," I say out loud.

"I was," she says, turning to face me with a forced smile.

That's when I realize I'm only wearing semi-damp black boxer briefs and she's only wearing a towel. Her skin is still wet with beaded drops of water, her long, blonde hair hanging almost to her waist.

I have an overwhelming urge to touch her other places too. Because she feels like mine. And I've touched her many times in the past. In every way imaginable.

But I control that urge because she's not mine now and maybe she never was.

She didn't belong to anyone. Not the way Sofia and Camille did.

We're staring at each other in the mirror when she breaks the now awkward silence and says, "Your turn."

She eases past me, the spell broken, and disappears around the corner into the hallway.

"Leave the door open," she calls back from her bedroom.

"Buddy system," I say, sorta grinning.

"Yup. Buddy system."

CHAPTER FOUR

It's both strange and totally normal to have Connor Arlington in my house. Strange because it's been ten years and normal because it feels like no minutes have passed at all since that last time we were together.

Which was the only time we were ever together alone. All the other times we were with Sofia. Or everyone. We did that a lot once we got used to the routine. But that last time was just me and him.

I admit that I planned it that way. I did. I wanted him to myself. Just me and him.

But I think he wanted it too.

I tell myself that, anyway. That he wanted me that night.

Maybe it's an illusion. Or a delusion, I'm not quite sure.

But then again, maybe it's real?

I'm not sure I can tell the difference anymore.

The shower starts and I stand still in my bedroom, listening and looking into my closet, as he turns on the water and pulls the shower curtain closed.

I took a bullet for him.

Wow, it's been a long time since I thought about that.

I find a t-shirt and a pair of shorts. My usual nighttime wear, even in the winter. But then I look in the mirror and second-guess myself.

Will I be sending him the wrong message if I bare too much skin?

Maybe I'll be sending him the right one?

Jesus Christ, Kiera. Get a grip. This guy has never looked at you that way. Everything we did was… scripted. I knew that then and I know that now. In three years he's going to be a US Senator. I don't care how preliminary the stages are in his campaign, he will win that election.

It's pretty much ordained.

So don't get lost in the fantasy. This is real life, not a stupid book.

The shower turns off, jolting me back into the present.

Was that the world's quickest shower or did I just lose time?

That stupid book. Just what the fuck is happening right now? Is it just a reminder? Just a subtle way to remind him that he's owned and that job in DC that will make him so powerful in the eyes of others is really nothing more than a puppet show?

But why a book? Why *that* book? Why publish it when everything was such a secret back then? It makes no sense.

I mean, I guess it makes a little sense. Our story, our true story, is in the hands of the public. They think it's a fiction, but would it be so hard to start a rumor that those people in that book are real? That the story is real? And hey, guess what? The star of that story is none other than Connor Arlington?

It's a very short leap, I realize. And in the twisted, dirty world we live in, it actually makes perfect sense.

"What are you doing?"

"What?" I breathe, turning my head to see him standing in my doorway wearing nothing but a towel.

"Why are you just standing there like that?"

"Nothing," I say, shaking my head. "I'm fine."

"You sure?"

"I'm sure."

"Because you say that a lot and it's never true."

"I said that once ten years ago."

"You said that ten minutes ago, Kiera. What the hell is going on?"

"Nothing," I say, stepping into my closet to make him disappear. "Just… get dressed."

He sighs across the room, then he must turn and walk away, because the floorboards creak.

I wait in my closet like some stupid person waiting in a closet. Unable to form coherent sentences, apparently. Because that was a bad one.

Maybe I should get out more? Maybe living alone up here in Vermont isn't the best idea after all? Maybe I'm turning into one of those weird reclusive writer people who have no social skills and everyone thinks lost their mind back in their twenties?

Except I'm still in my twenties. Got two more months of twenties to go, in fact. So if I'm this weird at twenty-nine, how bad will I be at thirty-nine?

I have an entire lifetime of weird habits yet to be collected. I cannot accumulate all my eccentricities before I hit thirty.

"Kiera," Connor calls from the living room.

I slide my eyeballs to the side, wondering if he's coming back here again. "What?"

"What are you doing?"

"I'm *fine*," I say, then cringe. Because seriously, my game is gone. I really need to get out of this house and find more game.

No. No more games. The last thing I need is more games. I play enough of those in my day job. All my characters are borderline insane, living these weird on-the-edge lives, playing with fire and—

"What the hell is going on?"

Shit. He's back. How long have I been in this closet?

"Would you just talk to me?" And then he's behind me. I can see him in the mirror. Some alternate reality version of him stares at me like I'm a—"What are you doing?"

"I'm just thinking." I sigh.

"Well, you look lost."

I turn around to see the real version of Connor Arlington and realize… none of this is how it's supposed to happen. "Why did you come here?"

He averts his eyes. Like he's ashamed. But he's also very used to being put on the spot, so he recovers an instant later. A career in politics does that to you. Makes you bolder, I guess. Better able to handle the tough questions. I picture him practicing his speeches. All his various handlers surrounding him, throwing out questions he's not expecting so when it happens with strangers he's got all the right answers on the tip of his tongue. He rattles them off instantaneously. Like shooting stars across the dark night sky.

"I'm sorry," he says. "I didn't mean to accuse you. I mean, I did." He smiles. It's one of those winning politician smiles. Bright white teeth and a secret hidden chin dimple. He's got this election in the bag for sure. Every housewife in New York state will be dreaming about that smile between their legs one year from now. "But it was wrong," he continues. "I shouldn't have jumped to that conclusion just because…"

"Just because I write dirty books for a living?"

He nods. "Yeah. I didn't know Sofia and Camille were writing that stuff too."

"If you did, you'd suspect one of them first instead of me?"

He sighs. He's sighing a lot tonight. "No," he admits. "No. I'd still have accused you first."

I nod. One of those "I get it" nods. I'm everybody's natural first choice when it comes to that nagging question titled, *Who wrote the anonymous, dirty, secret book without telling us first?*

I shrug. It's a long one. The kind that where your shoulders get stuck up by your ears because you're just not sure what to do with that information but deep down you know you can't deny it's the right conclusion.

Admission, I realize. It's a shrug of admission.

"If you're tired, I can just… hang out in the living room and… shit. You don't even have a TV."

"I'm not tired," I say. "It's not even seven o'clock."

This makes him laugh. "God, what a long fuckin' day."

I raise my eyebrows. Because it didn't feel like a long day at all. I wrote a bunch of words this morning. A cool, dark erotic story I've been working on the past few weeks. Then I put some music on and drank half a bottle of wine. Kinda drifted off and when I forced myself to get up the music was still playing and Connor Arlington was cursing his way down my snow-packed driveway.

"Do you… eat?" he asks.

And I huff out a laugh that is probably more genuine than any other laugh I've laughed in the last several years. "Yes."

"Well, I could cook something if you're hungry."

"I have Totino's Pizza Rolls," I offer.

His laugh sounds so nice, I forget about the book, and the past, and the problem. "Sure," he says. "Sounds great."

I inhale and hold my breath. Because I don't know what else to do with it.

And then Connor is up next to me, his hand on my shoulder. And even though that bullet-hole scar stopped hurting years ago, when his fingertips brush past it, I feel the pain of that night so clear…

"Come on, Kiera. Come out of the closet and I'll make you some pizza rolls."

"You were always good at that," I say. "And I never thanked you for it."

"Good at what?" he asks.

"Keeping my insanity in check."

"It's not insanity if it's real. We've talked about this before."

"Yeah, I know. That's why I'm thanking you, dumbass."

He smiles, unleashing that chin dimple on me. *Oh, lonely, sex-deprived-housewives of New York, you better get in line now, bitches. Because by the time you discover what a catch Connor Arlington is, it'll be too late.* "You're one of a kind," he says. "And I always knew that."

"Yeah," I say, blowing a stray piece of still-damp hair out of my eyes. "That was always my problem. 'Kiera has trouble fitting in.' Do you know every teacher in grade school put that on my report card?"

"It's a compliment if you ask me. Who wants to be like everyone else, anyway?"

"Not me," I say.

But on the inside that's not what I say at all. Because I stood in front of every single birthday cake from the time I was six and blew out those candles internally chanting the same wish year after year.

Make me like them. Make me like them. Make me like them.

But I learned that lesson early.

Wishes are bullshit and dreams aren't the future.

Dreams are just… fucked-up versions of your own sad reality.

I sit on the couch and watch him in my tiny kitchen. You'd think a competent guy like this wannabe US senator would have a handle on this whole frozen junk food thing by the time he was thirty, but then you'd have to assume he's just like us.

And he's not.

I've been to his family home. It's one of those historic mansions off the North Shore of Long Island where it takes almost no imagination at all to picture yourself at one of Gatsby's opulent parties. Drinking, and laughing, and dancing like a maniac. Drunk on money, and pretty people, and the idea that mortality is for the commoners outside the lavish garden walls.

It was his parents' thirtieth anniversary and all of the Dirty Ones went because the buddy system was in full force by then. We went nowhere alone. I slept in Sofia's room, or Sofia slept in Camille's room, or Sofia slept in my room, or Camille slept with both of us. And the guys were sharing a house on campus already, so they were all set. But by the time that anniversary party rolled around in the early spring of senior year things were… bad.

Or, if I'm being honest, good. I mean, no, they were bad—but I got good things out of that year and Connor Arlington's friendship was one of them.

We went nowhere alone and I liked that. My six-year-old self who had no friends really, really liked that. And we all know that adults are just six-year-olds in grown-ups' bodies. You carry that shit with you for life.

I met his mom and dad that year. All his siblings. Jack, Olivia, Stenton, and Baby Beatrice, who was seventeen at the time, but everyone still called her Baby.

This was no tent garden party with a string quartet. No. That's not how the Arlingtons do things. This was a first-floor mansion kind of event. In the ballroom kind of event. With a chamber orchestra kind of event.

There was a seven-course sit-down dinner for more than two hundred guests in the grand dining hall, an eight-tier champagne fountain in the foyer, and more than fifty parking attendants taking special care of Bentleys, and Porsches, and Jaguars, and of course, the Rolls.

There were balloons. So many lavender balloons. Maybe thousands of them. And they flew in lepidopterists from Central America with hundreds of glass-wing butterfly caterpillars, which were timed to hatch inside the atrium the day of the party.

It was the most magical evening. A dream party, really. Which is stupid because everyone knows that there's a nightmare behind every dream.

Right?

"OK," Connor says, wiping his hands on one of my flour-sack dish towels. "Thirteen to seventeen minutes from now we can eat."

He grins at me and just for a moment I see him that night of his parents' party. Fresh-faced and clean-shaven for the first time in months. His tuxedo the blackest of blacks and his lavender tie the color of the balloons. We were in the atrium just staring up at the reflective transparent butterflies as they floated in the night air like creatures of some dream world yet imagined. One landed on his tie, gently flapping its wings. And then there was a swarm of them surrounding him. Surrounding us. All six of us, because Louise wasn't there. She was never there for stuff like that. We were the chosen ones. Like this party was for us and everyone knew it.

"Is this all of them?" Connor asks.

He wandered over to my bookshelf while I was daydreaming and is plucking a book from my stack.

"Most of them," I say. "I lost track a long time ago. The novelty of collecting my own books on my own shelf wore off after… oh, book thirty-two, I suppose."

He shakes his head at me, but walks over to the couch, still holding the paperback, and plops down just a mere foot away.

He's got no shirt on. Just a pair of cut-off sweat shorts. He apologized for that over and over again, but he didn't figure he'd be spending the night at my house tonight, and if I have a t-shirt that will fit him, he'll gladly put it on.

I don't. Have a t-shirt for him, that is. No men have been staying over and leaving garments behind. So he's shirtless.

"What's this one about?" he asks, holding up my book.

"Sex," I say.

"Come on. I know you better than that. There's a great story in here. What is it?"

"Read it and find out."

"I'm gonna read it out loud if you don't tell me."

I smile at him. Because that brings up some of the good times. When he used to read to us. Me and Sofia, mostly. Camille was never into that, but that's her loss. Connor is a fantastic narrator. I could listen to him read a grocery list. Or the dictionary. And sometimes, if I was in a mood, he'd do that to make me smile. Just pull out whatever. A philosophy textbook, an essay I wrote for lit class. A poem from my notebook.

Not that notebook. The ones I used to always carry around. The pretty ones.

And he read a book once too. I just can't think of which one at the moment.

But if I ever get the chance to have him read to me again, it's not going to be one of *my* books. "It's about a girl and a guy. Two guys, actually."

"Two?" He laughs.

"Yeah," I say, blushing a little. "My girls like two at a time."

"OK. Go on."

"And she is… broken."

"Aren't they all?"

I squint my eyes at him.

"I mean, in these books, right? Dark romance. The girl is always broken."

"Oh. Yeah. Yes. They are. They have to be to do the crazy shit I make them do, right?"

He nods. "So why is she broken?"

"Oh, you know. The usual. She was kidnapped and sold to human traffickers—" He laughs. "It's not funny. Shit like that really happens."

"I know. Sorry. Go on."

"And of course, there's gotta be some good old Stockholm syndrome to make the story sexy. Everyone knows Stockholm syndrome is sexy, right?"

"Naturally."

"So she falls for her kidnappers and they have lots and lots of dirty sex and then they save her and have a HEA."

"HEA?"

"Happily ever after," I say. "Duh."

"Right, right." He stares at me for several eternal seconds, smiling that gonna-charm-the-housewife-yoga-pants-right-off-you smile. "Anything else? Like… is there romance? Or it's just dirty sex in a slave dungeon?"

"No, they have to have a date. Every romance has like… a date night, you know. Where everything's perfect. But of course that's right before that big, black moment when it all falls apart and looks hopeless. So all that happens too."

His charming smile fades. Slowly, like those butterflies must've after his parents' party. "Sounds a lot like real life to me."

I nod. "I guess that's why people like it."

"Is that why you write it?"

"It's my job, Connor."

"That's it?"

"That's it."

"Somehow I don't buy that excuse. I mean, you could write mysteries, or thrillers, or poetry. But you write this."

"I guess… I was just groomed for it."

"Don't do that," he says.

"Do what?"

"Let them tell you who you are. Because that's not who you are."

I smile. Breathe out a small huff of contempt. "That is who I am. They knew that when they chose me to be in this little gang we're both a part of."

But he's shaking his head the whole time I'm talking. "No. That's not why. They didn't just pluck you out of obscurity one day and say, 'I think she'll do.'"

"Then why me, Con? What did I ever do to deserve that year?"

"You were just born, Kiera. Just like me. Just like Sofia. Just like Bennett. Just like all of us. You were just born."

He's had that theory forever, it seems. But we didn't have all the pieces back then. I still don't have the pieces, but something tells me that now… he might have more than he's letting on.

So I say, "Why now, Connor? Why did this happen now? And don't tell me it's about your upcoming campaign. That's not it. You've had campaigns in the past."

"But I didn't win them, right? I lost those other campaigns. This is a message telling me in no uncertain terms that if I want to win, I'll have to opt in."

"Opt in to what?"

"The puppet show."

"So why do it? Why run at all?"

"Because we all have a destiny and this one is mine."

"So that's how this works, huh? You get to tell me to be strong and resist, but if I spit your words right back at you, you just give up?" We stare at each other for several long moments. "Way to disappoint a girl, Connor Arlington. Good job."

CHAPTER FIVE

I'm used to seeing that look in the eyes of women. Hell, my parents, my friends—pretty much everyone is disappointed by me eventually.

But I always thought Kiera kinda respected me. At least half as much as I respected her that year. And yes, I'm a dick for shutting her out since then, but I was just following her lead. She left early, not us. She cut ties, not us.

We would've made a place for her in the city. We would've surrounded her. The buddy system, right? And she's not poor. Not by any means. Not even by New York City standards. This cottage is sitting on a very nice-sized estate.

"Why don't you live in the main house?" I ask.

"It's not mine anymore."

"What do you mean?"

"I mean, when my mother died four years ago she left me the cottage and the house went to the estate."

"Yeah, but that's just lawyer talk for tax breaks, Kiera. You are the estate."

"No," she says. "I'm not. It's some kind of endowment."

I squint my eyes at her. "To you," I say.

She shakes her head. "To Essex."

"The fucking college owns your estate?"

"I don't really know. Like I said, it's complicated. All I know is that I got this cottage and the five acres surrounding it."

"That makes no sense."

She shrugs. "I'm satisfied with it. No mortgage, no never-ending upkeep costs."

"So who lives there?"

"No one, as far as I know. I don't go down that way much but I don't think anyone's been in there since my mom died."

"Something's not right here. Where's the will?"

"I dunno. Boxes in the attic, probably."

"You should have Bennett look at it. There's no way your mom would just rip your family estate away from you and leave you with this cottage. Was it even fixed up when she died?"

"No," she says.

"Yeah, no. I'm calling bullshit. Didn't your estate lawyer explain this shit to you?"

"Honestly, Connor, who cares?"

"I fucking care. It's like she cut you out or something. It's so fucked up and your mother wasn't fucked up like that. I mean, my family—hell, yeah, I could see them doing something like this to me, or Jack, or Stenton. But not Olivia or Baby, for Christ's sake. Never."

"That's kinda sexist."

"So? No one cuts their daughters off. Not unless they're huge fuckups. And you are not the definition of huge fuckup."

"Maybe she didn't like my books?"

I just laugh. And then she laughs too. Because Antoinette Bonnaire was always Kiera's biggest cheerleader. I didn't know her well, but I knew that much from the moment we first met. She was one of those parents who were invested in their kid, and not for the wrong reasons like mine. "I don't think that's it." Antoinette was the mom everyone wanted to fuck too. It's rude, I get that. But it's still true.

Hayes, and Bennett, and I had the other kind of mom. The kind who stays home with the kids and throws lavish charity parties. The kind who wears tailored designer suit sets with two-inch heels. The kind who are invested in their kids because they are an extension of themselves and not because they have maternal instincts.

Kiera's mom wore… romantic things. Lacy things with ruffles and low-cut necklines. She smelled good too. Not the way our moms smelled good, but the way sexy women smell. Her hair was always long and unruly, like Kiera's. And even though she was going gray when I first met her, you couldn't tell through the multi-colored strands of blonde unless you really looked.

No one was looking at her hair, I'll tell you that right now. You couldn't just look at one thing when you caught a glimpse of Antoinette. You had to see the whole package.

Kiera is so much her mother. And I mean that in a good way. All the good ways.

"Who cares, anyway?" Kiera says, still in the conversation. "I don't. I don't need that house."

"It doesn't matter if you need it. It's just… yours."

"We have bigger problems right now. So just drop it."

"I want to look at the will. You think it's in the attic?" I stand up, but she grabs my hand and tugs me back down.

"We're not looking for that will tonight. Just…" But she stops talking. And I'm dying to know what she wants me to just do.

"Just what?" I ask.

She tugs her legs up to her chest, wraps her arms around them, and plants her chin on her knees, staring at me. "I don't want to think about it."

The timer dings on the oven. We both look over at the small kitchen, then look at each other. She smiles at me. "Pizza rolls, Connor. If you go up into my attic you're gonna miss pizza rolls."

Then she jumps up and walks over to the kitchen, puts on some black oven mitts, and pulls the cookie sheet out of the oven.

I watch her get plates and forks. Study the way she carefully slides the spatula across the cookie sheet, scooping up the little bits of food, and then places them on the plates.

I like what she's wearing. Little fluffy shearling shorts that peek out from under her long creamy white t-shirt. She's got on red, knee-high slipper socks with white snowflakes on them.

She could be that girl back in school. She looks the part. Untouched by the years. Still very youthful in the face. Her too-pale eyes still tricking me into believing they're blue, then green, then yellow.

I asked her once what color they were and she just shrugged. Very much like the way she shrugged off the fact that she has no idea who her family estate actually belongs to.

Kiera Bonnaire has never *needed* things. Not a big house or special eyes. She just accepts what the world offers. I always admired that about her. How detached she could be from everything around her. It's a skill I never mastered. Probably never will, we're just different like that.

But I wish I was more like her and less like me. Have wished that since the day she ended up in the tower with the rest of us.

"So," she said, standing at the top of the stone stairs all those years ago. "What the hell are we doing here?"

She didn't look around. She didn't take it all in the way Sofia did. She didn't pull back from it like Camille, who thought the whole place was creepy and disgusting. She didn't fall back against the stone walls like Emily, trying to disappear. She didn't place her hands on the walls looking for secret passageways like Bennett, endlessly curious and desperate to solve riddles, or furiously try to open the shuttered windows like Hayes. Who is as subtle as a fucking bull.

She just accepted that she was there and moved on.

What are we doing here?

Little did we know.

"You lost in time or something?" she asks now.

I blink the past away and stare up at her outstretched hand. Take the plate, fork, and napkin, then set it back down on the rickety white coffee table in front of the couch.

"You're not hungry?" she asks.

"How can you be so calm about this?"

"About what? Someone found our story and decided to make money off it. That's all I see."

"That's not what this is."

She forks one of her pizza rolls, blows on it, then pops it into her mouth, chewing fast like it's too hot. "Who cares what it is?"

"I care, Kiera. And so should you. They could be back."

"Why would they come back now?"

"I already told you—"

"Yeah, yeah," she says, popping another too-hot pizza roll into her mouth. She chews and swallows. "I get it. You're Mr. Important these days. But come on, Connor. You're not that important."

She tries to hide her smile. Because it's a joke. An old one too. She was never impressed with us. She's not into money, or power, or things.

And we all kinda hated her for that. For a little while anyway. Soon enough it became clear we couldn't afford to hate her. We needed her.

And she did need us, even though she never admitted it. She did. We were a team. We were the Dirty Ones. The buddy system. And we were in this together.

For nine whole months we were inseparable. Sometimes, in that last semester when class schedules all lined up and things were… comfortable, for lack of a better word, we'd all have lunch together. And we did things at night too. We'd all get together and drink. Hayes would be smoking pot, of course. Camille would dance in the middle of the room to the music only in her head and drag Bennett into her dream. And I'd read to them. Kiera and Sofia, but mostly it was to Kiera.

What did I read them? What was that book?

And then, after Camille was tired, and Bennett's hands were wandering, and Kiera and Sofia had droopy eyes from listening to me read, and Hayes was good and stoned and spouting ridiculous theories about why this was happening—which always started and ended with Kiera for some reason—we'd... we'd turn into who we were that year. We'd turn into the Dirty Ones. It called us together like a siren song and we responded like sailors drunk and lost at sea.

But I don't want to think about it. Not that part. Not now, when I have her to myself. "None of you are that important," I say, echoing her words from the past.

"Nope," she agrees. Still eating.

"It was you who was important," I say. Because I always had this nagging thought that the things that happened to us that year were about her. "It was you."

"Get out." She laughs. "I was nobody then and I'm nobody now."

"You were the writer, Kiera. We were your... subjects."

"Those weren't my words."

I nod my head slowly. "Yeah, they were."

I don't even know how to explain that game we played senior year. It wasn't a game, not really, because there were no winners. There was no prize on the line. If there was, it might make sense. Sure, we could lose. We all lost something, some several times over. Well, maybe not Hayes. Hayes just never got the memo that he was a victim. He's a fighter and he fought his way through senior year like it was the last round of a championship boxing match.

But it wasn't a game. It certainly wasn't fun.

Liar, the little truth-telling voice in my head whispers. *You're a liar.*

Because some of it was.

After the shock wore off and we—meaning everyone but Hayes—accepted what was happening, it did get fun. In the winter time it was fun. We'd had enough time to settle in. Understand how to play, so to speak. And some of us were OK with it.

Me, for sure. Sofia, at times. Kiera, always. Because she was just the observer.

I think that's why Hayes hated her. Probably still does.

She was our judge.

Her words on the page made us into fictional characters. We lived a different life in her book. So weird.

"Do you ever see Emily?"

"Emily?" I ask. Like she's some forgotten ghost that makes no sense.

"Yeah. I mean, I know she left school—"

"Left?" I ask, cutting her off. "She didn't leave, Kiera."

"I know that," she snaps, all attitude. "I was there, remember? I'm just trying to be delicate."

"Don't bother." I huff. "We all know what happened to Emily."

"I don't. Which is why I asked."

"She never got out, you know that."

"I haven't seen or heard from her in—"

"You know that, Kiera. Don't lie to me or yourself. We all know what happened to her."

"So she's still there? In the hospital?"

I nod, looking down at my plate of food on the coffee table, suddenly feeling sick. Because hospital isn't quite the right word. Hospital implies she had a broken arm or a bad case of the flu. And that's not the kind of place she was sent to.

"Maybe she wrote the book?"

"How the fuck could she? She didn't even make it through one round."

Kiera shrugs. "Well, someone took that book. I went back the next day after the last page was filled up thinking I'd hold on to it if it was still there, but it wasn't. So someone took it. Maybe they gave it to her? I dunno. I'm as in the dark about this as you are."

I search for the book, find it with my eyes, sitting on the kitchen counter, and then go get it and return to the couch. "We should read it."

"No," Kiera says. "We should wait until we're all together."

"Fuck." I laugh. "I'm sure Bennett has read it three times through by now and is making little notes in the margins. There's no point in waiting."

"I don't want to read it."

I just stare at her for a few seconds, trying to figure out if this is just typical Kiera defiance or if it's something else.

Fear, I decide. She's afraid.

And she has good reason to be. We all do.

"We should go see Emily."

"Why?"

"Because we owe her that much."

"I don't owe her shit." And I don't know what gets into me, but I reach over, pull her t-shirt down to expose the bullet-hole scar, and say, "And neither do you."

Kiera shrugs me off and scoots away from me, pressing herself up against the arm of the couch.

"She shot you," I say. "And if that was all it was, I'd still be fine with never talking to her again. Letting her rot out her sentence in that fucking nuthouse. But that's not all. Because she was aiming for me and you got in her way."

Kiera lifts an eyebrow.

"Fine. You threw yourself in the way to save me. Which is why I love you and hate her."

She looks down, trying not to smile.

"What? You're surprised that I love you? Go fuck yourself, Kiera."

She laughs now and I laugh too. "Go fuck yourself right back, Con."

"God," I say, smiling, but not feeling happy. "What the hell is happening?"

"I don't know. All I know is that we're stuck in a blizzard for a night with no phone, and no TV, and no way anyone or anything can get to us, even if they wanted to. So why do we have to think about this shit right now?"

I don't know if that's an invitation or just rational thinking. But I choose the former. Because I reach over, take her hand, and pull her warm body up next to me. She folds herself into my embrace. Molds her body into the shape of mine like a missing puzzle piece.

I feel it. That love I have for her. Was probably always there even before I knew she existed. Because that's the kind of love it is. Has always been.

She says, "I just want you all to myself for a little bit. Is that so wrong?"

I get lost in the past again. Because that's what she said near the end. She wrote it in her book, I know it. She had to have. Because the next week she got her wish.

And I got mine too.

"Pretty soon, maybe even tomorrow," she goes on, "Sofia will be here, or we'll be there, and you'll be with her again. Not me. So that book can wait, Connor."

I smile again. And this time it's different. "You're forgetting something," I say. "I was always with you, not her. Because you were always there with us."

"It wasn't the same," she says.

"No, it wasn't. It was definitely different."

"And there was a time when you had her and not me. So don't lie about it."

CHAPTER SIX

The tower was empty that night. I showed up on the usual day, at the normal time, and there was no one home. The door was locked, no candlelight was seeping through the always-shut shutters, and I knew what was happening without being told.

They were together without me.

I was still, and always would be, just the impartial observer. The outsider looking in.

Or maybe it was the insider looking out? I wonder if that perspective change matters?

But the book was there. Sitting on the flat stone that announced the entrance to the tower. Propped up against the door like a headstone. I remember thinking that. It looked like a headstone.

And when I opened it our pages were already filled out. In my handwriting, describing in full detail what Sofia and Connor were doing without me.

Except… it couldn't have happened yet. It was just a few minutes past eight. But there they were. Five handwritten pages that I never wrote.

Later I'd learn that the details were wrong, but it didn't matter. Whatever really happened with Sofia and Connor didn't matter either. Because the book was the law.

"I didn't write that chapter, you know," I say, feeling the urge to clarify this one more time. Because it happened a lot after that. Someone dictated our story. Made shit up and wrote it down. Like we were on the wrong path or something. And they, whoever they were, were trying to guide us back in the right direction. Those false words became real, even though the story was fake.

And it makes sense, I guess. Because the stories I write aren't real in my head, but the second I put the words on paper, they are. They become truth. And when people read them, that's how they see it too. Doesn't matter if it's fiction. The story is the story and if I say it happened that way, then it happened that way.

I am God when I write. Little Kiera Bonnaire, puppetmaster of the masses.

"I know you didn't write it," Con says.

"I was jealous," I say. "But I'd never write that stuff." It was some pretty kinky shit. That's for sure. Dark too. Which is the part we were getting wrong, I think. We became friends. We started to enjoy it. Camille and Bennett dancing, Hayes drinking and smoking. Connor reading to Sofia and me.

We had… fun. And fun was never the point of that year. Like, I don't really know what the point was because the whole fucking thing was irrational from start to finish, I just know it had nothing to do with fun.

He nods his head at my declaration of innocence, but it doesn't feel like agreement. "But you've written some of that stuff since then, haven't you?"

It's an accusation but for some reason I don't take offense. "Yup," I admit. "Lots of it."

"Why?"

"Because the dark side of love intrigues people, Connor. Love makes you do weird things and sometimes you want to deny that. When things are going good, and all your expectations are being met, and there is nothing but bliss—people want to deny that dark side exists. But how many of us have a love life filled with bliss?"

He draws in a deep breath.

"Almost no one. And since love and betrayal are powerful feelings that come with an overwhelming sense of emotional irrationality, people who don't normally like to vacation on the dark side still want to feel like they're normal. So that's what I write about. The tangled, messy, uncontrollable things we say, and do, and feel when the bliss is missing and the darkness comes from inside *us*, not them."

He thinks about this, his heart beating right next to my ear. It's a steady beat. Not too fast, not too slow. He's not tense and his arm is around me, his thumb doing this soft back-and-forth caress across my clavicle.

"Do you think," he says, then pauses. "Do you think you'd be writing this stuff if what happened to us never happened?"

"Maybe not."

"So why do you do it? Why not just write thrillers, or mysteries, or poetry?"

"Because what happened changed me, Con. Just like it changed you. And if I had a mass-market paperback thriller or mystery inside me, I'd at least give it a try. But I don't. I have this shit inside me. These words, these stories, these characters. That's what lives in my brain so that's what comes out on the page. And you know what?" I ask, shifting my body so I can sit up a little.

"What?"

"I like it. It pays well, I never get writer's block, and I have fans who look forward to the books. So why fight it? Why buck success and fight the natural progression of things?"

"Because this isn't you, Kiera."

"Like hell it's not!" I laugh. "Look, if this wasn't the real me, do you really think I could knock out six books a year? Do you really think I could find all these stories, and all these people, and all these words? No. It doesn't happen that way. That's just… not how writing works. People who fight the story inside them fail. I learned that a long time ago."

"Yeah," he says, turning his head away from me. "I was there when you learned it, remember?"

But he wasn't. Not really. He was only there for part of it. The part that happened while I was with him and Sofia. That's all he knew, that's all he knows now.

But there were other parts. The parts with Hayes and Louise. The parts with Camille and Bennett. Parts I played and he didn't.

My eyes involuntarily find the book, still sitting on the counter, and I wonder how much truth is actually in there. How many missing pieces will he add to the puzzle when we turn that last page?

"I'm tired," he says. "It's been a long day. For both of us. I'll take the couch."

And there it is… the dismissal.

You'd think I'd remember what that felt like because he did it a lot back in senior year, but his words tonight hurt me like a brand-new wound.

"OK," I say, untangling my body from his. The cold immediately rushes in with our separation. "I'll get you some blankets and a pillow."

I feel more sad than I have in a very long time. Even though we're together again, we were never meant to be. It was always him and Sofia. And do I really want to fight the outgoing tide when it's so much easier to give in to the natural order of things and just… float?

The hall closet contains blankets and pillows for the off-chance a guest shows up and wants to stay. I never use them, but it's nice to be ready for guests who need my couch for a night. I grab them and walk back into the living room, placing them next to Connor, who hasn't moved.

"It's cold in here," he says.

"Yeah," I say. "Sure is."

I turn the heat up a few degrees, but it won't help much. The cottage is old and drafty, even with the new insulation I put in when I remodeled it after college. Things wear out, wear down, it's just the inevitable decay that happens with time.

So I light a fire as Connor sets up a makeshift bed on the couch.

I didn't have any grand dreams that we'd share a bed tonight. I didn't. But I feel lonely just the same. And apprehensive about tomorrow. Because by tomorrow afternoon this storm will have passed, and the roads will be plowed, and we *will* be on our way to New York to face the others.

He's staring at me when I stand up from the fire and turn.

"Good night, Kiera," he says.

I just nod and walk away.

But then, just as I enter my room and disappear, he calls out, "Leave the door open."

"Buddy system," I murmur back.

The best thing about this cottage is the view from my bed at night. There's a large window and a long wall running perpendicular to it, perfect for bed placement. I didn't realize this when I put the bed along this wall, but the first night I slept in here after the remodel was finished, it hit me in the face like a very sweet surprise.

The angle of the bed and the placement of the window frames a gap in the thick trees surrounding the cottage, and in that gap there are stars.

Not tonight. Tonight it's just the constant fast-falling snow lit up by a hidden full moon. But the heavy flakes make a white curtain that dulls the blackness of space and makes me feel like I'm underneath a fluffy down comforter.

I stare at it, lids heavy and tired, even though five minutes ago the idea of sleep felt as foreign as the man out in my living room, so I allow myself to drift away…

When he comes up the stone stairs to the second floor of the tower his expression is one of expectant surprise. And by that I mean he knew this was coming. Some part of him knew that I'd get a night alone with him eventually.

It's only fair, right?

"What's going on? Where's Sofia?"

"She has the night off," I say, then add, "I guess," to make it seem like I didn't play a part in these unusual circumstances.

"Huh," he says, taking a seat on the long, crushed-velvet couch.

The couch was Camille's request. It's been here since the second week we played this little game. Camille got the point of the game before the rest of us because she and Bennett went first, so she took that little pad of paper sitting on top of the wooden box marked "suggestions" seriously.

This room is her imagination incarnate because that first night we came up here the whole floor was empty. Nothing but cold stone to fill up the darkness.

We each had a candle. There's no power in this building. It's some leftover relic of master masonry from back in the days of soldiers and forts. So that's all there was. Just seven people holding seven candles, standing in the dark.

But tonight the walls are covered in elaborate tapestries. The cold floors are warmed with threadbare Persian rugs. There's more than just one couch too. Louise asked for another one about a month into things. That's the one I'm sitting on. Thick pillows and soft cushions slipcovered in cream mold to my body like perfect summer-day clouds.

This couch is out of tune with Camille's vision of the room, but no one cared. Not even Camille, because that first crushed-velvet couch is about as comfortable as a church pew.

There are four more chairs, each situated on a diagonal so that all the seating is arranged in an elaborate circle built for conversation.

And oh, the conversations we've had up here.

That alone could fill a book.

Not a sexy one. Not an erotic one, like what was actually being written. But a fantastic mystery for sure.

How many nights did we sit up here in our circle of seven, trying to figure out what was happening? Who was doing this? What it all meant and how we'd have to pay the price for the hedonism that took place within these four walls?

Too many.

Hayes wanted a bar. Fully stocked with a long list of expensive liquor and champagne. The sound of ice dropping into cut-crystal glasses will always remind me of Hayes. Hayes and I were always drunk when we had our time together. Louise didn't partake, but she tried to opt out of everything.

Bennett wanted a Victrola you could make play by turning a crank. Old, crackly music will always remind me of Bennett. He would offer Camille his hand and she'd accept. He'd pull her into the center of the room and they'd dance in slow circles for hours sometimes. Putting off the inevitable.

Sofia wanted clothes. Gowns. Racks and racks of them. We played dress-up when I spent the evening with Sofia and Connor. It was so weird.

Louise wanted games. Monopoly, checkers, chess, backgammon, Life, Trouble, Hungry Hungry Hippos. Shit like that. Every fucking week it was another goddamned game.

She'd gone well past weird by that time, but it wasn't this place that did that to her. Louise was just naturally weird. Always asking us weird questions about shit.

What were those questions?

I can't remember. I just remember the games.

I asked for books. So by this time, at the end of the school year, we had stacks and stacks of them. No shelf—no one bothered to waste a suggestion on a shelf, not even Camille, even though she sometimes read them too. Always looking for a way to escape her fate. They just lined the perimeter of the room in tall towers like soldiers keeping the walls at bay.

Connor wanted nothing. He never once dropped a suggestion into the box.

I admired that about him. How he resisted the perks but never the acts.

He was into the acts.

We all were, even me, who was only there to write them all down in perfect detail.

I'd gotten good at my job by this time. My words flowed effortlessly as I chronicled what happened in the second floor of the tower. Maybe they weren't prose, but they were on their way.

"So…" Connor says. "What do we do?"

I smile at him from my couch. "What you always do, Con."

"Who's writing it down?"

"No one," I say. "Not this time. This time it's just…" But I can't fill in the blank. I'm young, and embarrassed, and even though the things I've witnessed and done in this room over the past nine months should've cured me of any lingering childhood shyness, I feel shy.

"Just what?" he asks. "Your turn?"

I shrug, eyes tracking him as he gets up off his couch and walks across the well-worn Persian rug to sit next to me. "You wanted a night alone with me?" he asks.

I look him in the eye when I say, "Wouldn't you?"

He grins, his hands already on my body. Already squeezing my breasts. That sweet spot between my legs is already throbbing with desire when a finger slides against it, pressing down and moving in small circles.

I close my eyes, confident that this is right when I reach for his hard cock and squeeze it through the fabric of his pants.

His mouth finds mine in that same moment. Open, hungry, tongue inside me. It's a kiss of lovers who know each other well. And we do. We've done this lots of times, just never alone.

I'm breathing hard. My fingers fumble with the button, then stumble over his zipper, but he's not having any problems finding his way underneath my panties. And the wetness I've been saving for this moment spills out onto his fingertips as he pushes them inside me, thrusting with an urgency I've only dreamed about.

"I was hoping for this," he says, talking into our kiss.

"Me too," I whisper back.

"Did you ask for a night with Bennett and Hayes too?"

I don't even freeze up at the question. And my answer is truthful. "No."

This excites him more. And when I pull his cock free of his pants, he's so thick and stiff, I want to do things to that cock. Dirty things. Kiss the tip. Put my mouth around it and suck. Take him deep into my throat.

But he's not ready to move on to that. Not yet. Because he pushes me backwards. Hard, making me bounce into the soft cloud-like cushions of the comfy couch, and then he roughly tugs my panties down, throws my legs over his shoulder, and opens them up. A gleam of mischief in his eyes. A wry, slanted smile cutting across his face. Grinning as he lowers himself between my thighs and licks me with one long sweep of his tongue.

I buck my back, not ready for the sensations that flood my body.

He eats me out like a hungry animal. Like he's been waiting for this opportunity as long as I have.

This is right, I internalize. This isn't the dirty game. That's what we play when we're together with Sofia and the others. This is something different. Something real. Something outside of all those other nights. Apart, and special, and good.

I think that the whole time he licks my pussy. The whole time I suck his cock. The whole time he fucks me. Even after we're done, when he's getting dressed. I think it as he zips his pants and adjusts his shirt. When he grins at me one last all-knowing time and disappears down the stairs.

But I stay in the tower. Hours longer. Writing down every detail. Reliving every single moment in my head and transferring it to the book where it won't be lost. Hoping one day, through some miracle, he reads it.

Then praying he doesn't.

I wake up in the real world with his real hands on my real body.

I reach for him, tugging him down next to me, fully aware that everything I've done is about to come back and kick my ass. But not caring one bit.

No regrets. No apologies.

Because it will all have been worth it.

CHAPTER SEVEN

After Kiera goes to bed I just run all this through my head over and over on an endless loop.

I wish I could say I never saw this coming, but we knew.

We all knew what we were doing. How we were active participants in our own inevitable decline.

I just hoped it would come later than this. Not when I was still a rising star. I figured it would all explode once I was established. Once my power was consolidated and I was thoroughly addicted to it and would do anything to keep it all from unraveling.

So maybe this is better? Maybe this is a choice? Maybe even a way out of that future someone else dreamed up for me.

Maybe if I never become that self-absorbed, power-hungry political hack the world will be a better place?

Maybe whoever did this to us understands me better than I understand myself?

Maybe they're actually trying to save me?

That's some altruistic fuckery on their part, for sure. But in the end, will I be a better person if I never enter the world of global puppeteers?

Honestly, lying here in Kiera's living room, staring up at the ceiling as I listen to her breathe through her dreams down the hall, I could go for that life. One where I leave the family name and the expectations that come with it behind. Forget the power I'll have. And the money that will flow. Because that's what it does when you already have it.

It just flows.

I could leave behind the family estate, like Kiera did. Even though she says she was cut out. I still find that hard to believe. Something weird is happening there.

Maybe I'll make things up to her and figure that shit out. Give her back the family estate.

It's not a big estate. The land is there. And the lake view with a boathouse and a dock. But the house is modest by my family's standards. Five or six bedrooms. Four or five thousand square feet. This cottage. And all of it's old, but not the same way that our estate is old either.

It's the Vermont side of Lake Champlain, for one thing. And it's not made of stone, or brick, or gold, for that matter.

Our mansion is so well maintained, our lawns and gardens so well kept, our stables and outbuildings so well updated, you'd never know the entire place was built over a hundred years ago when our old money was still *nouveau riche*.

The Arlington name is synonymous with wealth, and power, and privilege.

Bonnaire, on the other hand. Who are the Bonnaires, anyway?

I know Kiera was on some kind of free-ride scholarship. And it makes sense. Her family must've all gone to Essex over the years. This house is one ferry ride across the lake away, after all. But she never did explain her status.

By the time the game ended we'd pretty much figured things out. It was about controlling us. I know that for certain. Forcing us to understand that we have a part to play in the world and this book we were writing was… what do they call it in those secret societies? Oh, yeah. Mutually assured destruction.

We knew why we were playing, what it all meant, and who was who.

Except for Kiera.

We accepted her as the outsider. The necessary impartial observer who kept us in check. She wrote our fates in the book.

But we never looked too close, did we?

We saw what they wanted us to see.

A girl from a respectable family who could wordsmith. And standing next to just about anyone Kiera Bonnaire looks like a shiny new thing, doesn't she?

But standing next to us… she is dull, and small, and average.

I like that about her.

Not that she is those things, but that she's not. Not in the real world. It is only our surreal fantasy life that makes her look like second best.

I get up off the couch and walk over to the book shelf, randomly pluck one out, and take it back to the couch, switching on the little lamp on the side table as I sit.

Disappearing, it's called. I read the back cover to get a sense of the story. It's not a kidnapping book, like I first thought, but a story of a girl who slowly goes crazy when an unseen tormentor takes over her life, but she later falls in love with him.

It's just another metaphor for what happened that year, isn't it?

So typical of her books. Why does she write this shit? And I'm not talking about the sex, even though flipping to a random page gives me enough pornographic entertainment I feel myself getting hard after reading a few paragraphs.

I'm talking about the *theme*. I might not have read her books but I saw them on the internet. I understood what they were. Her body of work is all darkness and secrets. It's all rough sex and no fairytale endings. There are no princes, no castles, no fireside declarations of eternal love.

It's nothing but villains, and dungeons, and cold stone walls that mutter, *This is what you deserve.*

But the answer is obvious. She, like all the rest of us, pretends none of it mattered when in reality what we did that year as the Dirty Ones has shaped us into the people we are today. And she is these characters. They are her, inside and out.

Who would I be if that year never happened? Would I be better? Or worse?

I decide… I'd be my father. I'd be my brother Jack. I'd be my brother Stenton. And while I love them all in a son and brother kind of way, I don't really *like* them in the way that counts.

Worse, I decide. I'd be a worse person if I was never a Dirty One.

Who will I be when this next mystery sorts itself out? Better? Or worse?

Remains to be seen, I guess.

I could give up the opulence of Long Island's North Shore. The lavish parties and extravagant charity functions coordinated by useless housewives to help them feel whole again. I could walk away from the expectations and political aspirations. After all, being a US Senator wasn't my fucking dream, was it?

What was my dream?

Did I ever have one?

I know I go along. I get it. I've always known that it was easier to say yes to my father than it was to say no. And I had role models, didn't I? My brothers showed me the way. I didn't make a decision, I realize. I just emulated them the way I was supposed to.

Am I so used to my station in life that I need to ponder the meaning of my existence by having an existential crisis? I mean, that is practically the definition of privilege, right? People who are so well situated, so comfortable they need to make up crises to justify their worth to the world.

I toss the book aside and get up. Walk to the edge of the hallway and listen.

She's mumbling things in her sleep. Having a bad dream, or maybe a good one.

I walk towards her open door and stop, peering in as my eyes adjust to the almost inexplicable brightness that finds its way into the room.

I never understood that about winter nights, but it makes sense, I guess. The snow reflects the moonlight, even though the moon is hidden by the cloud cover. It's some physical law of the natural world explained by the words 'refraction,' or 'reflection,' or some shit like that. Concepts I don't get and don't want to.

Except when I find myself in the spotlight-like beam of that elusive brilliance and start to question my own sanity.

Which is where I am now.

Why am I here and what am I doing?

Kiera sighs in her sleep, turns, her body wrapped up in the thick, white comforter. Her face is flushed and her mouth is open, moaning slightly, like she's in the middle of an erotic experience.

I walk towards her bed, pull the covers back, and get in, my legs sliding against hers, my hand on her shoulder as I gently shake her awake. "Kiera," I say. "You're dreaming."

She reaches for me. Pulls me into her. Hands already on my developing hardness, squeezing me the way she does. Did. Does, apparently, because she's doing it now.

"Come here," she says. "Be real for me, please."

I decide we're both having the same crisis tonight.

Two fucked-up people. And five more waiting, somewhere else, to make our dirty-secret past something in the present again.

I kiss her. Open-mouthed. The way we used to.

And she kisses me back, just as hungry for a repeat performance as I am.

Fuck that snow-covered spotlight outside. Fuck the coming morning. Fuck the inevitable consequences.

I want her.

And she wants me. Even if it's only in a half-awake state, I'll take it.

I pull her on top of me. Her hips grind against my cock as we kiss, our tongues twisting together like old friends who haven't seen each other in ages. Lifetimes, maybe.

She gropes at the waistband of my briefs, so I help her pull them down my legs, then get to work on her shorts. They come off easy, the soft shearling brushing against my own skin as I drag them over her knees and let her take care of the rest. Her shirt comes off as she sits up, straddling me now, her pussy already wet from her dream, and I wonder for a second if she was dreaming about me, or was it someone else? Someone I don't know. Some nameless, faceless man who has captured her attention in the years I've ignored her.

But then her tits are resting on my chest as she leans back down, still hungry, and we get lost in another kiss.

And all the faceless, nameless other men disappear and leave only us in their wake.

She lifts up her hips, reaches between her legs, and pushes my cock inside her. I slip in like an old friend slipping back into some long-forgotten, but easily picked-back-up conversation, and she folds over my shaft. Hugging it and squeezing it as her hands grip my shoulders. Her nails digging into my skin.

We begin to rock.

It's not the rushed, frantic fucking like the last time we were together. It's the opposite of that and I can't stop myself. I cannot stop myself from wondering who taught her to be so seductive and sensual, because it sure as hell wasn't me.

"Stop it," she whispers into my mouth. "Stop thinking."

And even though I'm not the kind of guy who takes commands in the throes of sex, I listen. I obey. Because right now is not the time to answer questions. There's no mystery that will be solved in this moment.

"It can wait," she continues, rocking back and forth faster now, her long hair brushing along my chest like a sensual bonus thrown in for free. "Forever," she says. "If it has to."

We fuck like that for a long time. Slow. Methodical. Then, when we both feel that the end is near, I flip her over, straddle her knees, and thrust myself back inside and take her the way I took her last time.

Rough. Urgent. With the sense that this is the last time I'll ever see this girl who turned into a woman while I was looking elsewhere.

There is no talk about contraceptive. No safety on our minds.

It's just heat. It's just sex. It's just…

I come inside her, not giving any fucks. And she spasms at the same time, moaning as she wraps her long legs around my middle and squeezes my cock with her slick, wet pussy.

She's wrong, of course. The part about forever. Things don't wait until you're ready for them. That hidden light behind the clouds will turn into the brightness of tomorrow quick enough and then nothing will ever wait again.

It's just another illusion.

Because reality trumps mystery and illusion every time.

I wake to the sound of banging and for one delusional second I imagine it's her. Kiera. In the kitchen making breakfast. I feel like I had that dream a lot over the years, I just never remembered it.

Except that's not what's happening.

Someone is legit banging on the door to the cottage.

We both sit up in bed in the same moment and look at each other. "Stay here," I say, sternly, pointing my finger in her face. She slaps it away, but doesn't move. Just pulls the covers up to her breasts and huddles back into the pillows while I find my boxer briefs, pull them on, and then grab a blanket on the floor and wrap it around my body because it's fucking freezing in this place.

The banging continues through all this preparation, and when I pull the front door open, the icy wind cuts through my body and erases all memory of the night before. His fist is poised to bang again.

"Ay up," the tall, gruff man says. He's wearing those thick Carhart overalls and a matching jacket, only halfway zipped. His head is covered in an ear-flap cap, and his thick, gloved hand is holding a black envelope. He nods over his shoulder. "It was a bad bastard, wasn't it?"

"What?" I manage, stuck on his thick Vermont accent for a second.

"The storm," he says. "She kicked ya asses bad, fer sure. But I got ya done first. And I wouldn't of bothered ya, but I was told to drop this off at the door when I was done."

He shakes the envelope, trying to hand it off.

I adjust the blanket, already shivering from the death-like cold, and take it from him. "What is this?"

"Got a call last night," he says, leaning back on the heels of his work boots. "Told me to get you out first thing the mornin'. Wasn't sure I'd make it, but the bastard quit early so here I am."

For a second I'm not sure who this bastard is, but then I shake myself awake and realize he's talking about the storm. The storm is the bastard.

"So yer good," he says, then does a fake hat tip to me, and turns to his waiting truck, snowplow on the front, and disappears in a steamy mist of exhaust.

I close the door and turn to find Kiera behind me, also covered up with a blanket. "Who was that?"

"Snowplow?" I say, unsure, even though that's the only clear part about what just happened. "He left this."

"What's it say?" she says, looking at the envelope.

"I guess we're gonna find out," I reply, lifting up the flap and taking out the matching black card inside. It's not a folded card, more like a thick postcard. And there's only one sentence written in metallic gold marker.

Be there soon.

CHAPTER EIGHT

"Weird," Connor says, looking confused. But it's pretty clear I'm not confused, nor am I interested in discussing this new development. So he amends. "Unless this is normal."

I turn and walk back down the hall.

"Where are you going?"

"Back to bed," I call back. I flop down on the mattress still huddled in my blanket and watch Connor's silhouette fill the doorway.

"You're coming to New York with me, Kiera. There's no way around it. Last night was nice, but we have a real problem happening here and we need to deal with it."

Last night was nice.

"It's still dark out, Connor. I'm not getting up yet. Let's just go back to sleep."

He shakes the card still in his hand. "What's this all about?"

I shrug and lie back on the bed. Turn my back to him and snuggle into the thick down comforter, trying to get warm again. "Just a friend who looks out for me. That's all."

"Oh," Con says, like this is a surprise.

I kinda smile at that. Because he can't help it. He can't help who he is or the perspective of the world he's cultivated. I live outside his sphere, and when you live in a sphere like the one he does, that pretty much means anyone outside of it doesn't exist.

"A guy?" he asks.

"Yes," I say, closing my eyes.

"Oh," he repeats. "So you're seeing someone?"

"No. He's just a friend who looks out for me. That's all. Come back to bed."

Honestly, I don't expect him to get back in bed with me. Connor Arlington has always had a possessive streak in him. With me, with Sofia. Probably with every woman he's ever dated. So I figure he'll skip bed and put his life back together, starting with the suit hanging over the radiator in my laundry room, and just be on his way because I'm no longer holding him captive at the end of a snow-packed driveway.

His body is both warm and cold when he flips up my blanket and slips up next to me. His legs are chilled from standing in the open doorway, but his chest is warm when he wraps his arms around me.

"Kiera," he whispers.

"What?"

"You don't have a boyfriend, right?"

I can't help the little laugh that escapes. I turn over, facing him, and find he's serious. "I said no."

"So this guy who thinks you need saving from the storm… he's what? A friend? An ex?"

"A friend," I say. "That's all, I promise. Are you jealous?"

He reaches up to move some of my unruly hair away from my face. "I've missed you. I don't think I realized that until I got here."

"Well, good? I guess. I mean, you know where I live. You could've come by any time you wanted."

"I know. And I feel a little sick that I never did that. But last night was nice and I don't want any hopes I have to be shattered before I get a chance to sort this whole mess out."

"What are you hoping?" I ask, still grinning. I know it's wrong to smile when he's being so serious, but it's more out of shyness than self-assured confidence. Because I have always liked this man. But I have also understood that our spheres were never going to intersect in any real way. We're too different. We live almost three hundred miles apart and I have no plans to upend my quiet life and move to New York City just to be with a man. Even if that man is Connor Arlington.

"I don't know. A chance, I guess. To start over, maybe?"

"You don't like our past?"

"Well, if I had the opportunity to meet you all over again under different circumstances, then yeah. I'd choose that."

I think about this for a few moments. "We'd never fall back into this level of comfort if we didn't share that past."

"I know. I get it. But still." He sighs. "I'm sorry."

"For what?'

"That whole fuckin' year. I… I could've handled it differently. I could've made a choice, ya know? Committed to something. For once in my life."

"What kind of choice? Like… opt out?" I almost snort-laugh. "Because we tried that and we both know what happened."

He sighs again. Closes his eyes and flops over on his back, covering his face with his hand.

"Hey," I say, scooting closer to him and resting my chin on his shoulder. "Emily made her own choices."

"I know that. But I have always felt that I could've done more."

"How?" I ask, propping myself up on my elbow. "She tried to shoot you, for fuck's sake."

"Yeah," he says, lifting his hand away so he can peek at me with one eye. "And shot you instead."

"That wasn't your fault. I should've…" But I can't even bring myself to say it now, ten years later. So I shake my head and say, "No. I did what I did and I'd do it again. I'm not going to second-guess that moment."

We're quiet for a little while after that. I finally flop back and join him in staring at the ceiling.

"Sometimes," he finally says, "I wonder what would've happened if you died."

"What?"

He turns to look at me. "I didn't want you to die. I'm not saying that. I just find myself asking what if? What if our book was never written, ya know? And we could write our own story."

"I think we both know that if I died, someone would've replaced me."

"No," he says. "I don't think so."

"How could you even think that? I mean, Emily was immediately replaced with Louise."

"Yeah, but you were the writer."

"So? Sofia could've taken my place. Even Camille could've done what I did."

"I don't think so, Kiera."

"Wait," I say, propping myself up again. "You're saying… I was the central figure in that stupid game? Me?" I laugh. And it's loud.

"Why is that funny?"

"I think it's obvious, Con. I mean, come on. I'm nobody compared to you guys. I've done nothing with my life."

"You're a *New York Times* bestselling author, Kiera."

"So what?" I bark out another laugh. "That means nothing. I'm not running for office, or doing legal things like Bennett, or… whatever it is that Hayes does. I mean, Sofia writes smut like me, for sure. But she also writes literature. She's legit. And so is Camille."

He shakes from a silent laugh. "Camille isn't even published. She's not in your league."

"You don't even know her," I say. "In our dirty little world she's a very big deal. And people love her for many different reasons. And not all of them have to do with her books. She does good deeds and shit."

His guffaw echoes off my ceiling. "Camille?" He laughs again. "Camille DuPont? That Camille? Because I just want to make sure we're talking about the same girl."

"Yes," I say. "If you only knew. She's not who you think. Her secret life is quite altruistic."

"OK," he says, still chuckling. "I feel like I've entered an alternate universe now."

I flop back into the pillow and shrug. "Maybe you have."

"And Sofia? Is she some shining example of good deeds now too?"

"No," I say, unable to stop the smile. "She's still Sofia. But she was nominated for the Women's Opportunity Award in Literature six years ago. She's legit, ya know?"

"And yet you're telling me she writes smut on the side?"

"Is that weird?"

"Uh… yeah. I just can't picture Sofia writing that shit." He regrets his word choice immediately. I can tell, because he sighs. "I didn't mean it that way."

"Whatever. I'm good at it and it pays the bills."

He ponders this for a few moments.

"So that's why you feel inferior? Because this… *career* you have is more of a job than a life's work?"

"I never said I feel inferior. And I'm certainly not putting down my talent. I'm quite talented in my own sphere of influence. I'm just saying that what happened back in school wasn't because of me, that's all. In your sphere of influence I'm pretty much a nobody."

"I don't know." It comes out tired. "For some reason I think we're missing something. Some hidden knowledge that could explain all this bullshit."

"Look, it's really not that complicated. You guys—you, Bennett, Hayes, Sofia, Camille, and Louise, but before her, Emily—you guys come from families that matter, OK? You guys are the princes and princesses of Old Money America. This is not hard to understand. Whoever made us do all that shit did it to control you guys."

"OK," Con says, holding up a hand. "I get that. Hell, I even accept it. But there's more to it than that. There has to be, right?"

"Why can't it just be greed?" I huff. "I mean, greed accounts for almost every bad thing that ever happens in life. Whoever is pulling our strings, they want the power you guys represent. That's it. That's all there is to it."

"But why you?" I laugh. "And I don't mean that in a mean way, Kiera. I'm just saying, of all the people we went to school with, why did they choose you?"

"Who knows? They knew I come from a family of writers. And not just any writers, erotic writers. My grandmother wrote smut, for fuck's sake. And I'm pretty sure her mother wrote it too."

He turns to me, and this time he's the one propping himself up on an elbow. "Wait. What? What the fuck did you just say?"

"You didn't know that?"

"No. You come from a long line of female erotica writers? This is a real thing?"

"Yes, my grandmother was Nicole Baret. She wrote this weird urban legend, subculture book called *The Longing* back in the day."

"Where is this book?"

"I dunno. There used to be a copy in the attic up at the main house. I found it once when I was a teenager."

"And your mother? She knew about this book?"

"Knew about it? Hell, modeled her whole career on it. Did you ever hear of a book called *The Seduction of Sadie*?"

He smiles and flops back down into his pillow. "Get the fuck out of here."

"Yeah, that was her."

"Your mother? That woman with the apron who worked in the kitchen at school?"

"She only did that for special events. You know that. And only because she likes to bake sexy desserts."

"Oh, my God. My world has been upended." He laughs. Loud.

"Why?" I laugh with him.

"I mean, actually… I can picture your hot mom writing erotica, but holy shit. I'm so glad I didn't know this before now. I read that book. Like, us guys used to sit up in our rooms at boarding school and read parts of it out loud trying to make the girls horny."

"Did it work?" I ask, unable to hide my smile.

"Fuck, yeah, it worked. Trying to get a group of girls to look at porn was like pulling teeth. But read them passages from *The Seduction of Sadie…*" He stops to chuckle. "Fuck, yeah, it worked."

We lie there in thoughtful contemplation for a little while. I don't know what he's thinking about, but I'm busy picturing a fifteen-year-old Connor Arlington sitting up in a boarding-school dorm room, pulling out *The Seduction of Sadie* as his A-game.

"I wish I knew you back then."

"Why?" He laughs.

"Because. I'm jealous of those girls in your dorm room. You're the best read-alouder I've ever met."

He turns, slides one arm underneath me, wraps them both around me, and kisses me on the lips. "It was just practice," he whispers into our kiss. "For you."

I know it's bullshit. I know this is just Con's sweet-talk talking. But I don't care. "Better be careful," I say. "You're making my heart all melty."

He kisses me again. "Mission accomplished then."

"Shut up. If you didn't accidentally see that book at the airport you'd be back in New York waking up next to some other woman you've been reading aloud to instead of me."

He smiles into the next kiss. "You're wrong, Kiera Bonnaire. So. Fucking. Wrong."

His hand slides up to my breast, reminding me that I'm completely naked. And is it weird that I forgot? That I'm so comfortable with him after one night, with ten years of separation between us?

No. I don't think so.

I reach down between his legs and bring his cock to life. He growls approval into my mouth, kissing me a little more urgently. Harder.

I love him. I have always loved him. And I know this is never going to work out for us. I know there is no conceivable future where the US Senator marries an erotica author, but I don't care.

I'll take what I can get. And right now, this is all I got.

A loud banging on the front door make us pull apart. "What the fuck?" Connor says. "If that's the snow plow guy coming to deliver another secret message, I'm gonna be pissed."

He throws the covers off, jumps out of bed, and grabs his discarded blanket as he sweeps through the door and disappears.

I grab my comforter, wrap it around me, and peek my head out into the hallway just in time to see Connor throw the door open.

Hayes Fitzgerald barges past him in a rush. "Get your shit, we need to get back to New York. Now." His eyes meet mine from down the hall and he nods his head at me as I wander into the hallway. "Kiera," he says.

"Hayes," I say back.

"Get dressed. You're coming too. I've got a helicopter waiting. Bring enough clothes for a few days, at least. Maybe a week."

"What the fuck are you doing here?" Connor asks.

"The book," Hayes says, turning to face him. "Everyone's meeting at my place at noon. So let's get this show on the road."

Connor looks at me, questions written all over his face.

"It's cool," I say. "We should go. Besides, I'm due for a trip to the city." Hayes shoots me a look, but I just shrug at him. "What?"

"This is serious shit, Kiera."

"I wasn't joking," I say, narrowing my eyes at him.

"OK," Connor says. "Can we table the inevitable Hayes vs Kiera bout for later? Let's just get dressed." He takes my hand in what I can only assume is a possessive gesture and tugs me back down the hallway to the bedroom. "Better pack heavy," he says. "Just in case."

"Just in case what?"

He smiles at me. Leans in and kisses me. Whispers, "In case you want to stay longer after we sort out the bullshit."

He pulls away, glancing down the hallway to where Hayes is waiting, then heads the other direction to the laundry room.

I throw on a pair of leggings, because leggings are my life these days—so sad—and I'm just slipping another oversized sweater over my bare breasts when the reflection of Hayes comes up behind me. Our eyes meet in the mirror. "What?" I ask.

He just shakes his head and leaves.

CHAPTER NINE

To understand Hayes Fitzgerald you have to accept two things as true.

One, he does nothing half-ass and this helicopter is just another example of what Kiera was talking about.

I admit that reluctantly because I want her to be wrong. I want to think that status in high society has nothing to do with friendships and love, but in what reality does Kiera Bonnaire find herself the guest of honor in a twelve-million-dollar luxury helicopter?

An alternate one, was her point.

Not her actual one.

Except here we are. Sitting on butter-soft leather seats watching the local New York news on a pop-up console sitting between the seats across from us. Hayes, in one of those opposite seats, is switching between glaring at me and watching the screen that sits between Kiera and I. Yes, this helicopter has two pop-up TV's because everyone should get the chance to news out like crazy when they get the fast-lane ride in the city.

The second thing is that Hayes always has an end game. Even the smoked-up drunk-y version of Hayes always had an end game.

But here's the catch. You almost never know what that end game is because he's a sneaky fucker. He's one of those guys who looks at life as a challenge. Something to be studied from above and planned out with a purpose.

Bennett is sorta like Hayes in this respect because he likes puzzles. The difference between Hayes' end game and Bennett's puzzle-solving is this. Bennett is playing Tetris on his phone while he waits in line and Hayes is playing chess with champions on a global stage.

Both games require an ability to see ahead and make predictions, but you can't really strategize Tetris. It was built to entertain. Your screen is only so big and there's the added complication of all your failures compounding at the bottom of the screen.

Bennett is OK with that. He's playing against himself and mostly because he's bored.

Hayes isn't. He's playing to win.

So… who am I in this scenario? I'm the one who doesn't play at all.

Sad, I know. But I don't like games. I like truth. And I have come to realize that the whole world is filled with nothing but lies and illusions, so what's the point, really? Why bother with games of strategy when I can just watch these fuckers tire themselves out and sleep well at the end of the day?

I get it. I do. I realize this is not a great outlook.

But I have spent my whole life wanting nothing because I already had it. And sure, you could point to all my friends and associates and say, *Well, they had it too and yet they have managed to be ambitious.*

I am not them. I am just me. I am just… ambivalent to the whole thing. I have no purpose.

So that's why I'm gonna be a senator, I guess.

There's no risk. None at all. It's not my money paying for this shit, it's my father's. It doesn't even matter if I win or lose, there's gonna be another chance, right? I mean, I've lost several campaigns already and no one cares, not even me. I got the backers. I got the funds. I got the name.

So I'll just keep doing it because I got nothing better going.

It's busywork, I decide. My whole life has been nothing but busywork.

Except that year I spent as a Dirty One.

That year… it was fucking amazing.

Sure, Kiera got shot, Emily ended up in the nuthouse, and now our whole sick, sexy story is sitting on the *New York Times* bestseller list, but who cares? Connor felt energized, Connor felt needed, Connor felt complete.

I'm a pretty sick dude.

Inside the helicopter we're all wearing headsets, but there's no sound on the TV, so the silence is awkward. Especially since I can't really read Hayes at the moment.

I count him as a friend but that doesn't mean I get the guy, ya know? He's a complete enigma. His family isn't related to the famous Fitzgerald, at least that's what they say. Because the famous Fitzgerald family was pretty average as far as high-society thinkers go and God forbid anyone in our world be average.

Upper-middle-class working families, like Kiera's, I suppose, are legit on their own level, but she's right. We don't mingle. Mostly because there is not much occasion for it. I mean, maybe Kiera's mother made enough to pay for her Essex education outright, but sixty thousand dollars, give or take, is a lot of fucking money to most people. Even if she was well off, you don't easily give up that kind of cash every year unless you have so much of it, it barely matters.

Hayes, Bennett, Sofia, Emily, Louise, and Camille—we're all the same. They're all like me deep down. Maybe they really believe in their purpose, but I doubt it.

Only Kiera is different. She might be the only intriguing thing I've ever encountered in my short thirty years on this earth.

Hayes clears his throat so I look up at him. "So…" he says.

I glance over at Kiera, who is curled up in the giant leather seat, seemingly asleep with her head pressed against the window and her headset in her lap.

I look back to Hayes. "So what?"

"You two have a nice night stuck in the snow?"

"It was you, wasn't it?"

"I'm gonna need a little more clarification if you want a straight answer to that question."

"The snow plow. It was you."

He nods. "Figured I'd shatter the illusion and bring you two back to reality. Because we've got problems."

"So wait a minute, you and Kiera…?"

"Kiera and I… what?"

"You're *friends*?"

"Why wouldn't we be friends?"

"Well, you're Hayes, for one. You don't have friends."

"That's not true. I have you. Sofia. Bennett. Camille. I wouldn't call Louise a friend, but that's her choice. I tried, she just wasn't interested."

"Hold on. You're telling me that Kiera has been in your world this whole time?"

"Again," he says, sighing into the mic of his headset, "I don't know why that surprises you. We went through a lot together and we came out of it stronger. You don't just throw that away, Connor."

I just stare at him.

"You really didn't know we were all still in contact?"

I blink at him now. "Wait, *all* of you? And Kiera?"

"Of course. Sofia and Camille are her peers. They talk online regularly."

"Get the fuck out of here."

"You think," Hayes says, almost snarling the words, "that the world starts and stops when you enter and leave a room, don't you, Connor?"

"No," I say. "I'm just surprised that this is the first I've heard about it."

"Well, all the ladies, present company excluded, are living double lives. They don't just shout that shit from the rooftops."

"But you knew."

He shrugs. "I asked."

"How did I not know about this secret life stuff?'

Hayes actually laughs. "Come on, Senator. You know why."

"I'm not a senator."

"Yet. But then again, I guess that outcome depends on this outcome."

Yeah, I think to myself. *I think it does.* And as much as I was trying my best to include the others in my paranoia—looking for connections with Kiera's writing and then her family—this is about me. I'm sure of it. My puppetmasters published that book. They put it out there so I'd have a very clear picture of what my future looks like.

"Has Kiera ever ridden in this helicopter before?" I ask.

"Of course. I pick her up for lunch at least once a month and we… go places. Do things. See people."

I don't even know how to process that. "So she has a secret life too."

"It's not a secret, Connor. That's the point you seem to be missing. Just because you're oblivious to something doesn't make it nefarious."

"I didn't say nefarious. I just said—"

"I know what you said." He cuts me off. "And you're still missing the point."

"Which is what?"

"The world does not revolve around you."

I tune him out after that. And he must not object because he makes no more attempts at conversation. If that's what you call the exchange we had.

We land on his front lawn. Which probably needs clarification, because it's one of those long expanses of open space facing the water. And it's so far away from the mansion, there's a road and a car waiting when we get out, leaving our bags behind for other people to deal with, ducking our heads under the rotors while holding our coats tight against the freezing wind and salty mist blowing up from the crashing waves of Huntington Bay nearby.

The car ride is short, and no one says anything. If Kiera heard any of our conversation in the helicopter, she doesn't let on. Just gazes out the window as we make our way up to the massive, castle-like Fitzgerald family mansion.

Castle is a good descriptor. Because the imposing Gothic structure is all stone and comes complete with two flanking towers, gargoyles glaring down from tall, pointed-arch windows, a high-pitched, slanting roofline, and a massive twelve-foot door that makes you wonder if it's gonna come slamming down on your head, drawbridge style, when you approach.

The only thing he's missing is a moat, but perhaps that's in the works.

We enter single file for some reason, Hayes taking point, and then we discard our outerwear into the waiting hands of the slew of servants and look at Hayes for direction.

I don't care how important you think you are, when you enter this palatial mansion, you get a little overwhelmed. There are so many rooms I wouldn't have the slightest idea of where to go.

"Follow me," Hayes says, leading us to one of the nearby grand staircases. "Everyone's already here in the third-floor library."

The fact that he has to tack the 'third-floor' qualifier onto the word 'library' should tell you all you need to know about this place.

"Jesus, Hayes," Kiera says. "You should've told me we'd be taking a hike when we got here. I'd have brought a protein bar to snack on while I climbed the seventy billion steps up to your third floor."

He shoots her a good-natured grin over his shoulder and not for the first time since our little conversation, I wonder what kind of relationship they have.

Friends, she said.

Good friends, from the looks of it.

"Don't you have an elevator in this place?" I ask as we round the corner of the winding second-floor landing.

"Several," Hayes says. "But it would take longer to get to one than it would to just climb the stairs. The library is right at the top here."

Kiera and I are both breathing hard by the time we stop in front of the massive double doors. Hayes reaches for both door handles, then looks back at us, grinning, like we're in for a sweet surprise.

And I guess we are, because when he opens the doors the first person we see is Emily.

CHAPTER TEN

"Hi, Kiera," she says in one of those artificially sweetened voices. "It's nice to see you again."

"What the hell is she doing here?" I ask, whirling around to glare at Hayes.

"She's part of the game, isn't she?" Hayes says, glancing at Connor to see how he's taking it.

From the look on Con's face, I'd say… not well.

"I wanted to come," Emily says, reaching for me. I step back but she's a quick little bitch. Her long fingers wrap around my upper arm and grip tight.

It's not like I'm afraid of Emily, because I'm not. But for fuck's sake, the girl shot me ten years ago and has been locked away in a mental institution ever since.

Two large men dressed in white scrubs step forward and pry her fingers off me, pulling her back to a more socially acceptable distance.

"And she came with guards," Hayes adds the obvious.

"I wanted to say I was sorry," Emily continues. "I didn't think things through." She talks slow, enunciating each word like she's drugged and needs to think very hard about what she's saying. "I didn't think things through," she says again. "And—"

"I think that's enough for one day, don't you, Emily?" another man says, stepping forward. He is so obviously her doctor he doesn't bother introducing himself to Connor and me.

"No," Emily says in her thick voice. "I have a present."

"Jesus," I hear Sofia mutter.

That's the first time I notice that everyone is here except Louise. Camille is standing near the tall, pointed-arch windows at the far end of the library, holding a drink. Looking every bit the socialite she was born to be with her light blonde hair pinned up, long curling strands hanging down, artfully framing her sweet, heart-shaped face. She's wearing a winter white linen suit, with wide-legged pants and a tight, cropped jacket trimmed in lace that makes her look like an updated version of Daisy from *The Great Gatsby*.

She is backlit by the dull gray sky outside and Bennett is nearby, leaning up against the stone wall, looking uncharacteristically frazzled in his expensive suit as he runs his fingers through his hair.

"Can someone get her out of here?" Sofia says.

"No," Emily protests. "I came bearing gifts."

"Yes, Emily," her doctor says. "It's time to go now. You've seen all your friends and they have work to do."

"I'm part of their work," she says. "And I have a gift!" Her voice rises a little in building agitation.

Sofia crosses the room to stand next to me. She feels like power in her red dress. It's silk, I could see that even from a distance. And tight, accentuating her curves. She's wearing a tightly cinched, thin black belt textured like alligator skin, and lots of jewelry. A set of bracelets clink together musically on her wrists, and a diamond choker encircles her throat. "Get her out of here," Sofia says. "This is ridiculous. Kiera had no advance warning and it's not fair to ambush her this way."

It comes off protective and I shoot Sofia an appreciative glance. She sends me a tight smile back and then I'm unsure if she was protecting me, or herself. Because she seems a little un-Sofia-like in this moment.

"My present," Emily demands. "I must give her my present."

Bennett huffs from across the room. "Let me guess, it's another bullet."

"That's not funny," Camille says.

Bennett shoots me an apologetic shrug.

"It's time to go, Emily," Hayes says, stepping forward to take her arm. "But it was nice seeing you. And you can come back again."

"Again?" I ask, looking at Hayes like I just discovered he's a traitor. "She's been here before?"

"Later, Kiera," Hayes says, leading Emily towards the door.

"But my present," Emily is still protesting.

"You didn't bring a present," her doctor explains. "And it's time to rest now."

There's a small confrontation as the two—nurses? Guards? Whoever they are—reach for her arms when Hayes hands her off. Emily skirts away, running to the other side of the room, pressing her back against the wall.

I sigh. Because I feel like I'm caught in a movie or something. The mansion, the people, the crazy girl with her weird doctor and tall, male nurses who look like prison guards. It feels like we've all been written into a script and now we're each playing our parts.

Emily has her hands out in front of her, trying to ward off the inevitable capture, when a phone rings.

It's a very old-fashioned, loud bell of a ring. And when I look down I spy a black rotary phone on the small table next to me.

Everyone stops in this moment. Even Emily and her captors. We all just stare at the phone like this little plot twist is the whole point of the scene.

I reach for the handset, more out of desperation to make the unbearable ringing stop than anything else, and bring it to my ear. "Yes?"

Static on the other end.

"Hello?"

"It's an inside line," Hayes says, reaching for the phone. I hand it to him and he says, "What?"

I hear someone talking but I can't make out what's being said.

Everyone draws closer to the center of the room. Even Camille and Bennett. Until we're a circle of people surrounding Hayes.

"I see," says Hayes. "Yes, open it up first, then call me back." He hangs up.

"What was that about?" Connor asks.

"A package was just delivered."

We all look over at Emily, wondering if this is the promised gift she was so insistent about.

But she's gone.

CHAPTER ELEVEN

"Are you fucking kidding me right now?" I say. "Where the fuck did she go?"

"She won't get far," the doctor says, pointing at his two apes, then the door. Indicating they should go collect his patient.

"This house has like two hundred rooms," Sofia protests.

"Ninety-seven," Hayes corrects her, which makes Sofia huff.

"We'll find her," the doctor says. "Don't worry."

"Don't worry?" Sofia yells. "She tried to kill us ten years ago. That's the whole reason she was locked up in the first place!"

Hayes takes over, ushering the doctor out of the room after his guards, and whispers something the rest of us can't hear. Then he closes the double doors and twists a key in the lock with a loud click.

I look at Kiera, who is standing close to me, mouth open. Either appalled at the way this whole thing is playing out, or shocked that Hayes just locked us in. Hard to tell which.

"That's just great," Camille says, making herself a fresh drink over at the bar cart. "We're locked in a room while a murderous crazy person runs free through a mansion. Will Mrs. Peacock kill us with the candlestick in the library? Or the wrench in the billiard room? They're never going to find her. She could be anywhere."

"Forget her," Hayes says. "We have business to discuss. Camille, I'll take one of those as well. Anyone else need a drink before we get started?"

I glance at Camille, wondering how she's taking her new promotion to bar maid, but she doesn't seem to care because she's already lining up five more glasses on the bar cart and is muttering, "We'll need an entire police department to flush someone out of hiding in this ridiculous place," as she drops clear cubes of ice into each glass.

"Let's just all take a seat, shall we?" Hayes, ever the host, says as he pans his hands over the seating arrangement.

There's two couches facing each other, and two chairs acting like bookends on either side.

I take Kiera's arm and lead her to the closest couch. She sits, me next to her. Bennett takes the other couch, Sofia takes the chair to my left and Hayes settles in the chair on Kiera's right, reaching for the book we've all come to talk about.

Camille is holding a tray of drinks, passing them out like she's done this before, as Hayes opens the book and begins to read.

"'They told me to write what I know so that's what I did. I wrote dirty. I wrote erotic. I wrote the truth. And then they called me a liar. But it's not me who's lying. It's them.'"

He closes the book and places it back on the side table.

"We know that part," Camille says, now finished with her duties, and settles herself on the couch, very close to Bennett. She puts a hand on his knee and he looks at her, smiling.

Kiera and I exchange a glance, both of us asking the same silent question.

"So who was it?" Hayes asks. "Who wrote this?"

Everyone shakes their head simultaneously, muttering out denials.

"Kiera?" Hayes says.

"Come on," I say.

"It wasn't me," Kiera says. No hint of animosity because it's not necessary. It's very apparent that Hayes isn't accusing her, just asking out of obligation.

"Sofia?" he says next.

"Not me," she deadpans back.

"Don't bother asking me," Camille says, heading Hayes' next question off before he can ask it. And then she meets my eyes. Tilts her head up a little like she's trying to be superior and boost her confidence, since I seem to be the only one who has no details about her secret life. But it makes me frown a little. Because I didn't know about Sofia, either. But she didn't get all haughty about it. "I do write erotic novels," Camille adds. "And it's a good idea, so maybe I wish I had, but I didn't do it. I did not publish that book."

"Well, I sure as fuck didn't write it," Bennett says.

Then everyone is starting at me. "Get fucking real," I say. "Why would I sabotage my life with this bullshit?"

"That's not a denial," Hayes says.

"I didn't do it," I snap back.

Hayes sighs, takes a sip of his drink, and then says, "It wasn't me either. So that leaves us with…"

"Fucking Louise," Camille says.

"I was gonna say a mystery," Hayes clarifies.

"It has to be Louise," Sofia says. "She's the only one who didn't come."

"That doesn't mean anything," I say. "She was never really one of us. And has anyone even talked to her since school? Because I sure as fuck haven't."

We all look to Hayes, because Louise was his partner back then, but he shakes his head no. "I've tried. Many times, but she won't even take my calls, let alone see me when I've gone to her family estate."

"She still lives at home?" Sofia asks.

Hayes nods. "Yup. No apartment in the city. I've had people on her for years. She's a goddamned recluse."

The sound of running feet outside in the hall makes us all turn our heads to stare at the door.

"There she goes," Camille quips, laughing into her drink. I definitely get the impression that Camille started drinking somewhere around daybreak. Two more sets of running footsteps follow, this time pounding ones. "And there they go, chasing her."

"This is crazy," Kiera says. "How the fuck is this even happening?"

"Well, I call Miss Scarlett," Camille says. Then she smiles at Bennett and hums, "You can be Professor Plum."

"This isn't a game," I snap, shooting Camille a look. "And you need to stop drinking. The last thing we need is you stumbling around drunk."

"I don't take orders from you, Connor. Everyone knows Hayes is running this show and he doesn't care if I drink. Do you, Hayes?"

Hayes ignores her and picks the book back up. "We need to read this book and see what's in it."

"You didn't read it yet?" I ask.

"No. We should do this together. Besides, only Kiera knows everything that happened. The rest of us have no clue."

Camille snort-laughs at the unintended pun.

Hayes continues, still ignoring Camille. And it makes me wonder what kind of relationship the two of them have. Hayes was always in everyone's business back in school. More of a floater, like Kiera, I reluctantly admit, than a true partner. Because we all knew Louise refused to play along.

And then I have a sudden, hot flash of jealousy. Because Kiera was there for all of it. And if Louise wasn't playing along like she was supposed to, I have to wonder if Kiera picked up her slack.

When I look at Kiera, she's looking straight ahead, either lost in thought at all the things she witnessed—all the things she wrote down in our book—or just refusing to engage because we're all thinking the same thing about her and Hayes.

"Maybe it's just… fiction?" Sofia asks.

"Come on," Camille says. "That's wishful thinking and you know it. Give me the fucking book," she says, hand outstretched. "I'll start."

Clearly Hayes wants nothing to do with the reading of this book. Nor do any of the rest of us, because he hands the book over without comment.

Camille smiles at him, then her tongue playfully slips between her lips and lightly dances across the edge of her top teeth as she looks over at Bennett, before settling back into the couch cushions.

At least she's not still squeezing his leg.

Camille opens the book, flips the page, pausing on what I assume is the dedication.

"What?" Sofia asks. "What's it say?"

Camille takes a deep breath, then on the exhale says, "'The future belongs to those who believe in their dreams.'"

"Why do I know that quote?" Bennett asks.

"Eleanor Roosevelt," Sofia says.

"No." Camille snorts.

"Yes. That is a quote from—"

"I mean, no. He knows it because it was written in the first book too."

"Oh," Bennett says, playing with his phone like he already lost interest.

It's telling that none of us actually opened the fucking book in the last twenty-four hours to read the epitaph on the very first page. Almost as telling that we're going to allow Camille to be the one who delivers the story. Camille is no one's first choice for anything under normal circumstances. And it hits me then that I should not've been surprised to hear that Camille ended up as some do-gooder erotica author. She's always been a weird mixture of good and evil.

I guess the part that surprised me the most about what I've since learned about Camille is that she's successful.

Which maybe makes me an asshole, but I call it like I see it.

"Prologue," Camille says. "'I'm gonna warn you. Our story isn't for everyone. It's not even for us. So if you're looking for the fairytale and the stupid fucking prince on his dumb white horse, you've got a hold of the wrong book. Move along. This is not your story, this is not your life, and this is not your opportunity to dip your frightened little toe into the dark pool of water and "try new things" and then pull it out and decide… *#NotForMe*. When you go in with us you go all in. So make a decision before you turn this page. Because I'm making one promise with this book. Just one. It's the truth. We are the Dirty Ones and this is our story.'"

That's the part I read to Kiera last night. The back cover copy.

"Nope," Bennett suddenly says in Camille's pause. "Louise didn't write that."

There's a collective sigh in the room. Because it's true. No one who knows Louise even half as well as we don't, would ever imagine those words coming from her pen.

"Then who?" Kiera asks.

But we're all thinking the same thing again. We are nothing if not a collection of group thought.

Kiera.

That's Kiera's voice.

"It wasn't me, you guys. I swear to God, I didn't write this."

"Well, no, Kiera, that's not true at all," Bennett says. "You actually did write this. Maybe not this copy, but you were the writer back then. You wrote all of it."

I just look at Bennett like… *What the fuck, dude?*

He shrugs and says, "Hey, I'm just stating the obvious. Kiera was the one with the notebook and pen, OK? That's all I'm saying."

"I had to," Kiera says, defensive. "We all had to play our part."

"We're not accusing you," Sofia says.

I glance at Hayes, mentally telling him to stop this before it starts, but he's watching Kiera intently. Logging every reaction. Every expression. All her little tells. When he speaks he's not looking at Camille, he's looking at Kiera, even though his words aren't directed at her. "Keep going."

"Are we really going to read this whole fucking book out loud?" I ask before Camille can start again. "I mean, shit. How many pages is that? Four hundred? It'll take days."

"Then it takes days," Hayes says. "Because we need to know what's in here and we need Kiera to corroborate that it's real. She's the only one who—"

"Then let her read it," I say. "I'll take her home and—"

"No," Camille spits. "We need to sort this out together. No one leaves until that's done."

I glance at Hayes again. Because he's awfully accommodating to Camille today. And that's not normally part of his MO. He's always had an in-your-face attitude about being in charge of us.

"Keep going," Hayes says, shooting me a warning glance.

But just as Camille opens her mouth to speak, the phone rings again.

This time Hayes gets to it first, picking up the receiver from the nearby side table just as Kiera is reaching for it.

Why is she reaching for that phone?

"Yes," Hayes barks. Listens, as we all do, leaning forward like that's gonna help, which it doesn't. "Yes, OK. Bring it up then."

"What was that?" Sofia asks.

"The package was a notebook and a pen. There's a message inside."

I look at Kiera and find her pale.

Everyone is silent as we wait. Even Camille has lost her words.

Hayes gets up, walks over to the door, unlocks it, and steps outside to collect our gift.

CHAPTER TWLEVE

"It's not even true," I say, taking advantage of the pause.

"What's not true?" Connor asks.

"That I'm the only one who knows. You guys were all there too. You don't need to corroborate anything. Bennett and Camille know what happened to them. Sofia and you know what happened to you guys. Hayes knows what happened to him. I'm not the only one who knows this shit, OK? It's not true."

All of that comes out defensive. I get it. I look guilty as fuck right now. But I didn't write that book and I'm not going to let circumstance dictate how this all plays out.

"Why would I write this story? I'm already successful. I'm a *New York Times* bestseller, for fuck's sake. I make plenty of money and I have more stories in my head than I know what to do with. I didn't need this book!"

"Need has nothing to do with it," Bennett says.

"Dude," Connor interjects. "What the fuck are you doing?"

"I'm just saying. Whoever wrote this book didn't do it for money."

"No?" I spit. "Well, it sure as fuck made a lot of it so far. You don't get to number three on the *New York Times* by not selling books. And I'm telling you, I'm not poor. OK? Maybe next to you guys I appear poor, but I've got more money than I need. I didn't write this book."

"Who did you leave the book with when you left that last night?" Bennett asks.

"Ben," Connor says. "Come on, man. Let up a little."

"We all want to know," Camille adds. "And we all deserve to know too. It's our story as much as it was hers."

"Well," Hayes says, coming back in the room and locking us back in. "They didn't catch her yet, if anyone's wondering where the resident psycho is."

"Great," Sofia says.

"Candlestick in the library," Camille chortles. "I'm calling it now."

"Fuck her," I say. "Show us what's in the box."

We all look at the slim box Hayes is holding. He hands it to me and says, "It's for you, so go ahead and take a look."

"For me? What the hell?"

"It was Emily," Sofia says. "She planned this whole thing. The book, the visit, all of it. This just proves it."

I shoot Sofia a grateful look. Because it seems like only she and Connor are on my side right now. It's comforting to know we're still a team, I guess. Even though everything that comes with being teammates is about to be read aloud for everyone to hear.

"Open it," Camille says.

"We already know it's a fucking notebook," Connor says.

"There's a message," Camille retorts. "And I want to know what it is."

Hayes says, "Read it out loud, Kiera."

"Jesus Christ," I mutter. My fresh hell is just getting started.

The box is shiny and black, wrapped in gold ribbon. And it's tied in a way so that you can lift off the lid without pulling the bow apart.

Inside, predictably, is a notebook. It's softcover with a linen spine, filled with handmade papers. One that looks very much like a notebook I'd own. One that looks very much like the notebook I wrote our story in.

Blank, thank God. Because if this was our book I was gonna die. I'm holding out hope that *The Dirty Ones* that Camille is holding isn't our story at all. That it's just some weird coincidence. And this untouched notebook is a much-needed reprieve so I can pull myself together.

The small envelope inside is white and written on it is 'For Kiera' in fancy calligraphy.

I pull the card out and read. "'Time to start a new story.'"

"Great," Bennett says. "That's just fucking great."

"No," Sofia whispers. "No, I won't do this again." She stands up, takes a moment to collect herself by smoothing out a wrinkle in her dress, and heads for the door.

Hayes catches her by the arm before she makes it halfway, pulling her back to her chair. "Sit down, Sofia. No one is walking out yet."

"I'm not doing this, OK?" She looks around, holding a steady glare as she finds each of our faces. "I won't do it. So if we all have to go down because of me, that's how it's gonna happen. I refuse to do this again."

"Chill, bitch," Camille says as she sips her drink with one hand and flaps the book around with the other. "No one is playing games this time around. Whoever did this to us is gonna get their payback. That's why we're here, right?"

Is that why we're here? Is it really?

"We know it's Emily now," Connor says. "She's the one who had the gift delivered."

"Come on, Connor. Use your brain for once. How the hell would Emily get her hands on a gift like this? Let alone have it delivered?" Hayes asks.

"Her fucking family?" Connor says. "She does have one, you know."

"They disowned her years ago," Hayes says. "I've kept meticulous records of all her visits and no one has gone to see her in over five years."

"God, no wonder she's so crazy," Sofia mumbles.

We all think about Emily's past decade for a few moments. And I'm sorry she's been alone in that place this whole time, but she did shoot me, for fuck's sake.

I should not have to feel sympathy for the person who put a bullet through my shoulder.

"Let's just… calm down," Hayes says. "We have to know what this book is if we want to understand what it means.

"We know what it means," Camille says. "It's a fucking threat, that's what it is. The notebook just proves it."

"You never answered our question," Bennett says, looking at me. "What did you do with the book on the last day?"

"I left it in the tower," I say.

"You just left it there?" Bennett asks.

"I was following instructions, Bennett." I'm losing patience with him. "They told me—"

"Who told you?"

"The same fucking people who told you to show up when you did, Bennett."

"And you have no idea who they are?"

"Jesus Christ, Bennett," Connor says. "Would you stop already?"

"I just want to hear it again. And that question isn't just for Kiera. I want everyone to tell me if they know anything about who started this bullshit."

"I have no idea," I say.

"Me either," Connor adds.

Sofia and Camille both shake their heads no.

"Hayes?" Bennett asks.

"No. But I have ideas."

"Who?" Connor asks.

"Dr. Eldridge, for one."

"The president at Essex?" Camille snorts. "Well, a lot of good that does. He died three years ago. So he's definitely not responsible for what's happening now."

"No," Hays agrees. "But he could've been a part of something bigger."

"Like… a secret society?" Sofia asks.

"Exactly."

"This is ridiculous," Connor says.

"It would be," Camille says. "If it wasn't real. But it is, Connor. Bennett and I have talked about it a lot over the years and we think it's definitely got something to do with the college."

"And the alumni," Bennett adds.

For some reason this makes Connor look at me. "What?" I ask.

"Your mother went to Essex?"

"Yeah, so? Everyone in this room comes from an Essex legacy."

"And your grandmother too?"

"What are you getting at?"

"Did you guys know that Kiera comes from a long line of erotica authors?"

Pretty much everyone—including Hayes, who should know this because he's always been so up in everyone's business, but clearly doesn't—stops to stare at me.

"So what? I come from a long line of filthy writers. I refuse to be judged. Especially when Camille and Sofia both write the same shit I do!"

"We're not judging you, Kiera," Connor says.

"Sure feels like it," I say. "Because I seem to have a target on me. Again," I add.

"You weren't the target back then," Camille offers. "Connor was."

"OK," Hayes says. "This is pointless. Let's just read the book." He walks over to Camille, snatches the book out of her hand, and tosses it to Connor, who catches it out of instinct. "You read it, Con. You always were the storyteller."

"Hey!" Camille objects.

But Hayes shoots her a shut-up look that makes her cower back into the couch cushions.

"Fine," she huffs, closing her arms defiantly. "Whatever."

"Read it, Connor."

Connor looks at me, then settles back into the couch and opens the book.

CHAPTER THIRTEEN

We all knew there was a tower *in the woods next to Essex College even though no one actually saw it. Maybe it was just local lore, maybe there was some truth to it, but everyone had convinced themselves there was a tower and that rumor was passed down to the incoming freshmen every year.*

But all anyone really knew was that there was a fence on the south property line. A twelve-foot-high wrought-iron fence that maybe went all the way around the mythical tower, or maybe not. No one knew that either because the fence had been there for so long the underbrush and brambles kinda ran through it. The woods were unkempt and thick. Like something out of a nightmare. So you couldn't even get close to the fence to try to follow it to see where you might end up.

The other thing we knew before we became the Dirty Ones in senior year was that there was a gate in the fence on the south side of campus. It was even more impenetrable than the fence. Perhaps it really was electrified, perhaps not. No one I knew was ever brave enough to touch the damn thing because of the high-voltage warning sign.

Then there were the cameras. All over the place, but most notably right there on the gate. If you approached the gate and started fucking with it by poking a stick at the locking mechanism, a siren would bleep a few times. And if you didn't get your ass back where you came from in ten or fifteen seconds, it turned into a full-blown warning that sent even the wildest, most daring students running.

"Who cares?" Camille complains. "No one wants to hear this shit. We all know there's a tower and a gate. We've all heard the alarm. We don't need convincing. Just get to the good stuff, Con!"

"There is no good stuff," Sofia whispers.

"The sex, I mean."

"That's not good stuff," Sofia counters. She looks at me for just a moment, then averts her eyes to the wall of bookshelves off to her right.

I want to say something about her little comment, because it's not my fault we were forced to do those things. And she didn't fucking complain most weeks. Most of the time we actually did have fun. There *was* good stuff, and she can deny that all she wants, but I was there. She's not fooling me. So what if we made the most of a bad situation? That's what smart people do. So fuck her and that thinly veiled accusation. She was no more and no less a victim of what happened than anyone else.

"Whatever," Camille says, saving me from commenting. "No one wants to hear about the gate."

"Did you write this?" Bennett asks.

"Who?" I say.

Ben nods his head towards Kiera.

"No," Kiera says. "I didn't set the scene in the first chapter, for fuck's sake."

"Well, what did you write?" I ask.

She shrugs. "I described the tower. Two-story, made of stone, about fifty feet in diameter… stuff like that. But I never wrote anything like this opening."

"Because it's boring," Camille says.

"OK, let me skip ahead," I say. "Because there's like five more pages of description."

"Well, then we know I didn't write it." Camille laughs. "My characters start having sex on page three."

Sofia rolls her eyes, but no one comments.

Camille is good and drunk.

"OK," I say, and begin reading again.

The invitations were beautiful and it was exciting for several reasons.

One, we now knew there really was a tower.

Two, we'd been singled out from the entire senior class.

Three, we'd been given the combination for the lock to open the gate.

And, four, we were supposed to go there that night.

At least that's how I felt when I got mine. How the others felt, who knows. All I really know is that we all showed up at midnight.

Seven senior students.

We were given pseudonyms in the invitations. Miss and Mr, then our initials. So, for instance, I was Miss KB.

"Holy shit," Bennett says.

"Shut up," Hayes snaps. "Just hold your fucking comments."

There was Miss CD, Miss SA, Miss EE, Mr. BY, Mr. CA, and Mr. HF.

We didn't call each other that, but that's how I was instructed to write the story.

"This is bad," Bennett says. "And fuck you." He points to Hayes. "I don't take orders from you. This is fucking bad. She names the college. All people have to do is cross-reference every student in every senior class—"

"Calm the fuck down," Kiera says.

Which makes everyone kinda look at her. Because that's Hayes' line.

"It's two letters," Kiera continues. "There's got to be several people in each class with these initials. Essex College is over a hundred years old. No one will figure it out. And besides, it's a private institution. They're not gonna just hand over academic records. It's fine."

"Is that why you wrote it this way?" Sofia asks. "So you could justify it?"

"I didn't write it."

"Well, this book says otherwise," Bennett adds, joining Sofia's side. "This is very clearly Kiera's point of view."

Camille gets up and is halfway to the bar cart when Hayes snatches her by the wrist. "Sit down, Camille. You've had enough."

I expect Camille to start spitting venom, but she is oddly subdued and just turns back to take her seat next to Bennett.

"Should I keep going?" I ask. "Or have we heard enough?"

Kiera says, "I've heard enough," just as Hayes says, "Keep going."

I sigh and keep going, scanning the next few paragraphs, then turning the page. "It's just a bunch of stuff about how empty the place was and how she was excited."

"Skip that," Camille says. "Just get to the first real night."

"That was the night—"

"Shut up," Hayes tells Bennett, shooting him a warning look that says the next time he opens his mouth there's gonna be consequences. "Let him fucking read."

They were paired off. CA with SA—

"OK, just say our names, for fuck's sake. The initials are too confusing." Hayes again. I nod, exhale out a long, frustrated breath, and continue.

They were paired off. Connor with Sofia. Hayes with Emily. And Bennett with Camille. I didn't have a partner. I wasn't supposed to do anything but write down what happened each night in explicit detail.

There was no explanation for this and we spent the entire year wondering why it was set up this way. Everyone agreed it was going to be used to blackmail us at first. But by the end of the year, we were wavering on that.

But I'm getting ahead of myself. Because there was an incident that changed everything the very first night. I was charged with reading the instructions written in the letter waiting in the second floor of the tower and it is transcribed exactly below.

Congratulations, Dirty Ones. You have been selected to climb the tower. All those who make it to the top will be rewarded with success. Don't worry about failing. It's not an option.

All but one of you have been assigned a partner.

Those of you with a partner have been assigned one night per month.

On that night you will show up here, read the instructions left for you, complete the task, and then leave.

One of you will show up every night, with the partners, to record what happens. There is a present in the storage room just inside the entrance. Go get it now. Come back upstairs, and open it in front of the group. All further instructions will be inside the gift.

Sincerely,

Tower Keeper

So I went down to the storage room, found an exquisitely wrapped gift in black paper and gold ribbon, brought it back upstairs, and opened it up.

Inside was a notebook. About two inches thick. Canvas spine, lined pages inside, about three hundred of them. About the length of a novel.

Which is appropriate, because that's what I'd written by the end of the year. Every page was full, every character had an arc, every plot twist revealed… except one.

Why? Why did the Keeper make us do this?

But don't worry, dear readers. All the questions will be answered before you turn the last page.

Back in the tower that night Hayes took the book from me and read the first page out loud.

It was nothing more than assigned dates. Saturday night at midnight.

I spent one entire year of Saturdays up in that tower recording the actions of the partners.

This book is that book. This is our story and every bit of it is true.

But again, I get ahead of myself. There's more to this story than you think. There are more twists than you could ever imagine. There's more drama, and fear, and violence than you probably need.

But hear me, reader. And hear me well.

This is the truth of what really happened to us at Essex College in our senior year.

There was no furniture in the tower that first night. It was bare, and cold, and dark because there was no electricity. Just a few candles lit up in the center of the room. We were sitting cross-legged around them. Except Emily. She was pacing in circles around the perimeter of the room muttering to herself.

The rest of us were mostly still stunned that we were here, but also a little excited because this was a secret society. And we were in the midst of initiation.

Emily suddenly said, "No, thank you. I'm going to pass." And she left.

The rest of us sat there a little longer, discussing what this was. What we might get out of it, how it might be an honor to be invited in.

It's Skull and Bones, right? We play along, we get in, we meet new, interesting, powerful people, and we go on to ascend to positions of power and live fascinating lives.

No one gave another thought to Emily's sudden exit.

We thought we'd come on our assigned nights and there'd be others here to welcome us. To explain things. To tell us what this is.

We were wrong.

Hayes and Emily were the first assigned pair the following week. Emily didn't show. Apparently she was serious about passing on the opportunity. But I did and Hayes did. And there was a box in the middle of the room with three candles on top.

Hayes opened it up, took out the note, read it, passed it to me. And this is what it said.

Take the gun out of the box and shoot Emily with it. Then return the gun to the box and show up on your next assigned date. Tell no one what you did. Everything else will be handled.

"I'm not shooting Emily," Hayes said.

"Well, I'm not shooting her either," I countered.

"So we quit?"

I nodded. "I'm not sure what this is, but I don't think it's good."

"Agreed. So… we're out?"

I nodded again. "We're out."

"We should tell the others," Hayes said. "I mean, if they want to continue, fine. But they should know this is some crazy shit."

We left. We didn't even blow out the candles, just left.

And when we got back to the dorms, Emily was waiting for us.

I stop and close the book. "I don't want to read this part." And sure, it's a copout. Typical me, right? Take the easy road, refuse to engage, just go along and don't make waves.

But I don't want to read this book.

Everyone is silent. Not even an inappropriate joke out of Camille.

Hayes sighs, then says, "Look. We all know what happened, we just need to—"

"I don't," Sofia says. "I never understood that night."

"Well," Hayes says. Then he pauses. Thinks. Says, "She had a gun too, Sofia. Presumably it came in a box with a note that said something like, 'Kill Connor and you can be out.'"

"But why Connor?" Camille asks. She's sober now. At least, she looks sober. Like those few pages were enough to clear her flooded bloodstream of every drop of alcohol. "Why not you, Hayes?"

He shrugs. Starts to say something. Changes his mind. Starts to say something else. Changes his mind again. I feel like getting up, walking over to him, and shaking him by the shoulders. "I don't know," he finally says. "It's logical that Emily would be instructed to shoot me, as I was instructed to shoot her. But she went for Connor, instead. No one ever saw her note. We don't even know if that's how it happened. Maybe… we don't know anything."

"We could ask her," Camille says. "If we could find her."

All six of us turn to look at the locked library door. "Is she still out there?" I ask Hayes.

"Presumably," he says. "I'm sure someone would've called to let me know if they found her."

"I still don't get it," Sofia says. "Why you, Con?"

"Maybe she was after Hayes. He and I were rooming together, remember?" I say. "And Emily already had me cornered with the gun when Hayes and Kiera got to the room." I look at Kiera. "Why did you come back to our room?"

"I was afraid," she says, looking nervously between me and Hayes. "There's no way I was going back to my room alone. I didn't have a roommate, remember? The whole fucking thing freaked me out. And that walk back to campus, in those creepy-ass woods…"

"I told her to stay with me," Hayes says. "She was shaking so bad she couldn't even talk."

"Emily was talking incessantly when we entered," Kiera says. "Like weird shit. Do you know what she was saying, Connor?"

I shake my head. "It was incoherent. Something about 'not for me.' 'Not me.' Or some shit like that. And then you guys came in and she pointed the gun at both of you."

"And told us to get over by Connor. She wasn't playing games," Kiera continues. "And at the time, I figured she was talking about the note and the box, and the gun. That game. But... thinking back on it now, I think she was talking about something else."

"Like what?" Bennett asks. He's been mostly silent since Hayes told him to shut up.

"I think she knew," Camille says. "I think she knew what that place was when she got there and that's why she was pacing around the room."

"And she was always crazy," I say. "I saw her on move-in day, walking around campus talking to herself."

"Maybe she knew she'd be asked to join?" Sofia asks.

"Because someone told her?" Kiera adds.

Everyone looks at me for the answer to that, but I have no clue. So I just shrug.

"Anyway," Kiera says. "Hayes and I moved over by Connor and she was muttering something about being sorry, but she had to do it. She had to get out. And then she pulled the trigger, but she missed us and hit the wall. Then she aimed again and I jumped in front of Connor and took the bullet in the shoulder.

"And then," Kiera continues, "after the police left the next day and hauled her off to jail, you came up to me and said, 'Make sure you go on Saturday. Because if you don't you'll be next.'"

"I didn't want anyone else to get hurt," I say.

"And that's when the suggestion box showed up," Camille adds. "So… fuck it. I was scared. And we had to…" She glances over at Bennett. "We had to do our *task* on the cold, hard floor. So fuck it. If I was stuck in this stupid game, that was the last time I was going to do anything on the floor. So I asked for a couch."

[illegible]

didn't want anyone to get hurt, and

and finally, when the [illegible]

[illegible]

[illegible]

on the cold, hard floor [illegible]

[illegible]

[illegible] the floor [illegible]

CHAPTER FOURTEEN

***Task.*.** It's a small, four-letter word that is almost never used in a sexual way.

Except when one of us says it.

I hate that word. I've never written it in any of my books. Ever. Never uttered it out loud after my last night up in the tower. I hate it.

But here it is again.

Task.

Sofia gets up from her chair and sits down next to Camille, pulling her into a hug. Camille wilts like a too-hot flower, and allows herself to be embraced. They huddle together, entwined arms and crossed legs. One of them sniffles. Sofia pets Camille's hair. Camille rests her head against Sofia's shoulder, sighs deeply, then closes her eyes.

And not for the first time I feel jealous for who they are to each other. I picture them in New York City, in their separate but nearby penthouse apartments. How they probably bump into each other at the corner market or coffee shop. How they brunch on Mondays the way most people do on Sundays because they are writers. Authors.

And authors do things like that. They have weird quirks, and live in bustling places where a story is born on every block, and collect other strange writer friends who relate to them.

They complain about word count together. They bitch about plot holes, and commiserate over characters they loved but now hate, and sigh over missed opportunities after publication.

It's true I speak to them, but rarely on the phone and never in person. We bump into each other on Facebook a few times a week, but that's just typing. Writing is what we do.

I don't ever go to the city and meet up with them. It's just too much bustle for me. I like my little cottage. I wish they all lived close by. Even Bennett. I'd even put up with Bennett at Monday brunch.

But they couldn't get out of Essex fast enough. I left before graduation, but my home was a forty-five-minute ferry ride across the lake. Hell, I can see the damn school from my back yard and I bet, if I climbed up on my roof, I could see the tower.

I wonder if they think I'm weird for staying?

I lived in the main house for several years. And then I started fixing up the cottage, and my mother got sick, and… yeah.

Now I'm alone.

"They sent me a note," Bennett says, breaking the spell of quiet.

"Who?" Hayes asks.

Bennett shrugs with his hands. His eyes catch mine, then pass over and rest on Connor. "Whoever."

"What kind of note?" Camille asks.

"It was instructions about what to do if I wanted to get out. Like Emily and you guys." He juts his chin first to me, then at Hayes.

"They told you to shoot me?"

"No," Bennett says. But it comes like a moan. "No. They told me to rape you."

I think the room gasps. Not us. We make no sound at all. But the room exhales something in the shockwave of Bennett's revelation. Something leaves in that moment. Any leftover childhood innocence, perhaps. Any hope that this might all make sense one day is just… gone.

I look at Camille, picturing her in a new way. Picturing her first as the girl who asked for a couch because all she wanted was to get up off the cold floor, and then as the girl who almost became Bennett's go-free card, but didn't.

No wonder she was drunk when we got here.

We should all be drunk. We should all be a mess, like Emily. We should all be locked up in the fucking nuthouse after what happened to us.

But we aren't, are we?

We are all successful, thriving, happy—as far as I can tell.

Just like they promised we would be.

Camille untangles herself from Sofia and re-tangles herself with Bennett. "You were so nice that night."

He was, I realize, thinking back. Because I was there. I saw the whole thing. Was forced to write it all down in the book as it happened. He was slow, and never raised his voice above a whisper. It took all night to finish their task. All night lying on that cold, hard floor to convince Camille that they had to do this.

And me, my shoulder aching from the surgery I'd had just one week earlier. High on painkillers, sitting on the cold stone floor, leaning against the jagged stone wall, trying to balance the notebook on one bent leg because I couldn't use my left hand. Scribbling…

Bennett draws in a deep, deep breath and when he lets it out he says, "I wanted there to be no misinterpretation. I wanted you to feel loved. I wanted to make sure you felt… I don't know. Not good, because I know you didn't feel good. You were scared to death. But I wanted you to know that I was being careful. Not for them, either. Not so they'd know my answer. But for you. Because if you were my partner in this nightmare, then fuck them. We were getting out together or not at all."

Bennett's place in my friend hierarchy just jumped about ten thousand levels at this admission.

"Sofia and I were up next," Connor says, glancing at her. She offers him a small smile.

So by this time the room had a couch. I asked for a chair and blankets because I was cold too. I didn't want to sit on that floor any more than Camille wanted to fuck on it. I think Bennett asked for the bed—or maybe that was just thrown in with my chair. Either way, by the time Sofia and Connor came to the tower it was partially furnished.

Camille definitely had it the worst, I decide.

Well, that's not true. I did get *shot* my first time out.

"I got a note as well," Sofia says in her soft, almost whisper-like voice.

"Shit," Connor says, raking his fingers through his hair. They lock eyes for a few seconds and everyone can feel Connor's fear over what that note said.

"It wasn't about you," Sofia admits.

"No? Who then?"

Her gaze shifts to me. She sighs. "They told me to make you…"

I wait for it, but she doesn't finish. "Make me what?"

She swallows, closes her eyes, shakes her head.

"Sofia, spit it out," Hayes says. "What did it say?"

"They told me to make Kiera join us."

I furrow my brows. "And what did you get out of that? They were gonna let you go? Because…" I pause to look over at Hayes for some reason. I don't know why, exactly. But I don't want him to know what happened between Sofia, and Connor, and me.

Too late now, that little voice in my head sneers. *It's all written in the book.*

Right.

"Because," I continue, "I did join in and you guys still had to show up every month for your night."

I don't look at Hayes. I deliberately ignore him.

Sofia is still shaking her head. "No, it wasn't a get-out deal. It was a let-you-live deal."

I look at Connor, but he's looking at Sofia. "What?" he says.

"Don't you get it? They were going to kill her. And I really thought they would, Con. I did." Her eyes meet mine again. "I'm not saying those things I said to you were fake, Kiera. I want you to know that. I mean, I didn't really know you that first night, so maybe some of them were lies. But…"

She doesn't finish.

Everyone goes silent again. We are stuck in some bizarre alternate reality. One where everything we thought was true isn't. One where the one thing we all thought we had in common wasn't even real.

Fake.

Everything about that year was fake.

I stand up.

"Where are you going?" Connor asks, grabbing my wrist.

But I yank it away and walk over to the windows.

"Kiera," Hayes says.

But I just shake my head and say, "I thought that was real. I thought I took one thing away from that horrible fucking year. I thought we were real."

"We were real," Sofia says.

"Fuck you," I say, looking out at the trees and the houses that are, in reality, so close to this stupid mansion, but also worlds away.

"I had to. I thought they were gonna kill you. And you were still recovering from a fucking gunshot, Kiera. What else could I do?"

I spin around, angry. "You could've told me. I would've been fine if I knew. But you kept the lie going. You built on it, for fuck's sake. You told me you loved me, Sofia. And so did you," I say, snapping my attention to Connor. "And I believed you both."

"Kiera," Connor says. "Everything I ever said to you was real. I didn't know Sofia was faking it."

"I wasn't faking it," Sofia says, her voice uncharacteristically loud and harsh. "Not at the end."

"Jesus Christ," Bennett says. "Hold on here. You guys were having a threesome? The entire year?"

"Who wrote in the book?" Camille asks.

God, I can't believe that just a few minutes ago I felt sorry for her. "I did," I say, practically growling out the words.

"I want to read that," Camille says, getting up and snatching the book off the couch next to Connor.

Hayes intercepts her. Snatches the book from her hands, and points his finger at her. "Don't be an asshole, Camille. I'm warning you now."

She laughs. "Oh, we both know you're going to read those chapters, Hayes. You've always had a thing for Kiera. I bet it stings, doesn't it? Knowing she was with them the entire time."

"That's enough," Connor says, who is standing now, leaning into both their faces. "I'm the reader, remember?" He takes the book from Hayes and sits back down on the couch.

Camille smirks at me from across the room, does this little dance-y wiggle thing with her body—like a shrug, but sassier—then says, "I can't wait to hear Connor narrate his part in all this," and takes her seat next to Bennett.

"I think we should take a break and have dinner," Hayes says, walking over to the phone and picking it up.

"Oh," Camille cackles. "I bet you do need a break."

Hayes ignores her, just tells whoever is at the other end of that line to bring dinner up and send up servants to set the table.

"We're eating in here?" I ask.

There is a table, but it's meant for looking over books, not dining.

"Emily is still out there in the house somewhere. So unless you want her to join us unexpectedly, yes. We're eating in here."

"Is there a menu?" Camille asks.

Hayes glares at her, but doesn't answer.

"I'd like to use the restroom," Sofia says. "Can you point me to it?"

"Any of those doors lead to a suite," Hayes says, pointing around the room at four doors, two on either side of the library. "But use these two by the windows. Because the other ones have doors that lead out into the hallway and they're locked from this side. I don't want anyone taking unnecessary risks with Emily."

Sofia shrugs, then walks over to the door I'm closest to, shoots me a look, and then disappears inside.

She wants me to follow her.

My first reaction is to shake my head in disbelief, but then… ya know what? Fine. Let's do this. Let's clear the air.

She leaves the door to the suite open after she enters, but I slam it closed behind me. She walks over to what I presume to be the bathroom and turns, looking at me from across the large, four-poster canopy bed. God, this room is pretentious.

"It wasn't all lies. That closeness, that… whatever it was—"

"Whatever it was?" I ask, unable to believe she just said that. Then I huff out a laugh.

"You know what I'm talking about, OK? I'm just having trouble finding the right words."

"Trouble finding words?" I laugh again. "You're a fucking award-winning writer, Sofia. And you write some of the dirtiest erotica I've ever read on the side. You're not having trouble finding words. You've having trouble thinking up *lies*."

"You can believe that if you want, but that's not how I feel. We were more than friends back then. My feelings for you and Connor were real. And most of them haven't changed."

"We weren't friends," I say. "We were never friends because we never had anything between us but a *deal*."

"That's not true," she says. "We talk to each other all the time."

"Online," I spit.

"So what? It's still a friendship. You live five hours away, Kiera. It's not that easy to plan a Saturday night with someone in another state. And anyway, you're happy up there in your little world."

"Oh, you did not just—"

"You've never said a word about coming to visit me. You never asked me to come visit you. Friendship goes both ways, so if you're feeling left out you might want to ask yourself what part you played in your own sad demise."

"There's the words," I say. "Found 'em, I guess. Better write all this down so you can use it in your next book."

"What?" She huffs. "What are you talking about?"

"I know you don't read my books, but I read yours. And I've noticed over the years you quote me quite often."

"I don't see how I can quote you if I don't read you. And so what? You're butt-hurt because I don't read you? I'm not into reading erotica."

"No, you're just into quoting me in conversation."

"I don't know—"

"Don't insult me, Sofia. Like I said, I read your books. I know I'm your main character every single time."

"Oh, my God." She laughs, swiping hair away from her forehead. "For someone who wants to be left alone up in your stupid woods so you can shun society, you sure do have an inflated sense of self-importance when it comes to your influence over other people."

"Is that right?" I glare at her. "You wrote this book, didn't you?"

"Fuck you! I didn't write that book. How would I even know what happened—"

"Obviously," I cut her off, "you have the original book."

"You're the only one who ever saw that fucking book, Kiera."

I give her one of those tight-lipped smiles. "You and I both know that's not true. You always made Connor read our previous chapter out loud each week."

She sighs and looks over her shoulder, wondering if anyone heard that. "What do you want?"

"You're the one who wanted me to follow you in here. I should be asking you that question."

"Fine," she huffs. "I use you, OK? Is that what you want to hear? Feel good now? I model all my stupid female leads after you."

"Why? Why do you do it?"

"You're interesting, OK? I think you're interesting."

"No, why do you write erotica at all? It makes no sense."

"It's therapeutic for me. That's why I do it."

"Liar," I say. "Such a liar. You write it because it sells. You wrote all that women's lit bullshit hoping people would 'get you' and when no one bought it, the awards weren't enough to fill up your giant ego and you got depressed. You're no different than any other writer in that respect. So you figure, hey, I'll write some erotica and then people will see my words, and gush on me in reviews, and I'll feel good about myself again. And you do use my words! I find them in every single book!"

"Because you're part of me, Kiera. And I'm part of you. I don't steal your words, I just borrow parts of *you* when it's appropriate."

"Because you've always wanted to be me," I snap. "You hate your stupid princess life, you hate that you never married, you hate that you had to share Connor in the tower—"

"Why are you being such a bitch? I'm standing here telling you my feelings were real. You're just looking for reasons to hurt me."

"Because... because... you hurt me first!"

We stare at each other for a few seconds and then we both laugh.

"You stupid whore," Sofia says. "I'm sorry, OK? Stop being an Emily."

I laugh again, even though it's not appropriate.

"When you didn't come for graduation I figured it was over. And..." She sighs. "That kinda hurt me, Kiera. You never said goodbye."

"Because I wasn't leaving *you*, dumbass. I was leaving Essex."

"Well, you failed. OK? Because you did leave me and you live right across the goddamned lake from Essex. And I wish you lived in New York. Do you think that Camille and I just... what? Got over what happened and moved on? No. We miss you every week. Not a week goes by that we don't sigh and say, 'I wish Kiera was here with us.'"

"Now I know you're lying." But I say that softly. And it comes out sad. "Because maybe you do miss me, but Camille—"

"Camille does miss you. We both miss you. We think you stay away because you hate us. And you only talk to us online so we'll help you market your books."

I gasp. "Fuck you! I don't care if you guys push my books! I just don't like the city, OK? It makes me nervous.

That place isn't my home. Like it or not, where I live is where I belong. I can't help that."

We both sigh with frustration. Then, after a few awkward, silent seconds, Sofia says, "It's not..."

But she stops and I get impatient. "It's not what?"

"I just... wouldn't know what to do with you alone."

"What do you mean?"

"Without Connor. I'm... not into you that way, Kiera. So... OK. Maybe I've been avoiding you in real life because I didn't want to have this conversation. I liked what we had. It was fun. And no matter what you believe now, I know I saved your life by following instructions and inviting you in. So when you got him all to yourself that last night I was so fucking jealous. Because I never got him without you. Even that one time we did get together without you, it was written in the book. It was dictated for us. You're the only one who got something that wasn't dictated!"

"Oh," I say, taken aback.

"And it always seems like you had it both ways. All the time. You were in the tower with us, but in a different way. You were at the same school and away from home, but one stupid ferry ride and you could be with your mother. You could be home, if you wanted to. And I couldn't, I was stuck there. I was jealous of you. How you got to be inside and outside in the same moment and I... I don't know. I was always miserable that year. Except for the time in the tower with you guys. So that last night when you and Connor were together... I was alone. And I was mad, OK? I was. So I've probably carried that with me all these years and I'm sorry."

"Everything OK in here?"

We both turn to see Connor standing in the doorway. He steps inside, closes the door behind him, and sighs.

"How much did you hear?" Sofia asks.

"All of it," Connor says, looking at me, then back at Sofia. "I think everyone just heard all of it. They're like twenty feet away and the two of you are yelling."

"Great," I say.

"I guess we should… talk about this?" Connor asks. "Because I don't want to have any kind of miscommunication. Kiera and I were together last night, Sofia. I want to be with her and give it another try."

I don't even know where to begin deciphering that declaration. He loves me? He wants to date me? He wants to fuck me on the side?

What is he talking about?

Sofia crosses her arms, nods her head, and presses her lips together like she's trying to hold something in. But then she huffs and says, "Well I don't want any miscommunication either. I don't want you *now*, Connor Arlington. I wanted you *then*. I'm not some sad woman pining over a long-ago relationship like some badly-written heroine, OK?"

Connor stares at her for a moment. Then he laughs. "Uh… OK. My mistake. I guess."

"So why are we even arguing?" I ask. "This is dumb."

"I'm sure you do think it's dumb," Sofia says. "Because you're the star of the show. I'm just someone he had to let tag along. And I thought we had something. And we didn't. But I thought… I thought we had *something* between us. Like I do with Hayes. I thought—"

"Hayes?" both Connor and I say at the same time.

"Yes," Sofia says. "I mean… I don't know what I mean. I'm so fucking confused right now. I have all these leftover feelings about you two. And him. And I don't know anything any more. None of this makes any sense. Not one bit. Not that year, not that book, not my relationships…"

Connor sighs. "It makes sense, Sofia. It does. It's just… complicated. But we all know what we mean to each other and that's all that counts."

"Well, I don't," I say. "I don't understand anything about any of you." Then I look at Sofia. "Hayes? Really? Because—"

"Connor loves us both, Kiera. But if he has to choose just one, he's going to choose you. And hey," she says, looking up. She's crying for real now. A tear runs down her cheek. "I'd choose him over you, that's what I was trying to say before. I like you, but he was all I ever wanted up in the tower. So what he just told me isn't any different than what I just told you."

There is so much silence in this room right now. The whole world must be one giant cacophony of loud because this room has sucked all the silence in.

God, how did life get so fucked up in the span of one day? I don't understand it. Why now? After ten years, why this day?

Why not that first year after we left? When everything was still fresh in our minds? Why not just keep it going if whoever did this wanted control? It makes no sense. Because we all left school, went on our way, and managed to even stay friends. I don't talk to Bennett or Connor much, and no one talks to Louise at all, but we came out of it pretty OK, considering. Sofia and Camille and I are still friends online. Hayes and I are probably what you'd call *good* friends. Which is why I don't completely understand what Sofia is trying to say about him right now.

And that makes me feel guilty because I don't like Hayes that way. At least I never thought I did. But I sure have spent a lot of time with him. Especially these past few years since my mother died.

Suddenly my feelings are all messed up.

I don't know anything. Nothing is what it seemed. These last ten years have just been one long lie.

No. Many long lies. And it makes me wonder how we can even look at each other now. After the things we did that year.

But we can. And there's friendship there. And maybe even love. Maybe I do love Connor? Maybe I've always loved Connor? I don't know, but if we've made it this far and we don't hate each other then… then… we won that game in the tower.

So I say that. "We won, you know."

Connor is walking over to Sofia now. He sits on the bed next to her and takes her hand in his.

"What are you talking about?" Sofia sniffles.

I walk over to the other side of the bed and look at them. I love them both, in different ways. I guess that's still the same. "Our… situation?" I say, for lack of a better word. "Up in that tower. It was a love triangle. They set us up to fight, ya know. To hate each other. But that's not what happened. We didn't fight. We had a good time. So we won."

"I guess that's what I love about you," Sofia says.

"What? What do you mean?"

"Underneath all that I-hate-everyone bullshit, you really are an optimist. Because we're not fine. We're so far from fine, it's sad. Someone wrote a book about us, you guys. We're in those pages."

"We haven't even gotten to our part yet," Connor says. "We don't know—"

"We do," Sofia snaps, pulling her hand out of Connor's. "They had the part about Emily. It's our initials. This is our book, just told a different way. It's like… creative non-fiction or some shit. True, but some events and names have been changed to protect the innocent."

"Innocent." Connor actually laughs. "None of us are innocent. What we did at all the parties that year—"

"Just… no," I interrupt. "I don't want to talk about that."

"It's gonna be in the book." Sofia sniffles. "Everyone's gonna know. Hell"—she fakes a laugh—"everyone already knows. That stupid book has probably sold thirty or forty thousand copies already. What's the point of even being here?" She looks at Connor, then at me. "There is no clever plan, no crazy scheme that will fix this, you guys. They're gonna find out who we are and what we did, and all our lives will be ruined. Why did I even bother using a pen name for my erotica when my real name now has this story attached to it? Everything is fucked up and—"

Connor places two fingers on her lips to make her stop. "Shhh," he says, putting his arm around her and pulling her into a sideways hug.

Sofia turns into him, kisses him on the lips. Connor just sits there, unsure, I think. But that hesitation only last a second or two. Because when the three of us are alone in a room… we know exactly what to do.

And that's exactly what he does right now.

He kisses her back.

CHAPTER FIFTEEN

I don't know why I do it.

That's a lie. I do it because I like it. I like her. I don't want to spend my life with her, but Kiera and I in a bedroom with Sofia only ends one way.

I pull back from Sofia, placing my hand on her cheek as I look over my shoulder at Kiera, who is standing on the other side of the bed.

She licks her lips, meeting my gaze. Then swallows.

"Come here," I whisper, patting the bed. "Come sit next to me."

She hesitates. Breathes in deep like she needs courage. And then, instead of walking around the bed, she climbs up on it, crawls on all fours across its width, and sits on her knees, wedged in between Sofia and I.

Sofia looks up at Kiera, reaching for her breast. Their eyes lock as Sofia makes contact. Her palm cupping first, then lifting her breast up as Sofia turns to get better access.

I should stop her. I should stop this. I know she's only doing it to make me happy. To make me want her.

But the problem is, it's working.

"Kiera," I say. "You don't—"

"Shhh," she says, breaking eye contact with Sofia just long enough to hush me. Then she picks Sofia's hand off her breast and places it over my cock, making her squeeze me through my pants.

Fuck. I am so fucked.

I close my eyes for a moment, and in that moment Sofia swings her leg over mine and sits in my lap.

"Kiera," I say.

"Shut up," she says. "Shut up and play along. What's it gonna hurt now? Nothing. It's not gonna hurt anyone."

But us, I don't add. We're the ones who are gonna get hurt. We're the ones hurting ourselves now. Playing this game is dangerous. In so many ways. Things are gonna come out tonight and…

"Just one more time," Sofia says, placing both her hands flat on my face. And when I open my eyes again, she's staring down at me. "One last time, Connor. And we can all move on, OK?" She hums out the words against my lips, kissing me at the same time.

Kiera, still behind me, reaches around my upper body and loosens my tie until the knot falls apart and she pulls it through my collar with that soft whoosh of friction on fabric. Sofia continues kissing me, one hand lifting up her dress and slipping between her legs, the other working the buckle on my belt.

Kiera is unbuttoning my shirt. Her face pressed into the side of my neck. Her mouth right next to my ear, whispering something dirty about Sofia's pussy.

God, I've missed them. Thirty seconds in and I'm rock hard and ready to fucking blow.

This is why, I think to myself. This is why we went to the tower each month that year. And this is why, two months in, we didn't need the tower anymore. We fucked everywhere. In our rooms. In classrooms. The library, hallways, the women's locker rooms, the pool, the chapel, and my parents' house. That night of their anniversary party.

We had no right. No right to feel the way we did that year. And I still carry that guilt with me ten years later.

Sofia has my pants open and she's pulling out my cock. Pressing it up against the soft silk covering her belly, rubbing it back and forth.

"Stop," I say. "I'm gonna—"

"Shhh," Kiera hushes me again. "Just one last time." She echoes Sofia's earlier plea as she kisses my neck, pressing her breasts up against my back as Sofia lifts her hips up, knees pressing deep into the mattress, and positions herself over my tip.

I moan when she lowers herself down and the tight lips of her pussy hug the tip of my cock. I slide in easily. She's so ready and slick.

And then Kiera, still with her tantalizing mouth up against my ear, is whispering just like she used to. Whispering the words she'll write down later in the book.

"What the fuck are we—"

But Sofia is kissing my protests away before I can finish. And Kiera is dictating, "She's so wet for him. And he's ready for her too. His cock thick and engorged with blood as he slides up inside her pussy."

I don't think I can take it. And it's not fair. Because they know the two of them together make me powerless.

I grab Sofia's hips and rock her back and forth in my lap. Trying to find the spot that drives her wild. She's panting hard now, breathing into our kiss as I begin to rock her harder. Thrusting her forward and back, my cock so deep inside her she squeaks out a small cry of pain.

"She feels him," Kiera says. "In her belly. Because he's deep inside. Deep enough to touch her soul." Her words pure sex.

Sofia's knees grip my hips as she breaks away from our kiss and throws her head back, exposing her throat.

Kiera picks up my hand and places it there, pressing against her neck. My thumb finds that shallow dip in the top of her breastbone and my fingers squeeze into her soft flesh.

"His claim of ownership fills her up—"

Sofia is moaning. Too loud. Because Hayes, and Camille, and Bennett are on the other side of the door and now they're gonna know.

She goes still, stiff. And I know she's close when she holds in her breath, like she's trying to hold in her climax, and then the explosion of pleasure comes out as a whimpering whine as she bites her lip.

I kiss her so she doesn't draw blood and leave a telltale mark of what we're doing. I kiss her hard as Kiera continues to narrate, and just before I come, Kiera pushes Sofia off me with a show of force, takes my cock in her hand, cupping her palm over my slick, wet tip covered in Sofia's come, and captures me.

"Fuck," I whisper, trying to be quiet. Always trying to be quiet because everything we did was a secret. "Fuck," I say again. Because Kiera is massaging my semen up and down the shaft of my cock.

I am there again. In that place. In our dorm rooms. In the hallways, and the classrooms, and my parent's house that night of the party…

A hard knock at the door jolts me out of the past.

"One second," Sofia calls, voice throaty and sexy with lust.

"Jesus Christ," Camille says from the other side of the door. She tries the doorknob, but it just jiggles back and forth because I locked it on my way in.

I knew.

There is no escape from the past.

"Come on," Camille yells. "We're fucking hungry."

Sofia has a towel from the bathroom and she delicately and slowly cleans herself, then cleans me too.

What am I doing?

Kiera is buttoning up my shirt, whispering, "They like the danger. They like the idea of getting caught, and when they don't—"

I laugh.

"When they don't, it just makes them want to try harder."

Sofia disappears into the bathroom, and by the time Kiera has knotted my tie around my neck, she emerges, smiling that smile as Kiera slips past her, fingertips trailing along the red silk covering her belly, and disappears into the bathroom to clean up.

I just stare at Sofia, enjoying her smile. No, I don't love her. Don't long for her, don't dream secret dreams about her. But—

Kiera emerges and says, "Go," pointing to the bathroom. "Clean up and we'll meet you out in the library."

I get up and walk forward, leaning in to kiss Kiera. Taking my time as I do it. Placing my hand across her soft cheek.

"Go," she whispers into our kiss.

Kiera closes the door and then I listen as they let Camille in.

"Fucking perverts," Camille says loudly. "So tacky, Sofia."

And then I hear Kiera's fading response as she leaves the room. "Fuck you, Camille."

I smile as I splash cold water on my face, watching in the mirror as I grab for a hand towel and dry off.

"What are you doing?" I ask the reflection.

But the only answer I have is… "What I'm supposed to."

It's a weird response. I think I realize that. But it's all I've got.

I finger-comb my hair, which is messed up from Kiera's wandering hands, and straighten my tie.

Satisfied, I pull the door open and step back into the bedroom.

"I hope it was worth it," Hayes says.

He's sitting in a chair just off to my right.

"Jesus Christ, Hayes. What are you doing?"

He's sitting casually, one ankle propped up on one knee, head tilted to the side, eyeing me cautiously. "Probably a question you should be asking yourself, don't you think?"

"It's none of your business."

"Not yet," Hayes says. "But it will be soon."

"What the fuck is that supposed to mean?"

"Just wait," he says, getting to his feet. "Come on. Dinner's ready downstairs."

"I thought we were eating here?"

"Camille protested. So we're going to the dining room."

"Did they catch Emily?"

"No. They're bringing in dogs."

"That's fucking ridiculous."

"Well." He shrugs. "Ninety-seven rooms, Connor. What choice do we have? She could be hiding anywhere. It'll take days. Believe me, I pulled this trick millions of times as a kid."

I picture Hayes as a small, trouble-making boy, playing a solo game of hide-and-seek with his… parents? No. That almost makes me laugh. His nanny. And the other servants. Hell, he probably had the entire kitchen staff looking for him too.

A mini-manhunt for wild, little Hayes.

Yes. That's something that definitely happened.

"It's cruel what you're doing," Hayes says, hand pausing on the doorknob.

"What are you talking about?"

"Kiera. Leading her on like this. I heard you, ya know. We all heard what you said to her."

"I'm not leading her on."

"She's not yours, Con."

I laugh. "She kinda is, dude. Always has been."

"No," Hayes says. "I mean, she's not your future. Sofia has always been your future. Or someone like her. Do you really think they're gonna let you settle down with a middle-class woman who writes erotica?" Hayes laughs. Too loud. "You can't really believe that."

"Who?" I ask. "My parents? They want me to find love. All parents want that. And I think I love her."

"This has nothing to do with love, Connor. You know that. This is business. This is politics. This is your family name."

"They're not gonna care—"

"Why do you think we're all here? So we can just… fall back into old habits?"

"We're here because you made us come."

"The book, Connor. This is all about you."

"Fuck off, man. This is about all of us. Except Kiera. She's just an innocent bystander caught up in something bigger than she realizes."

"God, you're stupid."

I push his hand off the doorknob and open the door myself.

Everyone is looking somewhere else. Camille stares into the drink she's holding. Bennett at his phone. Sofia is studying artwork on the wall and Kiera is pulling a book out of a shelf, her back to me.

"Ready?" Hayes says, following me out of the bedroom.

"How long do we have to stay here?" Bennett asks. "I have plans tonight."

"With who?" Camille snaps. She is definitely drunk. I thought for a second, earlier while she was talking, she might be sobering up, but I was wrong. She's going to drink her way into unconsciousness, hoping she wakes up tomorrow morning with no memory of any of it.

"My father," Bennett says. "I can't cancel."

"You can and you will," Hayes says, unlocking the library doors and throwing them open. "Let's go. And stay together, for fuck's sake. If ever there was a time to use the buddy system, this is it. The last thing we need is one of us going missing."

There's a nervous moment where we all look at each other without actually looking at each other, then—like I can almost feel this sense of... *forgetting*—we drop it.

We're good at that, I realize.

We line up like kids. And it's funny, kinda. Because we were all kids together. Except Kiera. But the rest of us went to the same schools all growing up. I think Sofia and

Bennett came to all of my first seven birthday parties. Hayes was there on and off. Camille was shuttled off to Paris from age six through twelve, so I didn't see her much. Louise was never one of us. Still isn't. But Emily was. She was with us in upper boarding school. I didn't know her well, but looking back I probably could've predicted her situation. Something was never quite right about that girl.

Going down the wide, stone steps, I am reminded how pretentious this house is. I mean, yeah. We all—except Kiera—came up in a pretentious mansion. But this place feels like a fucking palace. Ninety-seven rooms. I just can't even imagine it. My family estate is big. I've never counted the rooms but there's definitely no more than forty. Fifty absolute tops. And that includes all the little rooms.

Hell, the room count in this house could just be suites, for all I know.

Down at the bottom of the steps there's a group of doctors and nurses conversing quietly. Presumably about Emily's unknown whereabouts.

How do they even know she's still inside? I mean, how many doors does this place have?

"Where do you think she is?" Sofia asks me as we pass the search team and follow Hayes through a wide room that is still technically the foyer, but I know from first-hand experience that they've held balls in this hall.

"Probably a thousand miles away by now."

"God, I hope so."

We're all silent after that. Just the sound of footfalls across the polished marble floors as we follow Hayes into a wide hallway that leads to the south wing where the actual ballroom, kitchens, and formal dining hall are located.

"Where are we going?" Bennett asks. "Do we really need to eat in the dining room? It's stupid."

It is stupid. We all know this. Because the table seats twenty-six people.

Which means when we finally get there, there's six place settings at the far end and the rest of the long wooden monstrosity is bare.

"Wow, Hayes," Camille chortles as she crunches ice from her now empty glass and picks up a little white card with a name written on it in scripted calligraphy. "Seating arrangements? Really?"

"It's just how the staff does dinner, Camille. And you're the one who insisted on eating down here."

"I'm tired of being cooped up in that stupid library. You have a bazillion square feet in this place and we're stuck in three thousand of them. It's not fair."

Kiera is next to me now. "Do you think she's just… clueless? Or does she say that shit on purpose?"

I smile at Kiera. She makes me happy and even though this whole book thing sucks and will suck even harder in the coming weeks when the full intention of this development becomes clear, I'm glad I went to her house yesterday. I'm glad we've reconnected. And I don't care what Hayes says, we can be together. It's taken me a while to see that, but now that I have I'm not gonna let her go again.

"Definitely a little of both," I say, answering her question.

"OK," Camille says. "I need to make a revision. Miss Peacock, in the dining room, with the revolver." Then she cackles a drunk laugh as everyone stops to stare at her. "What? That's funny."

"Not really," Kiera says, unconsciously rubbing her shoulder where the bullet went through.

I take Kiera's hand, then shift my feet when I notice Sofia watching us.

Maybe… fucking around with them both upstairs was a mistake after all.

My problem—and theirs too, if they feel like being honest—is that I lose all sense of control when the two of them are alone with me in a room. And I have to wonder, did they condition me to feel this way? Or did I do that to myself?

I've heard friends talk about cheating. How a woman they barely know can supersede the one they know so well. Can overtake their thoughts and consume them from the inside out. Take away everything they thought they ever wanted and replace it with divorce papers, and custody battles, and failure.

And they don't care. They can't stop. This woman, these women, they eat them up and spit them out.

Lust, I guess. It's just lust.

But that's not what this is. It isn't like that. It wasn't like that. Sofia and I were forced into a situation that required we work together. And by work together, I mean fuck.

Kiera was just… there. Watching. Writing down what we did. So when Sofia wanted to invite her in… hell, it was just hot. That's all. That's the only explanation I have for it. Having her in the room with us was hot. Even Sofia got into it.

"Please," Hayes says. "Take your seats."

"Can I get another Scotch and water?" Camille asks one of the servers as we all take our assigned seats. Hayes is at the head, Kiera on his right, me on his left. Then Sofia and Bennett on my side of the table and Camille next to Kiera.

"How about we hold the Scotch? Hmmm?" Hayes tells the server nearest Camille, who turns her head to glare at Hayes with contempt.

"Good idea," Bennett says from the end. Then, "Hayes, why do you have to sit way up there and make this all uneven? I feel left out down here by myself."

I can see his point. So does Hayes. But he's not giving up the head of the table. Not in his own house. This is his little plan, after all. He wants us to know he's in control.

"We should've brought the book," Camille says, pursing her lips. "Have a little trot down memory lane and get it all out in the open."

"We don't need the book," Hayes says. "We have Kiera."

I look at her, and she's looking at me. "I don't want to continue the conversation over dinner," Kiera responds. "We can pick it up later."

"No," Hayes says. "We don't have time. We need to come up with a plan and to do that we need to know what happened. How about I start?"

"Hayes," Kiera says.

But he puts up a hand to stop her. "Relax, Kiera. There's no judgement here. Right, Connor?"

Something is happening, I'm just not sure what. Something between the two of them.

"Yeah, let's hear it, Kiera," Sofia says. "What happened when Hayes and Louise came up to the tower?"

Kiera repositions the napkin in her lap, looking down at her empty place setting.

"Of course," Hayes says. "We have all been reminded that Emily took herself out of the game, but of course our… what did they call themselves in that first communication?"

"Associates," Camille whispers.

"That's right," Hayes laughs. "Associates."

"What are you doing?" I ask, suddenly pissed.

"Whatever do you mean?" Hayes replies.

"This fucking act you're doing. What is this? Did you plan this shit? Was it you?"

"Are you afraid of something?"

"No, asshole. I'm wondering why the five of us feel sick inside and you're sitting at the head of the goddamned table acting like you're one of them. Like this was all your doing. Are you like… getting off on this?"

"You're the only one getting off tonight," Hayes says, deadpan. "Oh, not true. Kiera and Sofia both got off with you."

Camille snort-laughs into her glass of ice water.

I look across the table at Kiera. "Is there a reason he's acting this way?"

"Why are you asking me? He's sitting six inches away from you, ask him."

"Yes," Hayes says. "There is a reason. And if you'd let me finish, I'd get to the point a lot quicker than if you keep trying to put off hearing the inevitable."

"Which is?"

But just as Hayes opens his mouth to speak, we look up to see six servers walking down the long dining room holding covered plates. Kiera, as the guest of honor on Hayes' right, is served first. If she's aware that her position at the table has meaning, it doesn't appear to bother her. The silver dome is lifted off to reveal a bowl of consommé.

"Would you like a bit of shaved white truffle, madam?" the server politely asks Kiera.

And for some reason I imagine her declining the fine delicacy. But she surprises me and says, "Yes, thank you," in an equally quiet voice.

This night is full of surprises.

I watch her as the server shaves off three slices, gently dropping them on to the top of her soup.

Kiera smiles and politely says, "Thank you," when the server backs away to stand behind her.

My dish is placed in front of me, and that's when Camille says, "Hey, where are my truffles?"

It's only then I notice Kiera was singled out for this privilege.

I look at Hayes, who nods to the server behind Kiera, and she dutifully slices off three small shavings of the aromatic fungus for Camille.

No one else asks. Bennett is already lifting his spoon of broth to his mouth. Sofia is still looking down at her place setting, ignoring everyone. And Hayes is motioning for Kiera's server to pour her a glass of wine.

"I hope I get wine," Camille says.

"Would you just shut up, Camille?" I say. "You're making a fool of yourself."

"Fuck off, Connor. I want wine. Why is Kiera the guest of honor here, anyway? I don't get it."

"Someone has to sit there," Bennett says, matter-of-factly. "Should we just leave the chair empty to make you feel better about yourself?"

I can't see Bennett because he's on the other side of Sofia, but just what the fuck? I mean, yeah, we all know Camille is difficult, but he's supposed to be in her corner tonight. That's how this works.

I catch myself in that archaic assumption leftover from college and take a deep breath.

Amazing how easily we slip back into buddy system mode.

"Fuck you too, Bennett," Camille retorts, holding her wine glass up to be filled. Hayes must OK this, because she gets her wish. But she's lost her shine, if she ever had it today. And I know Bennett's curt response to her objection hurts her more than she'll ever admit.

"Shall we toast?" Hayes says, lifting up his wine glass.

"To what?" I ask.

"To us, of course," Hayes says. "It's nice to be back together, don't you think?"

"No," Sofia says, leaning back in her chair and crossing her arms. "I'd actually like to go home now."

"Got what you came for, Sof?" Bennett asks, still spooning his broth into his mouth.

"Jesus Christ," I say. "What are we doing? We're supposed to be on the same fucking side here."

"We are," Hayes says. "And no, Sofia. You may not be excused. We have many things to discuss tonight."

Sofia sighs, her broth untouched as the servers swoop in and begin clearing away the dish. Only Bennett ate his consommé. And Kiera's white truffles are still gently floating on top of her broth. What is the point of a multi-course meal again?

Oh, yeah. That's right. It's a pretense, like everything else in this world we live in.

"OK, now that we're all in the mood. Let's move on," Hayes says. "We left off at Louise, didn't we?"

He directs that question to Kiera, who looks at me from across the table with downcast eyes. She doesn't answer him.

"Louise showed up at the tower—well, why don't you tell it, Kiera? You were the one who met her first."

Kiera isn't looking at me. Something is going on between these two. And I know what it is. I just want to hear from her, not him.

"Kiera," I say. "You can tell me anything."

I want to reach for her hand. Give her support. Comfort her.

But I can't for reasons I know—and have always known.

Hayes has deliberately separated us.

She opens her mouth to speak, but it's Hayes who talks…

CHAPTER SIXTEEN

"We killed someone that night."

"What?" Camille actually spits her wine across the table.

"Camille, goddamn it!" Sofia protests, wiping drops of wine spit from her cheek.

"Sorry… what?" Bennett asks. "Did you just say—"

"We killed someone that night," Hayes repeats.

"What the fuck are you talking about?" Connor asks.

I glance at Connor, but then quickly look away and take a deep, deep breath.

"Kiera?" Hayes asks. "Do you want me to tell it? I know it's hard for you."

I shoot Hayes a look that hopefully says, *What the fuck are you doing?* But he either doesn't understand my glare or he chooses to ignore me, because he says…

"Louise came to the tower…"

And then the story begins and I'm the one telling it.

Louise came to the tower. Hayes and I were already there, sitting upstairs in the partially furnished room. On the couch, I remember that much. So close to each other our legs were touching.

"So, how's this work?" Hayes asks. "You write shit down in that book and then what?"

"I leave it behind when I'm done."

"And they come take it?"

I shrug. "I guess. Someone does something with it. Because each week there's a new chapter heading."

"Can I see it?" he asks, reaching for the book in my hand.

"No." I clutch my notebook in one hand and push his hand away with the other, scooting farther down the couch so we're not so close. "I'm not allowed to show anyone."

"Or what?"

"Or maybe I'll get shot again, Hayes. And this time it won't be in the shoulder. I'm not fucking playing around with you, OK? Not when I already got hurt. I just want to do my part and get through this fucking school year. So back the fuck off."

He puts his hands up in surrender. "Chill, killer."

"Did I miss anything?"

We both turn to look behind us where a girl is standing.

"Who the hell are you?" I ask.

She smiles at me. Indulgently. Like I'm a small child she needs to be patient with. Then directs her gaze to Hayes.

"Hayes," she says. Like she knows him.

"You wanna tell us why you're here?" he asks.

"Same reason you are, I suppose." She says it like she's bored. Oblivious to what's been happening to us these past several weeks. "I'm glad you're not hurt, Kiera."

I squint my eyes at her. "I am hurt," I say. "Emily Medici fucking shot me last month. Or maybe you didn't hear?"

"I heard," she says. Her voice is harsh and matches her sharp face. Her hair is blonde and stylish. One of those cuts that has no personality built in, it needs to be added daily. Her curls are defined. Not tight ringlets, but soft and wavy. Like someone from those old, glamorous days. Back when women wore dressing gowns to bed and

fast-talked into princess phones that lived on vanity tables in large mansion bedroom suites.

Her clothes are old-fashioned as well. Some might call them classic, but it's not a look I've ever aspired to. A subdued mint-green swing dress made of chiffon with pleats in the skirt and an off-white belt. I have a hard time picturing her walking through the woods in the heels on her feet. Same color as the belt. She's carrying a little matching purse, for fuck's sake.

What does she think is happening here tonight? Some grand party?

"But you're OK now," she adds. And it's not a question. I'm OK now, is what she's saying.

I want to protest and say, No. I'm abso-fucking-lutely not OK.

But I am OK. I'm alive. My shoulder is healing. I've even stopped taking the painkillers to get through the night.

"So listen," Louise says, walking around the couch to take a seat in the chair off to the right of Hayes. "And don't ask a lot of questions because we don't have much time."

"What are you talking about?" Hayes asks.

"I know it's hard for you to take orders, Hayes. But we really don't have time. There is a man in the bottom floor of the tower and we need to take care of him."

"What?" I ask, standing up and looking at the doorway that leads downstairs. "Where? I didn't see anyone down there."

"Please," Louise says. "There is no time for a Q and A, Kiera. He's in the basement and in about five minutes he's going to leave. So we need to catch him on his way out." She pulls a pair of tennis shoes out of her purse, toes off her heels, and slips her feet into them. "I hope the woods aren't too muddy."

It occurs to me then, looking down at my own filthy shoes, then at Hayes'… she didn't get here through the woods.

Her new footwear now adjusted, she stands and sighs. "If you want any chance of escape, you'll just do what I say. Because I'm warning you now, if we take a stand they will ruin our lives. All of us. Camille, Bennett, Connor, Sofia. Us." Hayes opens his mouth but Louise puts up a hand. "Later, Hayes. I promise I'll tell you what I can once it's done."

"Once what's done?"

"Once we kill him."

"What the fuck are you talking about?" Connor growls.

"We killed him," I say. "We followed her downstairs to the first floor and she… opened this little hatch in the floor. And then we went down to the basement and there was a fight. He had a gun. But he wasn't ready for us. So we fought him," I say. "And killed him."

Camille laughs. She needs to stop drinking.

Bennett stands up, walks over to Hayes, and says, "Give me some cash. Now."

Apparently this makes perfect sense to Hayes, because he takes out his wallet, looks through it for a second, then places a hundred-dollar bill on the dining room table. "Sorry," Hayes says. "I know it's supposed to be a symbolic dollar, but I only have hundreds."

"Everyone, give me some cash. Right now," Bennett says. "Then I'm your lawyer and I can't legally say anything about what I hear next."

We just stare at each other like a bunch of dumbstruck idiots.

"Here," Hayes says, pulling out four more hundred-dollar bills. "This should cover everyone."

Bennett picks up the cash, pockets it, and then returns to the table, this time taking the empty seat next to Camille. He reaches for his wine glass, gulps it down and sighs, "OK, keep going."

Servers appear with our next course, but Hayes waves them away with one hand. "Later," he says. "Leave and don't come back."

And then, before I realize what I'm doing, I resume the story.

"What will we do with the body?" I ask Louise.

"Bury it, of course. We certainly can't leave it here. That will definitely send the wrong message."

"What the fuck—"

But Hayes interrupts me. "Kiera," he says. "Just... go along."

"Is this normal to you two? Because killing someone and burying a body isn't my typical Saturday night."

"No," Louise says. "Your typical Saturday night is coercing people into sexual acts and then writing them down in a book for some unseen group of people to take possession of."

"Fuck. You," I say. "You have no idea what's been going on this past month."

"Quite the contrary, Kiera. I'm the only who knows what's going on here. Unless you count Emily, but I don't. Since she's locked up in a mental hospital for shooting you. Which, I should not need to remind you, but will anyway, she was ordered to do by the people running this little scheme. So shut up and grab his feet. Hayes, you get the arms. I'll get the door."

And then she doesn't go to the door we came through, but another one on the far side of the room. Almost hidden behind a rack of gowns, of all things.

"There was a tunnel," Hayes says in the here and now. "Right, Kiera?"

I just stare at him for a second, trying to recall the details. This part seems very fuzzy in my head, but… "Yes," I say. "I remember it now. There was a tunnel."

"So we took him out the tunnel and came up in a cemetery," Hayes says.

"Very convenient," Camille chortles.

"Wasn't it?" Hayes says, smiling. "Almost like it was planned that way."

Camille's laughter stops abruptly. She reaches for the bottle of wine, but Bennett puts his hand on hers and whispers something I can't hear.

This seems to calm her, because she lets go of the wine and places her hands in her lap.

"This makes no fucking sense," Connor says.

"That's because you never got the whole story, Con," Hayes says. Cordially, I note. "Kiera and I were the only ones who sorta understood what was happening that year. Louise is the only one who knows everything. Unless you count Emily, but I don't. Because after what she did, no one would believe her."

"Which was the whole point," Bennett surmises.

"Correct," Hayes agrees.

"I'm sorry," Sofia says in her small, soft voice. "It still makes no sense to me now."

I sigh, so tired. I feel like I've been locked in this mansion for years instead of hours. "Essex is an exclusive club, Sofia. One only the world's best and brightest can attend."

"So how did you get there?" Camille asks.

It's a legitimate question, so I don't take offense. I don't even think she was trying to be mean. It's just… pertinent.

"My mother went there. And my grandmother."

"Oh, shit," Connor says, snapping his fingers and looking at me from across the table. "Did you guys know who Kiera's mother was?"

Hayes sighs. And then he's holding my hand under the table.

"Who?" Sofia asks.

"She wrote *The Seduction of Sadie*," Connor says.

Hayes is staring at me.

"What?" I say. Irritably. "It slipped out this morning."

"What else does he know?" Hayes asks, letting go of my hand, his cordial demeanor gone now.

"You knew?" Connor says.

"Well, I didn't know," Camille says. "But I know that book."

"And her grandmother—what was her name? Noelle?"

"Nicole," I say. "Nicole Baret. She wrote an erotic book too. Called *The Longing*. Also published. In the Fifties or Sixties." I wave my hand in the air. "I don't really remember."

"Erotica," Bennett guffaws. "You come from a long line of erotica writers?" His laughter echoes in the large room, bouncing off the ceiling in an eerie way. "Please tell me this isn't really about *books*. Because that's just… stupid."

"Anyway"—I sigh—"that's how I got in. Apparently, my grandmother filled out a legacy scholarship application for all her female descendants. My mother had nothing to do with it."

I say this last part specifically to Hayes. He gives me one of those looks that says, *Keep telling yourself that.*

"So this is about you," Sofia says, her soft voice hard now. "You did this?"

"She didn't do anything," Hayes says. "No more than you or I."

"I didn't do shit," Sofia spits. "I just showed up at school."

"That's all Kiera did as well, Sofia. Now stop it. We can't turn on each other. Not now. Everything depends on how well we can stick together from this point on. They're counting on us being divided. That's how it always worked in the past."

"In the past?" Bennett says.

But Hayes ignores him. "Look, there's a lot more going on here than you guys realize. But all you really need to know is that all this tracks back to Connor."

"Me?" Connor asks.

"Yes," Hayes says. "It makes the most sense. But we really need to get in touch with Louise to make sure. She's the one who knows things."

"Or Emily," I say. "Who is right here in this house and doesn't refuse to talk to us."

"Sneaky little bitch," Camille says. And for a moment I think she's talking about me. "Emily!" she screams. "Get your fucking ass out here now or I'm gonna hunt you down like Professor Plum and kill you in the dining room with the goddamned candlestick!"

Bennett guffaws again. "God, I love you sometimes, Cammie."

"Cammie?" Sofia and I say together.

Camille does one of those shrugs that come with a sideways turn of the head and a covert smile. "I like the sound of it."

Sofia and I roll our eyes simultaneously.

"Speaking of Clue," Camille says. "Who asked for the games? Up in the tower?" She looks across the table at Sofia. "Remember the games? Trouble. Parcheesi. Checkers. Who the fuck was playing checkers up in the stupid tower?"

I force myself not to look at Hayes.

"We were," Hayes says. "That's what Louise asked for in the suggestion box after… that night."

"She asked for board games?" Connor says. Then he looks at me. "That's what you guys did up there all year while the rest of us were fulfilling some freaks' sexual fantasies?"

"Yes," I say.

But at the same time Hayes says, "No."

I glare at him.

"Well, which is it?" Sofia asks. "Yes or no?"

"Both," we say, this time in sync.

There is silence around the table at this point. Everyone but Hayes and me is trying to put those two answers together in a way that makes sense.

"Is anyone still hungry?" Hayes asks. "Because I for one am not. Should we go back upstairs and—"

"I'm going home," Camille says, standing up and throwing her napkin on the table. "You need to leave anyway, right, Bennett?"

"I do, man," he says apologetically to Hayes. "I have an appointment with my father tonight. I really can't stay."

"Sofia," Camille says. "If you don't want to be alone tonight, you can stay with me."

We all look at Sofia.

"No," she says, her quiet voice back. "No. I'm going to stay here tonight."

"Are you staying?" Connor asks me.

"Yes."

"I think this is a bad idea, Bennett," Hayes says. "You should cancel on your father and stay here with us. We should all stay together. Buddy system, remember?"

"I'll bring Camille with me," he says, looking at her. "We'll buddy up, OK?"

Camille nods her head, forcing a smile. "We'll keep the candlestick close."

"I don't like it," Connor says.

"Con, you know my father," Bennett says. "You know I can't cancel."

"Do you think he knows what's happening?" Sofia asks.

I lean to the side so I can see Bennett better and catch him in a shrug. "I dunno, you guys. I can't imagine he knows what we've been through. Aside from Kiera, that is." He leans to the side so he can see me now. "The shooting, I mean."

I nod. "I get it."

"We should meet up tomorrow," Bennett says. "Maybe in the city."

"We'll see," Hayes says, not committing. Then he stands and says, "OK. Let's walk them out together."

I know what Camille wants to say. Something like, *We don't need your help to get to the car.* Or, *Back off, I'm not helpless.* But she holds it all in. Because we've been there. We all know how quickly things can change.

We make our way back through the house to the grand foyer. There are cops here now and we hear the familiar sound of radio-speak as we get closer to the entrance. There's a group of doctors and a K-9 dog walking briskly across the marbled floor, nose busy sniffing, as the officer follows down a hallway and out of sight.

"Any luck?" Hayes asks the doctor, who's talking to someone in a suit who appears to be in charge of the psycho hunt.

"She's been all over this place," the one in charge says. "They get a scent and then she… disappears into a wall. Mr. Fitzgerald, you don't happen to have secret passageways in this place, do you?"

"Don't be ridiculous," Hayes laughs, patting the man on the shoulder like that is some fantastic joke. "No, I'm sorry. But she is a very clever girl so I'm not surprised she's giving you the slip." Then he pauses. "Do you think she's still here? Inside, I mean. Or do you, perhaps, think she has vacated the premises?"

"Do you have an alarm on the doors and windows?"

"Of course," Hayes says.

"And did it go off?"

"No, but some of it isn't armed at the moment," Hayes replies.

The detective—I think this suit guy is a detective—says, "That's… typical? That you leave yourself so open and exposed?"

"Well, no." Hayes frowns. "But I had guests coming today. So the main part of the house—this center wing right here—is unarmed. All the separate wings are armed at all times because we rarely go in there."

The detective looks up at the ceiling where an elaborate crystal chandelier hangs. I look up too, unable to stop myself. But every time I'm in one of these mansions and I look up at a chandelier I imagine it falling from the ceiling and killing me.

Not that I'm in these mansions a lot lately. But I've been to everyone's family estate for events. Except Louise's.

That anniversary party for Connor's parents. All those lavender balloons and butterflies.

A birthday party for Sofia's great-grandmother. Four generations of wealthy Astors together in one room to celebrate the matriarch who started it all.

Bennett's younger brother's high-school graduation. A wild, extravagant rave complete with an in-person appearance of that rapper everyone loved back then. The glow-in-the-dark jewelry.

Camille's family Christmas. String quartet in the corner playing traditional carols and a hundred thousand dollars worth of champagne flowing through a fountain.

And of course, I've been here to Hayes' place many times. Not just for parties.

I stop imagining all the different times I could've been killed by a chandelier and focus on another K-9, sniffing its way across the lobby. Maybe it's the same one backtracking. Maybe not. It's just better than imagining myself being crushed to death by grotesque opulence.

"Ready?" Connor asks, snapping me out of my introspection.

I realize Hayes and Sofia are looking at me expectantly and Camille and Bennett have already left. "Sorry, drifted off there for a second. Yeah, let's go."

We follow Hayes up the stairs to the third-floor library, passing by several people still searching for Emily.

"It's kinda ridiculous, don't you think? That she's loose in this house and we're staying the night here?"

"No more or less ridiculous than anything else that's happening today," Sofia mutters, out of breath as we hike up the last flight of stairs to the third floor. "You don't think she came back while we were gone, do you?"

"I locked it when we left," Hayes says, taking out the key.

"I didn't see you lock it," Connor says. "You were leading the way."

"I have people, Connor," Hayes snaps, just as we reach the top.

The three of us just accept that because Hayes tries the doorknob. It clicks back and forth, locked. Just like he said. And then he unlocks it with the key and opens the doors.

If Camille were here she'd say, "So someone else has the key. That's comforting."

But she's not. And the rest of us don't have Camille's penchant for rudeness, so we stay quiet.

My bag is waiting near the entrance. I'd forgotten all about it. It feels like years ago that I packed that bag. "Do you need—" I start to ask Sofia, but I see she has packed a bag too. "Oh."

She smiles at me. But it's tight-lipped.

"I guess you were planning this, huh?"

"No more or less than you were, Kiera."

Connor and Hayes are over at the drink cart, pretending not to hear us.

"Can we not make this weird?" I ask.

"Whatever are you talking about?" she quips.

"You know what I mean," I whisper. "Staying the night here with Connor."

"You don't need to worry about me," she says, not bothering to whisper. "I'm buddying up with Hayes." She smiles at Hayes. He smiles back and raises his glass to her. "What we did was fun but there's more fun to be had."

I make one of those screwed-up faces at her.

"Come on," she whispers. "Hayes brought us all here for a reason."

"Yeah, to read the book and come up with a plan."

Sofia huffs. "We didn't get very far, did we? I mean, a few chapters of Connor reading out loud sent us right back into the past, didn't it?"

I want to deny it, but I can't.

She's right.

CHAPTER SEVENTEEN

"Want a cigar?" Hayes asks.

"No, thanks," I say. Something is off here between Kiera and Hayes. Has been the whole fucking day. Ever since he showed up at her house with that helicopter. And that story at dinner? How come they never told us about that guy they killed? I mean, for fuck's sake. That's something you share when you're playing the same fucked-up game of show-and-tell, right?

Unless… unless we're not playing the same game at all.

"I'm tired," Kiera says. "I'm going to bed."

"Me as well," Sofia says. "See you all later."

See you all later. Was that an invitation?

Sofia plays the quiet-demure part perfectly but I know her. It's an act. She's just as dirty as the rest of us. We did things together. Me. Her. Kiera. But we also did things *together*. At the parties we went to. All six of us.

"So what are you gonna do?" Hayes asks.

"About what?" I ask back, still thinking about the parties.

The first party we all went to was at Camille's family estate. It was Christmas Eve and for some reason we were all together. Ah, I remember why now. Bennett's parents were in Europe looking at colleges with his younger brother.

Mine were on the yacht in the middle of the South Pacific, halfway through an impromptu let's-sail-around-the-world cruise. They took all my brothers and sisters, but for some reason I don't recall now, I stayed behind.

Sofia's father had just died, so her mother wasn't doing Christmas.

Hayes's parents were too old to give a shit about holidays anymore. Well on their way to becoming the eccentric recluses they are today. And Kiera… why *was* Kiera there?

"About Kiera," Hayes says.

She certainly was out of place.

The DuPont family Christmas party was beyond extravagant. There was a champagne fountain in the center of the ballroom. Trickling waterfalls of Armand de Brignac flowed out like a river. I've seen my share of high-society parties and this one, for sure, was the most disgusting display of opulence I've ever witnessed. The gowns and jewels alone in that house were enough to fund small countries for a month. Beluga caviar—which I can't tolerate for many reasons, and the taste of it doesn't even make my top three—served on light-as-air crackers. Truffle cream canapés. A seven-course sit-down dinner of lobster bisque, prime rib, Florette baby leaf salad, rack of lamb…

"What about Kiera?" I ask.

The expense. It was so ludicrous to have a party like that when people all over the country were starving or homeless on Christmas Eve. Children would wake up with no presents. Hell, no tree. But that's the thing, ya know? It's so easy to forget about shit like that when you live in this world I was born into.

I remember we were sitting in a small seating area just off the ballroom. Kiera was wearing something very fancy. Something so not her. I don't remember much about it, just that it was short and sparkly. Camille was wearing a long light-blue gown with many layers in the skirts. I remember that because of what came next. Sofia was in red. Sofia is always in red.

Camille's little cousins—or maybe they were nieces?—came up to us while we were sitting there feeling out of place and muttering about how long we'd have to stay. They were dressed like angels and had a basket of gifts. Each gift had our name on it. Like they—Camille's family—knew we were coming and had gone shopping for each of us.

I realized that there were little angel cousins or nieces going around to everyone at the party with baskets of gifts. All the little boxes were from Tiffany's.

How ridiculous is that? Like it was some kind of fairytale party. Not real at all.

Sofia got a bracelet. Kiera got a necklace. I got cuff links and Hayes got a small luggage case that must've been mistagged "male" in the gift pile, but he kept it anyway. Said he was gonna regift it to his mom.

Camille appeared after that, face flushed with excitement and heat. I think she was dancing with Bennett because he came up with her. Then she ran across the room and turned, put a finger to her lips and said, "Shhh. Follow me," and disappeared around a corner.

Bennett followed immediately. The rest of us looked at each other. "Did she mean us too?" I remember Kiera asking.

Then Hayes stood up, tugging on his lapels, said, "Yes," and walked after Bennett.

Kiera and I looked at each other. I was thinking I wouldn't mind dancing with her. Wouldn't mind spending the rest of the evening just with her.

But she stood up and said, "Shall we?" as she held her hand out to me.

I took it and followed her.

We ended up in Camille's bedroom, which was more like an apartment than a bedroom. I'm rich too. I come from the same kind of family. But my family is in politics. We don't show off like that. Extravagant luxury and privilege was something we hid.

Camille was slow-dancing with Bennett in the middle of the room, even though there was no music on. Her head was on his shoulder, eyes closed as they shuffled their feet around the floor like two high-school kids at a dance.

Sofia was sitting on the edge of the bed, biting her lip. Looking at me, then Kiera.

I knew she was interested in me. Hell, we'd already had sex a bunch of times. But it was no secret I was interested in Kiera.

"Come sit down, Kiera," she said. Then she patted the bed to show just where Kiera should sit.

I glanced nervously at Hayes, who just kinda smiled and walked over to them as they sat, waiting for us, I think, and started taking off his tie.

He was different back then. Kind of a ringleader. Which isn't so different than he is today. But it's altogether different at the same time. I just can't put my finger on what's changed.

Once he had his jacket and tie off, he reached for Sofia's hand and pulled her to her feet. She blushed, looking at me over her shoulder as he turned her around and unzipped her dress.

It fell to the floor. Like a little silky red puddle at her feet. She had on white panties and no bra. The panties hugged the shape of her ass in lace, climbing up to her hips at an angle so her cheeks were just the right amount of bare.

Kiera was looking at Hayes then. Not me. Eyes and chin upturned, like she was waiting for instructions.

He held his hand out to her next. Stood her up, turned her around, and unzipped her dress and soon it was on the floor at her feet too.

I glanced at Camille and caught Bennett feeling up her breasts as they kissed. There was no way he was getting her out of that gown so easily, so he didn't even bother trying. Just lifted it up, his whole forearm lost in the layers of chiffon and silk, and started playing with her forbidden, hidden places.

I remember thinking, *What the fuck is happening?*

But then Hayes said, "What are you waiting for, Connor? Do you need an invitation? Do you want me to take your hand and undress you too?"

And I was young. Just twenty years old. I was a boy who thought about things boys think about. My cock was hard and I wanted Kiera. Sofia too. And maybe even Camille. Because by this time she was moaning into the magic Bennett was making between her legs.

Hayes had Sofia on her knees in front of him. I couldn't see what she was doing from where I was standing, but I didn't need to. He had one hand on her head and his belt was jingling.

Kiera was watching them as Hayes absently played with her breast. Then he turned a little and I caught a glimpse of Sofia, her hands massaging his cock as she took him into her throat. Hayes was pulling down Kiera's bra and that's when I snapped out of the spell and went over to them, unzipping my trousers as I walked.

Kiera's eyes met mine and then, without any prompting on my part, she dropped to her knees beside Sofia.

Hayes grunted out a laugh.

It took a lot of effort to drag my eyes off what Kiera was doing to me and look at him.

He grunted another laugh. "Not a bad way to spend senior year, right?"

Not a bad way at all, I remember thinking. Still think it now, which is sick.

But I knew it was sick back then too. Didn't care.

Minutes later we were all naked. Me, Kiera, Sofia, Hayes, Bennett, Camille—haphazardly strewn about Camille's king-size bed, fucking, and sucking, and licking, and kissing, and…

"You know it's never going to work," Hayes says.

I snap out of the past and look at him. He's already sitting down in the same chair he occupied earlier, one ankle propped on one knee. Same old casual attitude of the über-rich I've come to expect from Hayes. I join him, sitting as far away as I can get, in the chair opposite him.

We stare at each other. "Why are you so concerned with what I do?"

"Because she's half mine and you know it."

I laugh. Almost guffaw, but catch myself in time. "No."

Hayes shrugs and takes a sip of his drink. "Maybe we should read the next few chapters in the book while the ladies are pretending to sleep? Hmm?"

I look at the book sitting innocently on the side table next to him. "Go ahead. I've got nothing to hide."

"No. I don't suppose you do. But Kiera certainly does."

"Just fucking spit it out, Hayes. You've been hinting around all night that the two of you had a thing. And why you tried covering for her at dinner with that stupid murder tale—"

"That happened," Hayes says, sitting forward in his chair, suddenly serious. "Someone died that night."

"How did you kill him?" I laugh. "Bored him to death with your monotonous conversation? Because you certainly didn't shoot him. The whole tale is stupid beyond recognition."

"Louise had a weapon."

"Did she? Fucking Louise. The surprise of the night, I'd say. So how is it that Louise is suddenly this all-knowing superpower when she didn't have anything to do with us that whole year? She never went to the parties."

Hayes looks confused for a moment. "Parties?"

"All those fucking parties we went to. Camille's at Christmas. Sofia's old-lady birthday party. Bennett's brother's graduation. She never went to any of them. And I invited her personally to my parents' anniversary, so it's not that she wasn't invited."

"What the hell are you talking about?"

"The fucking parties! You know, where you slithered your way into my good thing."

He laughs. Loud. And I can't help it, I laugh too. "That's what you're thinking about?"

"I mean… yeah. That's what you're doing tonight, isn't it? Trying to make sure you're in on whatever we have going?"

"What do you have going, Connor?"

"Fuck if I know. I mean, hell. Yesterday morning I woke up and Kiera Bonnaire was the last person on my mind. Now here we are. Me. Her. Sofia. You. I mean, what are you fucking thinking about?"

"Oh," he says, trying to hide a smile. "I'm following now. The sex."

"Yeah, the fucking sex. God, what are you? Two? I have to explain things in little baby words? We fucked them all. At the same time. Like… what the hell were we thinking?"

"And now you're wondering if we're gonna do it again?"

"Uh, yeah, dude. I'm wondering."

Hayes tries to hide a smile in his glass as he takes another sip.

"Fucking say something!"

"Hearing you say 'dude' just kinda makes me happy."

I laugh. "Shut up."

"'We have here the future senator from New York. Mr. Arlington, what can you tell us today?'" He fakes the motion of a reporter holding out a mic for a statement. "'Uh, yeah, dude. I got big news. Better listen up.'"

"Don't be an asshole. I'm fucking serious. And I don't give a shit that you think I'm not. I am."

"Well, that makes all the sense." He sighs, rolling his eyes. "Look, I don't know what you think you're doing, but you can't be with Kiera. Senators don't marry erotica authors. And she doesn't even hide it. She uses her real name, for fuck's sake."

"So maybe I won't be a senator? How about that? Satisfactory outcome for you, Hayes? Do I pass your sudden fake big-brother persona now?"

"Good start. So how would Connor Arlington begin to untangle himself from those kind of expectations? Hmm?"

I open my mouth to say something obvious like, *Drop out of the race.* But I'm not even officially running yet. So the next logical answer is, of course, *Don't run.* But I'm not even the one coordinating this whole Senate run, my father is.

Hayes waits, patient as I figure it all out.

"I don't know," I finally admit. "But I will. I don't even fucking want to be a senator. Sounds like a long, dismal life of bullshit if you ask me."

"Indeed," Hayes says. "And that's exactly what it will be. Don't you see?" he says, putting his drink down and leaning forward, elbows on knees. "They're setting you up."

"For what?"

"For failure, Connor." Before I can respond he leans back and puts up a hand. "Before you say anything else, think about this. OK? You're gonna run that race. You're gonna win that race. Because you're the chosen one in this little group. You're the one who always falls in line. I'm too unpredictable, especially after I came to my senses a few years ago. Bennett is too dumb"—I laugh—"and I'm not saying that to be mean. He's too much like Camille.

Says the first thing that pops into his head without thinking. He's a political consultant's worst nightmare. That leaves you. And if you look back on your life between then and now, you'll see how it happened. There's a roadmap, Con. And you've stayed in your lane as you drove down that highway. Following it to perfection." He sits forward again, making sure I get this final point. "They're setting you up to win and for you, that means you lose. Understand me?"

"Whatever," I say. Because I don't feel like talking to him anymore. I just want to go to bed. Go in that room, climb under the covers with Kiera and forget everything that happened since Hayes showed up at Kiera's cottage.

We could've spent the whole day together. Stayed in bed, fucked a dozen times, pretended that book never happened. Pretended all of it was over.

"You know what?" I say.

"What?" Hayes asks.

"I don't even like politics. I don't even watch the news. My father has this intern guy called Richie write me up bullet points each morning."

"Then why are you doing it?"

But he knows why.

"Are you really that spineless?"

"Fuck you," I say.

"You get one life, Connor. How sad would it be if you lived it based on someone else's plan?"

I think about this. Have been thinking about it for a long time now. Years. But I never seem to be able to make a decision, one way or another. I just can't commit to it either way.

"If you can't find a reason to tell him no yourself, then think about Kiera. Because there's no way in hell the two of you end up together if you don't take a stand right now. In three years you'll be a senator, in ten years you'll be governor, and in twenty years you'll be running for president. Is that really how you want to live this one life?"

"I dunno," I say. "Doesn't everyone kinda want to be president?"

"No." Hayes laughs. "Almost no one wants to be president, Con. The only reason people want a job in politics is for the power. That's it. The paycheck is shitty, the job is shitty, and the constituents are unbearable."

It's true. I can't even argue his point.

Why can't I make a decision?

"Things happened that night, Connor. Things that were written in that book." He nods his head to the book. "And I really thought this was gonna be pretty simple. Everyone would show up here, we'd read the book, figure shit out, plan the next move. But for some reason we just all reverted back to the people we were." He stops to look at me. Like I'm supposed to say something. When I don't he goes on. "Why do we do that? And I'm not even trying to pretend I'm above it, either. I'm doing it too. Do you know why we do that, Connor?"

I can't even hold his question in my head. It just floats above me, shimmering like light, then disappears.

"Do you?" he asks again.

I shake my head. "No."

"Well, I do. And I was gonna explain everything tonight, but I'm not gonna do it without Bennett and Camille."

Do what? I want to ask. But I don't. I just sit here and say nothing.

Hayes sighs like he gives up.

"I'm going to bed," I say. "Where're you sleeping tonight?"

He juts his chin at Sofia's door. "Is that gonna be a problem?"

"Are you going to sleep with her? Or just sleep next to her?"

"I'm gonna fuck her," Hayes says. "That's why she's here."

I just stare at him.

"Problem with that?" he asks.

"Kinda," I say, even though I don't really care about Hayes and Sofia. It just feels wrong. Not how it's supposed to be.

"I thought you wanted Kiera?"

"I do."

"But you don't want to share Sofia, either." He shrugs. "Fine with me. But if that's how you feel then you need to go get Sofia out of that room and take her over to yours. Because she doesn't deserve to sleep alone tonight."

I wonder if Kiera would mind?

God, what is wrong with me? That's the dumbest question I've ever asked myself.

"Look, I don't know what I'm doing, OK? I'm here because Kiera's here."

"But?"

"But seeing Sofia makes everything complicated for me. This whole day is confusing. The book, us, tonight."

"You don't know what you want, Connor. So why not let me tell you, because I know more than you think. Just view this whole night… as a… you know. A *thing*."

A thing.

Meaning… meaningless.

"It's not though," I say. "I just don't know how to make that clear."

"That was always your problem, Connor. Always on the fence. Never willing to commit. You're gonna be the perfect politician."

"That's funny."

"Why? It's true. You're just a figurehead. That's all a politician is and you fit that bill to perfection. You're gonna let your father run your life, and call the shots, and one day you're gonna wake up after he's dead and realize you had one chance to turn it all around and that one chance was tonight. And you did nothing. Just... did what you normally do and went along."

I say nothing because he's right, of course. I am that man. I will be that man.

So I say... "OK. Tell me what to do."

And he does.

Kiera's room is dark, so I force myself to be still for a few seconds, allowing my eyes to adjust. When the crack of light leaking in from under the door goes from barely visible to a golden haze rising up from the floor I step forward towards the edge of the four-poster bed, unknotting my tie and pulling it through my collar as I walk.

"Kiera?" I ask, pulling my shirt out of my pants and unbuttoning my shirt. "You awake?"

She moans, rolling over, one of her pale breasts exposed from her top, one long leg bare as it sneaks out from under the covers. Her hair is wild, splayed out on the pillow and half covering her beautiful face.

I want to turn the lights on. Want to see her better. See all of her. Never take my eyes off this woman. I want to make this whole nightmare go away. Give her something better. Leave behind my old life with all its expectations and just steal away with her to some far-away tropical island. Stay naked with her forever and raise babies on the beach.

God, what the fuck is wrong with me? We've been back in each other's lives for less than forty-eight hours and all I can think about is throwing everything away?

You're in love, Con.

I hear the words in her voice inside my head.

You're in love.

Maybe I am.

I unbuckle my belt and unfasten my pants. Drag my zipper down, trying to be quiet.

I don't want to wake her. I want to ease into bed, slip my fingers between her legs, and kiss her mouth as she dreams. Make her come in her sleep.

I am one sick fuck and I don't care.

When I'm naked I place one knee on the bed and carefully swing my other leg over hers. She twists, flat on her back now. That one exposed breast caught in some stray ray of light that shouldn't be there, but is. Like a spotlight just for my own sick, hedonistic pleasure.

Thinking back on the party at Camille's house has turned back time for me. Taken me to the place I was, the person I used to be. The one who fucked her and Sofia—and sometimes Camille too. The one who didn't mind sharing with Hayes or Bennett because they didn't mind sharing with me.

It was an orgy. Group sex or whatever.

It was sick, and twisted, and very fucking erotic.

It was heavy breathing, and sweaty, naked bodies, and never enough.

It was never enough that year.

We fucked them all. Together.

It was sensuous, and uninhibited, and lecherous.

How did I ever walk away from these people? How did I ever live a day without them?

I place my hand on her one exposed leg and slowly slide it up to her thigh.

She moans again, mouth parted like she's waiting for my cock.

I picture those nights long ago. At the parties. How Camille would always be the one to invite us in. And how Hayes would be the first to take her up on those offers. How Sofia was meek, and afraid, and shy. And how she changed. How we all changed.

How Kiera used to whimper and moan as she came.

I want to hear that sound now. Right now.

I lean forward, crawling up her body, my rock-hard cock dragging across the sheets. Aching to be inside her.

CHAPTER EIGHTEEN

In my dream we're dancing. It's a party, but not one I was ever at with them. Everyone is here. Hayes, Connor, Bennett all wearing tuxes. Me, Camille, Sofia all wearing gowns. They are the gowns we found in the basement room that first night with Louise.

I stop dancing when I realize that. I'm partnered with Bennett for some reason, which is also confusing. So I look around, searching for Connor, then Hayes. Connor has Sofia pushed up against a wall, his hand hidden beneath the long flowing layers of her elaborate skirt. Her head is tilted upward, mouth slightly open. And he's whispering something in her ear.

I'm jealous, but turned on. So I lead Bennett over to them and take my place next to Sofia against the wall. Someone is kissing me. Bennett, or Connor, or maybe Sofia—but then I realize it's Hayes. His soft lips caressing the side of my neck. His soft words wrapping around the tender skin of my ear just like Connor's words wrap around Sofia. "Do you like it?" he asks. "I want you to like it."

"What are we doing?" I whisper back. "When did this become who we are?"

And Hayes says, "It's not real, so don't worry about it."

But it feels real. Camille is kissing Bennett now, her body pressing up against mine. Her soft, full breasts are bare. Somehow she's gotten herself naked. And in my dream I laugh at that. Because it's so typical of Camille to just take off her clothes and be indiscreet.

And then we're all naked. All twisted together in the sheets of some giant bed. Camille's bed, I realize. Now we're at her Christmas party. And there's butterflies in the air. Clear-winged butterflies like the ones at Connor's parents anniversary. Dozens of them. No, hundreds of them. Their soft wings flutter around my hot, feverish skin like a summer wind. Making a cool breeze that feels so good.

But it's not the butterflies. It's Connor, blowing air across my pussy as his tongue laps against my folds, looking for the sweet spot. And when he hits it, I buck my back.

But Bennett is there, whispering, "This is wrong. This is so fucking wrong."

And I reply, "Shut up," because I'm irritated that he's ruining the feeling of Connor between my legs. "Just shut up."

And then he and Camille are gone and I get this weird feeling that they've left us. They figured it out—this wrongness—and left us.

But Hayes is there, saying, "Shhh, they don't know anything. Don't worry."

But I do worry. Because I want to know what they don't know. And Hayes is the secret-keeper and he's close now. So close. "What don't they know?" I ask him.

But Connor steals the words from my mouth with a kiss and it's too much. I forget about my questions and how none of this makes sense and say, "It's just a dream."

And Sofia is touching me now. She was always so careful when she touched me, afraid she might do it wrong. But I used to tell her, "There's no wrong way." And that always made her happy for a little bit.

Which makes me think about her sadness. And her books. Those books she writes. The dark, sexy stories that steal your life away for days, or months, or years. And I say, "When did you change?"

And she just looks at me with her sad, sad smile that's on her face so often now, I've grown used to it. She says, "You know when."

But I don't. I don't really remember anything except that tower. And the book I wrote. And those dresses down in the basement. Why were there dresses in the basement?

"Kiera?"

It makes no sense at all. Why that guy had dresses. Did he have a fetish?

"Kiera?"

But they weren't dresses, were they? They were costumes.

"Kiera!"

I open my eyes to find Connor on top of me. Holy shit, this is real. "Where are we?" I ask, pushing him off and sitting up. "What's happening? Why are we—"

"Shhhh," he says. Just like Hayes. "You're OK. We're in the library bedroom, remember? At Hayes' house."

"Was there a party?"

"No," he says, pulling me back into his waiting arms and smoothing my sweat-soaked hair away from my face. "No. We were just here talking, remember? I came in to surprise you." And even though I can barely see him in the faint light leaking in from the window, I know he's smiling. I can hear it in his words. "But you were having a nightmare, I think." He pauses. "Were you having a nightmare?"

Was it a nightmare?

"No," I say. "Just a dream, that's all."

"Your heart is beating so fast."

I turn in the bed, tangled up in the sheets, so I can place my hands on his cheeks and whisper, "Sorry."

And he whispers back, "You don't need to be sorry. It was probably me sneaking into your bed that screwed up your dream."

"No," I say, my hands still on his rough cheeks. He hasn't shaved in days now. Two days I've been back in this world and it's already fucking with my head. But I don't care what Bennett says. It's not wrong. "How could something that feels so good be wrong?"

I realize I'm not talking to Connor anymore, but that dream version of Bennett.

"Where is everyone? Why are we alone?"

He makes that noise I love. It's kind of a laugh, but no real sound comes out, just air. "They went home, remember? We stayed."

"Where's Sofia? Is she alone?"

"She's with Hayes. She's fine."

I let out a long exhale of breath and it feels like relief.

"I just wanted you to myself for a little bit, that's all."

I think about that for a few seconds.

"Is that OK?"

I nod, knowing he can't really see me. But also knowing that Connor Arlington doesn't need to see me to understand me.

"There were butterflies, right? Those were real, weren't they?"

"What?" He laughs.

"At your parents' anniversary party. Did they have butterflies?"

"Yes," he whispers, kissing my neck, his hand exploring my breast. "Millions of them."

I close my eyes, relieved that some things I remember are real, enjoying his touch. And soon he's lifting up my lacy, Victorian nightshirt, dragging his fingertips up and down the line of my belly.

I want him to keep doing that forever. I want to stay in this bed with him forever.

But that book. And the whole reason we're here. And Emily, somewhere out there. Lurking. She's probably found a weapon by now. I'm pretty sure this mansion has one of those rooms where old families keep old weapons. Swords displayed on walls. Fanned out in pretty designs like this mansion was once a castle that needed defending and had an army of soldiers living inside the walls and now it's just a shadow of its former self and everything that once was is a relic to look at and not be used.

Something is wrong. Bennett was right.

I picture her climbing up a wall, balancing precariously on stacked furniture to reach a sword on display. Or maybe she found an old revolver in a glass case. I'm pretty sure there's cases and cases of dangerous things under glass in this museum. Clubs, or whips, or knives that were used in some long-forgotten battle over crops, or taxes, or some farmer's daughter's virtue—

"Do you want me to stop?" Connor asks, kissing the corners of my lips, his fingers pulling aside my underwear so they can slip inside me.

I'm wet for him. I used to be so embarrassed by that when we first met. How easy it was for him to turn me on with just a few kisses and the touch of a fingertip in just the right place.

All his fingers are in the right place now.

He's got at least two inside me. Pushing forward, then drawing them back out, slick with my desire. He goes slow. I've always liked that about Connor. How careful he is with his lovemaking.

He can be rough too. I like that as well. But it's the careful that touches my soul and makes me think I love him.

"No," I say. "Don't stop."

The sex we've had hasn't been exclusive. I don't have much experience in being Connor's sole focus in bed. Only these past two days and that one last time up in the tower. There was always someone else there. Always Sofia. Sometimes Bennett, Camille, and Hayes if we were all out together at the parties.

So even though we've had sex dozens of times in the past, this still feels new to me. This time with him. His body and my body. With no other bodies to interfere.

Connor's other hand plays with the nipple of one breast, pinching it up into a peak as he kisses me. First my lips, which makes me open in response—both my mouth and my legs. He mumbles, "Yes," into the kiss and inserts another finger inside me. Stretching the walls of my vagina the way his hard cock does.

I picture sex with him and Sofia. Feeling all the ways in which this is different. We weren't into each other much, but we were into him. Making him feel good. Letting him watch us kiss. Letting him tell us to do things like finger each other, or lick each other, or… whatever.

I liked that part. The part he played. The part she played with me.

The jealousy I felt in my dream comes back, but not as a real thing. Just something that was always sorta there, and sorta not.

Right now it's sorta not.

Because Connor is only looking at me. Only feeling me. Only has time for me.

I sorta miss her, actually. Things were less awkward with three, if that makes sense. Now I'm wondering, *Is this right?* as I reach for him and begin to massage my hand up and down the long, hard shaft of his cock. *Does he like it? Or would she do it better?*

He withdraws his fingers from my pussy and places his hand over mine, guiding me as I continue the up-and-down motion. His whole hand is wet. We jerk him off together and just thinking those words turns me on more.

Because Sofia and I used to do this too. And occasionally our eyes would meet and we'd move forward, towards each other, like we were being pulled together by some unseen force, and kiss.

That would always turn Connor on. We'd feel his cock jump between our hand. Hers squeezing the top of his shaft, her fingertips brushing across the tip of his head. Mine squeezing the bottom half, taking a break sometimes to cup his balls.

And one of us would eventually change position and go down on him. He'd place his hand on her head or my head, and I would pump his cock into her mouth, or she'd pump it into mine.

There was no jealousy in the dark of night, naked bodies pressed against each other. The insecurities only manifested in the light of day. During school, or lunch, or whenever it wasn't appropriate to show off who and what we were to each other.

"That feels so fucking good, Kiera," Connor says as I grip him tight and pump him harder. "I want to be inside you."

And back then I'd have to wonder who he was talking to and now I don't. He's only talking to me right now.

"Not yet," I reply back, my voice throaty and hoarse from lack of conversation.

We used to talk more when it was the three of us too. Dirty things. So many dirty things came out of our mouths.

"Her pussy is so wet," Sofia would say to him. "Your cock will slide in deep now, babe. Put it inside her."

And he would. He'd climb on top of me, or I'd climb on top of him. And Sofia would help. She'd take his cock and flick it back and forth across my clit, making me squirm and wait. Then she'd position him at my opening and play with me as we fucked.

Or I'd do that to her. Didn't matter.

In the here and now he pulls away from our kissing and repositions himself, taking my nipple in his mouth. Biting it with just enough pressure to make me gasp, but not enough to really hurt. He squeezes both breasts as his mouth moves down to my stomach, kissing as he goes. Dropping lower after a few seconds to continue the pilgrimage. Seeking just the right place I need to be worshiped. Soft, fluttery kisses on my lower belly. His hands parting the soft, wet flesh between my legs as his mouth descends, licking everywhere but the place I crave his attention.

Sofia, in those times she went down on me, did it the same way. And I realize we taught each other how we liked it. She taught him, and I taught her, and he taught us. And there is no difference, I realize. No difference at all between him and me, and him and her, and him and us.

When did that happen?

Why isn't she here now?

But just as that thought manifests in my head he touches me with the tip of his tongue, flicking it back and forth across that one spot on my body that feels it the most. Then he puts his whole mouth on me, sucking hard for a moment. With such ambition and determination, I moan, and squeak, and even cry out a little. But his fingers are there again. Pushing inside me just the way I like it. Pumping gently at first. Teasing me until I grip his hair. My hands making fists, demanding more.

He laughs. Right into my pussy. Because he knows me so well. After ten years apart, he's still the only man on this earth who knows me like this.

"I'm ready for you, Kiera," he says, lifting his head up a little to look me in the eyes. I'm still gripping his hair, but my eyes are open, because I like this view. The view of his body positioned between my open legs. His eyes seeking out mine as he runs his chin back and forth in the place I want his tongue.

It's scratchy, and it hurts a little. But I don't care. I want to feel what he's doing tomorrow when I walk. I want to be uncomfortable and sore, the way I used to be back in college. And Sofia and I would be sitting in class and our eyes would meet across the room as we squirmed in our chairs, and we'd know. We'd both leave the room and enter the night that came before. And that's how we spent so many afternoons in Masters of English Lit class. Dreaming about how we fucked him, and he fucked us, and we fucked each other.

And we would blush. Or she'd put her hand between her legs—discreetly, so no one would even notice except me—and I'd do the same. And every once in a while we'd come like that. In class, across the room, dreaming about the sex we had the night before.

Why isn't she here? When did I start missing her? How did I not know?

"Tell me when," Connor says.

"Now," I say, tugging him back up my body by his hair. "Right now." Because I can't wait another minute. I like the slow buildup. And with Sofia it was necessary so everyone got the attention they deserved. But alone… I can't wait any longer. If she was here I would. I'd make myself. And we'd do this all over again with her. Only I'd be pushing up next to her, helping the way she helped us. And we'd always come before he entered us. Sometimes more than once. We'd always feel wanted, and needed, and satisfied before Connor took his turn. And neither of us were jealous if he came inside the other. Because we knew we'd get our turn. It might take twenty minutes, or twenty hours, or twenty days, but we'd get our turn.

But when he enters me now I know he's all mine. I will get all the rewards. All the time. All the attention.

His cock is so hard, his balls so tight when I lift my knees up, spread my legs wide open, and give them the room they need to bounce against my asshole, I almost come. But I bite my lip, and Connor kisses them, nibbling along to take my mind off what he's doing to me. How he makes me feel, and the building explosion.

And it works. For now. Because I settle down and open my eyes so I can look at him.

His beautiful face, and his rough jaw, and the way he breathes hard as he thrusts himself deep inside, and then pulls out so slow, I grab his ass and try to force him to go faster.

He doesn't respond. Not the way I want him to, at least. He just does it the way I need it, not the way I want it. Because he knows. He knows everything about me. Inside, outside, everywhere.

He knows things I've forgotten long ago.

His hands are flat on the bed, his disheveled hair hanging down over his face. No longer slicked back like the man he was when he came to my cottage yesterday afternoon, but the lover he is now. In the heat of the sex. Our sweaty bodies sliding against each other, reminding me of hot summer nights I never spent with him. Reminding me of all the days and years we've been apart and how this moment right now makes up for all of them.

We are right where we're supposed to be.

He's gazing down at me with those brown-green eyes I can barely make out. But I don't need to see them to see them. They are burned in my memory. A part of me left over from times gone by.

"Talk to me," he says. "Say all the things to me."

"Fuck me harder," I say, smiling. Breaking the erotic spell, just a little.

"Not good enough," he says. "I've heard better."

Which makes me laugh. And that laugh feels so, so, so good. And I want to make him happy. I want to impress him with all the years I've spent writing erotic sex scenes. Imagining him as my hero in every single book. Putting words in his mouth, and my mouth, and playing out all my dirty fantasies on the pages with paragraphs and chapters, and books, and books, and more books.

So I say, "Flip me over and fuck me hard, Mr. Arlington. Because if you don't, I'll walk away wanting more."

"Maybe that's what I'm after," he whispers. "Maybe I don't want you to love it. Maybe I want you to need more so next time you'll see what's missing."

"I know what's missing," I say. "But she's not here and we are. So we'll just have to pretend."

"Tell me more," he says. "Tell me what you want her to do."

"If Sofia was here, and you were on top of me the way you are now, she'd be right next to me," I say. "She'd be on her side, head resting on my shoulder, looking up at you as you pushed your cock deep inside me."

"Fuck, yeah," he moans. "Fuck, yeah, she would."

Because that's how it was.

"She'd play with my breasts. Pinch my nipples, and kiss my mouth. Her hand would slowly find its way between my legs. To the mess of wet, sticky sex from our mingled bodies. And she'd play with it. Rubbing it on my stomach. Playing with my clit—"

"Jesus Christ, Kiera. That mouth is so dirty, makes me want to kiss it."

So he does. He kisses my dirty mouth as he fucks me. And when he pulls his head aside to bite my shoulder because the motion of our bodies is too much to maintain a kiss, I go on.

"She'd get me off with you inside. Make me come with her fingers. And wrap her legs around me any way she could manage so I could feel how wet she was for us. How ready she was for you—"

"Kiera—"

"And then you'd bite your lip the way you are now. Trying not to come because you wanted to make sure you had enough energy left for her, or me, if it was her turn and not mine."

"Kiera—"

"And when I couldn't hold it in any longer I'd let go. Just let it all go and explode. And she'd kiss me. And whisper, 'He fucked you hard, right? He fucked you good. And you loved it, didn't you, you dirty little slut.' And you—"

"Kiera, oh, my fucking God—"

"—filthy, filthy slut. Always trying to be the dirtiest dirty one."

"—shut up!"

I want to laugh, but I want to torture him more. "And then she'd start playing with me. Driving me crazy to make me come again. Or make me squirt on her fingers. And then she'd push you off me. Hard, roughly. And slither her way underneath you, and put your hard, slick cock inside her pussy and say, 'Come in me, Connor. Come inside me. Give me everything you have left.'"

He grunts, dropping his full body weight onto my breasts, panting hard, sucking in air like he can't get enough. And his body goes stiff and still and he explodes too.

We stay like that for a long time. Then he falls off to one side, one arm sliding underneath me, the other wrapping around my middle so he can pull me closer, even though we're as close as two people can be.

"I've missed you," he whispers, drowsy with sleep. "Don't go away again."

I smile as I enter the dream world again. A world of butterflies, and orgies, and dark rooms at the top of a tower where sex was a story written in a book by my hand. And there are fountains of champagne and gowns that are really costumes, and so many mysteries that make no sense.

But later… later there's a noise in the dark. The soft padding of footsteps. And in my dream I open my eyes and see Sofia, naked, climbing into bed with us on Connor's side. He turns, eyes still closed, and slides one arm underneath her. Pulls us both close.

And I think, *This is a nice dream.*

But then I hear another noise across the room and squint my eyes, trying to see what's there. Imagining Emily with one of those ancient swords from the weapon room I'm still sure exists.

But it's not Emily.

It's Hayes.

And this isn't a dream.

CHAPTER NINETEEN

My arm is already around Sofia before I even fully realize what I've done. But fuck it. This is what I wanted, wasn't it? It's always what I wanted. I was just never able to admit it before tonight.

And hearing Kiera dirty-talk Sofia into our lovemaking has me convinced that we can do this. We are meant to have this one last time together. All of us. And if being a senator means I have to choose, then fuck it. I want nothing to do with politics. I'd much rather go down in history as that deviant Arlington boy than Mr. Connor Arlington, US Senator from the great state of New York.

I can commit, goddammit. I will. To these Dirty Ones in this bedroom with me. Now and forever.

That's when I notice Hayes walking towards us on Kiera's side of the bed. I have a moment of panic. Like... maybe she loves him more than me. Maybe she'd prefer him instead?

And for sure, she's into this. She's staring at him as he approaches her, unbuckling his belt and then pulling it through the loops with a swooshing sound that makes me hot for some reason. I picture him slapping her ass with it and realize that actually happened once. Not sure when. Not exactly. Back in college, for sure, since that's the last time he was in a bedroom with me. But which party? That I don't know.

But he drops the belt and starts taking off his shirt, pulling it out of his pants and unbuttoning it from the bottom up, his eyes only on Kiera. But then, just for a moment, they flick to me. But back to her in almost the same instant.

Kiera hasn't moved. Her eyes are locked on his.

Sofia brings my attention back where it belongs. With her. She untangles herself from my embrace and climbs up on my body, her thighs straddling mine, and begins to rub her already primed and wet pussy up and down my half-hard cock.

I absently wonder if Hayes has been playing with her already. Of it that wetness is just for me.

I decide it doesn't matter. Not tonight.

Her long, dark hair sways across my chest as she lowers her lips to mine and begins to kiss me. I grab both ass cheeks, then slap them. Hard. Breaking the stillness in the room with the booming sound.

She says, "Ooooh." Like it hurt but felt good too.

I grab her hair in fistfuls, pulling her even closer, ready for a hard fuck now that the soft one with Kiera is over.

"Yes," she moans. "Just like that."

I have never felt the need to be careful with Sofia in bed. Which is ironic, because in any other circumstance she needs all the variations of careful. She is sad, and quiet, and introspective. She takes everything to heart.

But during sex she changes into something else. Someone completely different. Someone who wants to be thrown down on a mattress face-first and fucked hard in the ass. She turns into one of the dirty ones, just like us. And I never have to be careful of her feelings in bed, either. Because she is getting everything she ever wanted when we're in the filthy dream world of multiples. This is joy to her. Happiness fulfilled.

"Turn over," I say. But I don't explain more because I don't need to. She knows what I want because we've done it like this a hundred million times before. In the real. In the dreams...

She kisses me hard one more time, then carefully positions herself so her back is pressing against my chest. I don't know if Kiera will be into it, but it's worth taking a chance.

I play with her pussy until she's gushing wet, then drag that down to her asshole with one hand, fisting my now fully-hard cock with the other. It doesn't slip inside her asshole easily. And she moans and cries out two or three times. But in between those moans and cries she says, "Don't stop, don't stop," in quick, panting breaths.

And when I breach her tight muscles and finally get inside her, she squeaks out, "Yes, yes, yes," as I open her legs and turn my head to see Kiera.

She is fisting Hayes' cock, two-handed. But she sees what we're doing and she knows how to play her part. It's been a long time, but this is one fuck you don't forget.

I've done it to her too. They've been in opposite places before. So she knows what it feels like and makes her move. Dropping Hayes' cock and scooting her body into position.

But Hayes, never one to be left out, grabs her by the ankle and pulls her back toward him.

"Come on, man," I say.

He just smiles at me and drops a knee to the mattress, making us all shift in his direction. He's naked now and I wish I hadn't missed that. His undressing. But there's no time for regrets because he climbs over Kiera and takes the position that was meant for her. Pressing his fingers into Sofia's soft, primed pussy until she reaches for my arms, holding her in place, and digs her nails into my skin.

There's a second when I think Hayes and I will take her at the same time, but then he drops his face between her legs and begins to lick her. His hot breath on my dick, which is now so hard, it's like I didn't just get off a little while ago.

His other hand grabs Kiera by the waist and pulls her close. He says, "Get up. Make him lick you."

And she does.

God, I want to die as I watch her kneel on the bed, then crawl her way up to my head, straddle my face, and drop her delicious pussy onto my mouth.

I wriggle out of the death grip Sofia has on my arms because I want to grab Kiera's hips. I squeeze her flesh hard, rocking her back and forth across my face. Letting my tongue flick her clit when she lifts her hips up and grabs onto the headboard.

I stop fucking Sofia in the ass because my mind is blown. There's no way I can concentrate on how this feels. Her asshole clenching around the shaft of my dick while I suck in the sweet taste and scent of Kiera.

But I don't need to move to fuck her. Hayes does that for us. He's got his hands on her hips, gripping her the way I'm gripping Kiera, and he's thrusting her back and forth across my chest.

Kiera lifts up off my face, but I hold her tight, whispering, "No, no, no," as she tries to escape.

But she says, "Shhh," as she pries my hands off her, and turns around. Leaning forward on Sofia's belly in an awkward position, but I see what she's going for. One hand steadies herself. Flat on the mattress, the other reaches for Hayes, digging her fingertips into his hair.

There's some movement and repositioning as Hayes makes his cock available. And then we are a twisted tangle of sweaty, sexy bodies as Kiera's mouth covers the tip of his cock and begins to suck wildly.

She's not in range for me to lick her so I play with her instead. Overwhelmed by all the sensations in this moment.

Sofia, and Hayes, and Kiera, and Connor…

Like the old days, I realize. A memory coming back to me. Someone's party. Can't really remember, don't really care.

I just know we've done this before. The four of us. The six of us. All of us.

The Dirty Ones.

Sofia comes. From my cock in her ass or Hayes's magic tongue, who knows. Who cares. She just comes hard. And I wish I was the one licking her pussy right now. Licking her as her come slides out and I lap it up like sweet cream.

Then there's more repositioning. Hayes is next to me, shoulder to shoulder, and Kiera climbs on top of him, spreading the lips of her pussy with one hand as she slides over his cock.

The daylight is breaking outside. And Kiera looks like a dream in the soft, gray winter light.

She leans down, kissing Hayes, then shifts over, kissing me. Sofia is writhing again and when Kiera reaches over to play with her, she comes again.

And that's it, folks. That's all I can stand. I pull my cock out, slide Sofia over onto the mattress, and pump myself hard as I watch Kiera rock her hips back and forth on Hayes's cock like a mad woman who hasn't been fucked in years.

I spill all over Sofia's stomach and her fingertips are there, playing with it. Eyes closed, legs still spread wide as she brings herself to one final climax.

I flop down on the bed next to her and watch Kiera. How her long, wild mane of unruly blonde hair whips across Hayes' chest.

I can't see her face when she comes, but I've seen it enough to know what she looks like.

A beautiful, erotic, sex goddess. Writhing in the break of dawn.

He's about to come, I realize. And I think he's gonna do it inside her. Because he's kissing her mouth as he holds her face close to his. Unable to let her go.

And for a second I wonder… did I make a mistake? Will he take her away from me?

But if he does… then it was never meant to be. I'm selfish for wanting two women and both Kiera and Sofia deserve whatever it is that fills them up. And if Kiera decides that's Hayes then—

"Fuck you, asshole," I say, pushing her off him.

I don't know what I was thinking two seconds ago, but I do now.

I grab Kiera's hair and push her head down on his cock. She takes him deep, wrapping her lips around his shaft.

He comes in her throat. And the gagging noises she makes as she pushes him away turn me on.

The four of us sleep in fits of erotic gratification. Desperately tired but unable to forget that we are surrounded by naked bodies lathered in the scent of sex. Unable or maybe just unwilling to leave the dream behind.

When I wake up it's probably late afternoon. I realize two things.

One, it's Thursday and I'm still not at work. My phone is probably blowing up with messages, but oh, well. It's in the other room, so who cares.

And two, Hayes is gone.

Kiera and Sofia are twisted up like a couple. Arms and legs crossing over each other. Dark hair spilling over onto Kiera. Blonde hair spilling over onto Sofia.

They are Venus twins. Perfect, sculptured goddesses of sex.

And they are mine.

Are they mine?

God, why does everything always look so different in the daylight?

I ponder that as I swing my legs out of bed and begin getting dressed, hoping I'll wake them up and maybe we can go at it one more time before I have to face the repercussions of disappearing.

But they don't. Sofia is snoring softly, mouth slightly open. I can't even see Kiera's face. It's resting on Sofia's stomach, turned towards the window. Covered by her tangled mess of hair.

I settle for just pants and go looking for Hayes, needing to talk last night through.

He's not in the library, but the massive double doors are wide open. So I guess that means he's somewhere out there and not in one of the other bedrooms.

I walk out into the hallway and stop at the railing that overlooks the grand staircase. Look down. Listen for voices.

Nothing.

I see nothing. I hear nothing.

No cops. No dogs. No doctors.

Jesus Christ. Did all that shit really happen last night?

I don't even know where to begin looking for Hayes in this hideous mansion either, so for a second I think about going back to bed. But… no. We need to be clear on what last night was before the girls wake up.

So I start the long descent down the stairs, barefoot. The stone is cold on the soles of my feet but it feels kinda good. Like a firm root in the soil of reality.

When I get to the bottom and stand in the grand foyer, I have no clue where to go next.

I think the dining room is that way. But unless he takes his breakfast in the industrial catering kitchen or at that ridiculous monstrosity of a dining table, I can't imagine he's that way.

I turn to look at another wing of the house and wonder if he actually lives here.

Like… does he sleep in this fucking place? I can't even imagine it. It's like bedding down at the Met every night.

I shiver, shaking off the chills of spending a night in a place like this alone.

Do his parents even live here still? Like is there anyone here at this moment?

Servants, surely.

But there's literally no one around.

I turn into a hallway and walk for a little while, passing a music room, another library or maybe an office, an atrium that is loud with birdsong, so that's probably an aviary.

And then eventually I reach a huge sitting area. And by sitting area I mean Waldorf Astoria Hotel New York kind of sitting room. Like they throw afternoon tea here on Sundays. That kind of room. A dozen small round or square tables surrounded by low, upholstered armchairs.

I cup my hands to my mouth and yell, "Hayes! Where the fuck are you?"

Nothing but an echo.

I turn and look back the way I came, wondering if the girls heard me and I woke them.

Nah. No way that's even possible. They're like a half a mile of stairs and hallways away.

"Dude," I say, loud but not yelling. "Where the fuck are you?"

There is literally no hope of me finding him in here and that suddenly makes me think of Emily and her great escape last night.

No way they found her. No fucking way. I continue through the sitting room and come to another hallway. "Hayes!" I yell again. "Dude!"

Then the slapping of feet behind me makes me turn.

"Hayes?" I ask the empty hallway. "Is that you, man?" Knowing it's not.

I backtrack the way I came. "Hayes?" I ask the empty air again.

More slapping feet.

Does he have family here? Like little nieces and nephews or something?

No. Dude is an only child. I know that.

"Hayes?" I say, louder this time. "Hayes!" A little more urgent.

Because right now, I think I'm lost in his stupid house. I thought I was taking the obvious path when I came this way, but when I backtrack and walk past a pool, I know that's not the case. There are no birds, either.

A giggle makes me whirl around, and then there's a flash of disappearing nightgown around a corner.

"Who's there?" I ask. Then I roll my eyes at myself. I sound like a dumb girl in a horror movie. "Whoever the fuck that is—"

"Connor!" Hayes called.

"Dude!" I yell back. "I'm lost!" And then I laugh, too loud.

"I'm in the conservatory!"

Another laugh burbles up. Because I think of Camille and her stupid Clue references last night. I'm pretty sure people get killed with a candlestick in the conservatory.

Or is that the observatory? I'm not sure.

Another giggle behind me, but this time when I whirl around there's a girl.

"Emily," I breathe out. "Shit, you fucking scared me." And then I say, "This house is creepy as fuck, don't you think?" Because I don't know what to do.

This girl tried to kill me ten years ago. She put a bullet through Kiera's shoulder.

"I didn't do it," she says.

"Connor!" Hayes yells. Closer now. "Where the fuck are you?"

I look around, spy a billiards room, then hate Camille for her stupid Clue game references.

Emily did it with the pool stick in the billiards room.

"I'm by the pool table!" I yell back.

"Which one?" He's closer, but not close enough to save me from this moment with Emily.

Jesus Christ. This isn't happening.

I clear my throat and speak to Emily. "Um… what now?"

"I didn't shoot her."

"Yes, you did, Emily. I mean, you actually tried to shoot me, but you missed. Or rather, Kiera threw herself in front of the bullet to save me. So yeah, you absolutely did shoot her. I had blood all over me. I went with her to the hospital. Stayed with her all night."

"No, you didn't," she says softly, shaking her head of wild hair no.

"Yes, I did! For fuck's sake, why are you still here? What do you want?"

"You need to know the truth," she says.

"Connor!" Hayes yells. And he's very close now.

I turn and call, "In here!" And when I turn back, Emily is gone. "Where the fuck—"

"Dude." Hayes laughs. "What the hell are you doing?"

"Emily," I say.

"She's gone. They found her a few hours ago and took her back to the hospital."

"What?" I turn to look at the empty place where Emily was just standing.

"Yeah, crazy bitch. The dogs found her hiding inside a dumbwaiter. She's a mess."

"But—"

"Are the girls up?"

Shit. And now I remember why I was coming to find him. "No. Not yet. But just… you know, last night…" He waits for me to say more, so I do. "Um… well, just thanks, man. I appreciate it."

"Hey," he says, coming up to squeeze my shoulder. "That's what friends are for."

I smile, laugh a little, then turn with him and start walking back to the front of the house.

But I swear to God, I think I hear the ghost of Emily behind me.

Laughing.

Back upstairs the girls are still sleeping, so I gather up my clothes and get dressed in the library. Acutely aware of Hayes, sitting in what I now think of as his chair, watching me with thoughtful consideration.

"What?" I ask.

"Do you have a plan?"

"No," I say, tucking in my shirt, trying to pull myself together while wearing the same suit for the third fucking day in a row. "Well, maybe. I'm gonna go home and change." I laugh a little as I say it, because I know what he's talking about and my deliberate avoidance is pissing him off.

"Do you enjoy it?" he asks.

"Enjoy what?" I ask back, buckling my belt and reaching for my suit coat.

"This thing you have for being… ambiguous." He sighs, then says, "No. That's too mild of a word. You have a problem with commitment, Connor. And it worries me. Because it's like a disease. If you don't confront it it will fester and take over."

"Look, I said I'd get out of it, OK? And I will."

"That's not what I'm talking about and you know it."

I sit down on the chair opposite him and start putting on my shoes, trying not to meet his intense gaze. "I mean… what do you want me to say? I'm just not a good decision-maker. I'm never gonna choose." I shrug as I stand up, dressed, but certainly not put back together.

"I can choose for you," he offers.

I roll my eyes. "I already know who you'd choose."

"Who?"

"Kiera."

"Now why would I do that, Connor? Why the hell would I choose the girl you love? And anyway, Kiera and I have a good friendship. I wouldn't want to put a strain on it like that."

"Like what?" I look around for my coat, then shoulder into it.

"Singular expectations."

I point my finger at him. "See, you've got the same disease."

He shrugs. "I've always wanted Sofia."

I stare at him for a second, my head filled with so many things right now. Where I'm at, where I'm supposed to be, the days of work I've missed, sex with Kiera, sex with Sofia, sex with Hayes… "Well, is that what you're gonna do, or what?"

"No."

I wait for more, but whatever he's really planning stays locked inside that weird head of his. I sigh. Loudly. "Look, can we talk about this later? I gotta go."

"Here's where we're different," Hayes says. "You're only looking for satisfaction. You're looking for the easier way to make things simple. Do I want Kiera? Or do I want

Sofia? When, in actuality, you want both. But both is complicated. Both is a lot of work. Never mind the logistics of getting a girl who lives in Vermont to move to the city, there's also someone standing in your way. Me. I don't want the simple, direct route to happiness. If I did, I'd have gone on pretending that book didn't exist. If I did, I wouldn't have offered to take your decisions away last night and brought Sofia to your bed. If I did," he says, kinda angry now, "I wouldn't have joined the three of you last night. I'm not afraid of complicated, Connor. I welcome it. Crave it. I want everything and that's where I stand."

I… just… blink at him. "Everything?" I say, like a dumbass.

"Everything we had and lost," he says. "I want it all back. That's why I'm here, that's why you're here, that's why we're all here."

There is a lifetime of eternal silence as I internalize what he just said. A lifetime of good sex, and weird days, and exciting adventures in that eternal silence as well.

"Not like that, asshole."

"What?" I say, so thoroughly fucking confused.

"I want us, man. You know. Normal shit. We can put this all behind us now, Connor. And that's a beautiful thing, don't you think?"

"What are you talking about?"

He sighs. Rubbing a finger along the top of his eyebrow as he shakes his head. "We didn't even finish the book. How did my perfect plan go so sideways?"

I glance down at the book, still sitting on the small side table. "Who cares about the book? We know how it ends."

"Do we?" Hayes asks. "I mean, I do. I read it. Very carefully."

"What?" I say, so off balance at how this morning—hell, this whole week—has just gone completely sideways. "So you knew about it?"

He nods. "I was thinking I'd just take care of it myself"—he looks away, out the window at the view of the water—"but then you saw it in the airport. I figured it would do its thing, maybe stay on the list a week or two, at most. And be forgotten. Just like everything else that happened back in senior year. And I could wrap this shit up without bringing the rest of you into it. Let you go on with your lives. But…" He shakes his head. Looks me in the eyes. "Now I can't."

For some reason I feel hot. And my heart starts beating too fast.

"Because you saw it and called Bennett, and he called me, and he told the girls before I could do damage control…" He throws up his hands. "So here we are."

"You wrote that book."

He shakes his head. "I absolutely did not write that book. We all know who wrote the fucking book, Connor. It was Kiera, remember? We were all there when she wrote it. Hell, we helped. How do you not remember?"

"I remember. I was there," I say, echoing what he just said, but getting a weird feeling about it. He opens his mouth to say more, but in that exact instant, my phone dings a text.

I pull it out of my pocket and stare at the screen.

"Who is it?"

"My father," I say, looking back at Hayes. "He's pissed. I gotta go."

"How long are you gonna let this go on?"

"I'll take care of it, OK? I'm fine with telling him I don't want to run."

"And what about all the other stuff, Connor?"

"What other stuff?"

"Jesus Christ," he says, running his fingers through his messed up hair. It's only then that I notice him. I mean like… really notice him. See him. He's wearing yesterday's suit as well. No jacket, just his two-thousand-dollar once starched flat, white button-down shirt that is now rumpled. Half tucked in, half pulled out. His jaw has a shadow across it, which looks good and accentuates his hard features. Maybe even softens them a little, in a masculine way. If that makes sense.

"What other stuff?" I ask. "You mean the book? I'm not gonna bring that book up to my father."

"Why not?" His eyes are blue, I notice. I don't think I've ever noticed that before. Blue. Which contrasts sharply with his nearly-black hair. They hold my gaze and we stare at each other for a long time. Seconds that seem like years. "Maybe you should take the book with you and plop it down on his desk. Ask him what the fuck?"

"Why the hell would I do that?"

Hayes huffs out a little breath of air. "Why the hell wouldn't you is the better question." He pauses, rakes his fingers through his already tousled hair, and says, "It's not fair, Connor. To keep her as a mistress. She deserves better after all she's been through. Either love her whole or set her free."

My phone dings again.

"I gotta go," I say for like the hundredth time. Only this time there's no urgency in it. No frustration. No defensiveness.

"So leave." And his words come out the same way. No anger. No blame. No expectations.

"I'll be back. Where you guys gonna be?"

"I don't know, Con. I have no idea."

"Call me then, OK? And let me know."

But he just stares at me.

"Can I take one of your cars?" I ask. Because I just realized I have no way home.

"The helicopter is waiting," he says, waving a hand at nothing in particular. "I'll text the pilot and let him know you're coming."

"Thanks," I say, meaning it. "For, you know… everything."

He shakes his head as I walk out the library's large double doors, calling, "I'll see you guys later," over my shoulder.

I'm sitting in the cold seat of the helicopter, halfway to the city, when I remember Emily.

Did he lie about her?

Or did someone lie to him?

Maybe I made her up? Maybe she was never there? Maybe I'm going crazy? Because I feel like I'm going crazy. This book, and Kiera, and how yesterday turned into last night, and the memories… it's all very insane-asylum crazy.

CHAPTER TWENTY

When I open my eyes Sofia is staring at me, her hands tucked under her cheek, light brown eyes catching the light filtering through a pair of sheer drapes so it illuminates those little rings of yellow in her irises.

"Hey," she says, smiling at me.

"Hey." I smile back. "What time is it?"

She turns over to peek at a clock. Which I can see without moving, but I don't care. I like the way her neck looks when she stretches it like that. "Almost two-thirty."

"Is Connor still here?"

"I don't know," she says, turning back to me.

"Hayes?"

"Haven't seen him. But I haven't been up yet, either. So no clue."

"How long have you been awake?"

She shrugs. "Twenty minutes, maybe? Half hour? I dunno."

"So… you've just been lying here, looking at me this whole time."

She smiles again. "Give it a minute, Kiera. Let last night sink in. Then tell me you don't need thirty minutes to process."

"Point," I say. I turn over on my back to stare at the ceiling, thinking back on what happened last night. "Did I fuck Hayes?"

We both laugh.

"Yes," she says through a building fit of giggles. "Did you like it?"

"Mmm-hmm," I mumble, thinking I'm gonna need more than thirty minutes to process.

"You're not mad at me?"

"For what?" I ask, turning my head to see her.

"Being with Connor."

I shrug. "He's half yours, Sofia. Always has been."

"I know, but it felt like things changed yesterday. You two were pretty attached to each other."

"Yeah," I admit. Then I turn all the way back over onto my side so I can see her properly. "But that's just because we forgot."

She blushes. Closes her eyes for an extended second. And when she finally opens them again she says, "I forgot too. But Hayes reminded me. I figured he and I would be together, for the most part, anyway. But then Connor—"

"We'd finished," I say in way of explanation. "It was just your turn. That's all."

She nods. Silent. Then says, "Do you think this is weird?"

I nod back, then whisper, "Yes."

"Do you think it'll work?"

"I dunno, Sofia." Then I sigh. "But I've been sharing him with you for as long as we've been friends. I just want to know my place, that's all. And if I made you jealous that last night Connor and I were alone together in the tower, then I'm sorry. I didn't want him to myself to keep you away. I just wanted to know what it felt like to be the only one."

She stares at me for a few silent seconds. "Did you like it?"

I nod. "I did. But I think I like what we did last night better."

"You mean… with Hayes?"

I nod again. "It feels good to be back together. Do you think that makes me a bad person? You know, because of how it all started?"

"No. Just a normal one. I like being with you guys too."

"Hey," Hayes says.

We both sit up and find him standing in the doorway looking like a man who's been fucking three people at the same time.

Hayes and I have been friends for a long time and never once has he even tried to kiss me outside of senior year when we were all together. Not once. I don't know how I feel about him, or Sofia, or even Connor, for that matter. I just know I want them with me. Always. Every day. Every night. I never want to go home. I never want to go back to that sad, solitary existence again.

"Where's Con?" Sofia asks.

"Work," Hayes says. And it comes out kinda angry.

"Oh," Sofia and I say in the same breath.

We have no work to go to.

Well, that's not true. We're just stay-at-home workers with no set schedule.

Also not true. We have deadlines. Especially me, since I publish a lot more than she does. But they are my deadlines, not anyone else's. And I don't have to meet them if I don't want to.

The point is, we don't wake up and go to work. Not like Connor and Bennett do. I have no clue what Hayes does with his days. Not even one. So whether he's used to lounging around all day on a Thursday, I have no idea.

"Well, I need to go home and shower. You wanna come with me?"

At first I think she's talking to me, but then I realize she's looking at Hayes. And then… it hits me that she's talking to both of us.

"Yes," he says. "Get dressed, ladies. We have a lot to do today."

He turns away and disappears.

"What was that about?" Sofia asks.

"I dunno. The book? Maybe?"

"Shit, that stupid fucking book. I'd forgotten all about it. I wish it would just disappear. Just leave us alone."

I stare at her for a moment because I'd forgotten about her sadness. Which is the kind of sadness that permeates a person. That wraps itself around a person like a blanket. And she has always been a girl who snuggled up to sadness.

But in these few minutes since waking she was someone else. Someone unfamiliar to sadness. Someone happy and content who didn't need that blanket emotion to hold on to.

Sofia throws her legs out from under the covers and swings them over the side of the bed. She sits there for a moment, her back to me, long, dark hair hanging almost to her waist.

I reach out and touch it and she looks over her shoulder. Hunching them a little. And if I were in front of her, instead of behind, I'd see how that movement pushed her breasts together.

She has nice breasts. They're a little bit bigger than mine. Very round and firm.

She smiles at me, then stands up. I let her hair fall away from my fingertips and study her shape. The curve of her hips and the length of her legs. She bends over, flashing her pussy at me, and picks something up.

My nightgown, I realize.

Then she slips it over herself, shoots me a smile over her shoulder, and walks out of the room.

Fucking Sofia… isn't bad, I decide.

But all of this seems like something from the past. Like I'm still caught in a dream. Or a web of… of what?

The first word that comes to mind is lies.

But that's not true. It can't be true. We were nothing if not truthful. I made sure of it. I wrote it all down in the book.

I lie there for a little while—a few minutes, maybe—processing. Wondering about the past and trying to imagine the future.

"Are you coming?" I look over at the door and find Hayes peeking his head through.

"Hmmm?"

"Get dressed, Kiera. That wasn't really a question."

I laugh. "Fuck off."

"Seriously," he says. "I'm gonna drop you two off at Sofia's and then I have shit to do before Connor gets home."

"Home?"

"Sofia's house. We're gonna stay there for now."

"We?"

"Get up and get dressed." He leaves me with that. No explanation, just orders.

I don't mind the orders, but I would like to know the rules of this temporary arrangement. But that can't happen until we're all four together again, so I give in. Get up. Get dressed. Pack up my bag I brought and place it in front of the doorway as Hayes talks on the phone about… whatever. And Sofia takes extra long getting ready in her suite bathroom.

When we're all back on the same page, heading down the stairs—two house people carrying our bags—I suddenly remember something.

"Did they ever find Emily?"

Hayes ignores me. Or pretends he didn't hear the question. Or maybe he's just thinking about something else. So I ask again. "Hayes? Did they ever find Emily?'

"Yes," he says, straight away this time. "She was found early this morning. She's back where she belongs now."

"Good," Sofia says, letting out a long breath of air once we reach the bottom of the stairs.

"Has anyone talked to Camille?" I ask.

"I called her while I was getting my stuff together," Sofia says. "She's gonna meet us for dinner."

"Cool," I say. And I mean it too. Because this is the part I've missed living up in Vermont. Meeting for dinner and stuff like that. And Camille lives in the building across the street from Sofia. If I stay there with her—if we all stay there with her—then I can meet up with Camille all the time.

I feel unreasonably happy about this new perk.

When we get outside the frigid air reminds all of us that it's mid-December.

And then I have another thought. If I stay in the city I can go to Christmas parties. Surely Sofia and Camille have invitations to all the best Christmas parties. I'll get to go shopping, and buy gifts for people, and wake up to Christmas morning. Which I used to do with my mom, before she died. But these past two years have been very lonely for me during the holidays.

There's a car waiting for us. A driver opens the back door and since I'm the first to reach it, I get in and scoot all the way down. Sofia gets in after me, then Hayes.

We sit there, breathing out puffs of steam, as the driver closes us up and walks around the back of the car to get in the driver's seat.

There's a partition between us and the driver, so that's the last thought I have about him.

Now all I can think about is how good the heater feels, and how nice it feels to be pressed up against another body. One you're allowed to be pressed up against.

Sofia must feel the same way, because she leans over and rests her head against Hayes. And I do the same to her. So we are a sideways pile of people who are allowed to crush each other with body parts.

I want to giggle at that thought. I should write that down. What a fun sentence. Use it in my next book.

But then Hayes says, "How would you like to go to a party this Saturday night?"

Sofia says nothing so I answer for us. "Yes." It's like Hayes can read my mind.

"Great. I'll let Connor, Bennett, and Camille know attendance is required."

"Whose party is it?" Sofia asks. She must be tired because her words come out in a mumble.

"Louise Livingston's."

I have never loved New York City. I'm not a New Yorker. My little town of Charlotte, Vermont is my happy place. But I have to admit, being chauffeured down Fifth Avenue and dropped off in the valet in front of Sofia's pre-war building impresses me.

I've read her books. I read all about her version of New York. I've lived in the apartments and townhomes of her characters. I've walked through Central Park across the street and sat on the steps of the Met to eat lunch. I've experienced the splendor she writes about and even though none of those settings were her own personal apartment, I thought I'd prepared for the luxurious and opulent world she lives in.

I was wrong. I am not prepared at all. I get the doorman. I get it. I have seen these things on TV, and I've been to the city with Hayes several times over the years, so I'm expecting the greeting. "Good afternoon, Miss Astor." But after that things get a little surreal.

"Hello, Gregory," Sofia says, accepting Hayes' hand as he helps her from the car.

Gregory tips his head at Hayes. "Mr. Fitzgerald. How are you doing today?"

"Just fine, thanks," Hayes replies, reaching in for me.

"Hello, miss," Gregory says to me with a cheery smile. "Welcome to the Corinthian. You're a new guest for our Miss Sofia, aren't you?"

"Yes," I manage to say, looking up at her building like a tourist.

"Gregory, this is Kiera Bonnaire," Sofia says. "She's staying with me."

"Welcome, welcome, Miss Bonnaire! Anything you need, you just ask."

"Thank you," I say, feeling nervous for some reason.

Then Sofia leans into him, cupping her hand near her mouth like she's gonna tell him a secret, and whispers—not all that softly—"She's a famous author, Gregory. So if any fans come looking..." Sofia makes a *shhhh* sound with a finger to her lips.

"Mum's the word." Gregory beams.

Sofia beams back.

"We have two bags," Hayes says, palming a tip into Gregory's hand.

"I'll take care of it, sir."

Then Hayes is between us, placing his hands gently on the small of our backs, urging us towards the door. Gregory turns a key in a short pillar of stone near the entrance to the classic green canopy that covers the walkway leading to the entrance. And when we enter the lobby that's it, I'm done.

I know it's dumb. I just came from a mansion so big I can't wrap my head around it. But that was Long Island. This is Fifth Avenue.

It's art deco. Straight lines that bend in sharp corners. And glittering sun medallions made of inlaid marble on the floor. It's black, and white, and gold, and old. Every man is in a suit. Every woman fresh with perfect makeup and designer clothes, and necklaces that cost more than my cottage.

How is this real?

It makes no sense. So many rich people in one place, sipping afternoon tea in low velvet upholstered chairs with tiers of scones, and pastries, and pretty little finger sandwiches piled on silver trays. There are small gatherings of conversation. People whispering secrets, holding martini glasses, and drinking in the bar. Because this isn't an apartment building. It's a hotel. She lives in a hotel penthouse.

I knew that. I did. But I didn't understand it until this moment.

"You coming?" Hayes asks, pushing on my back a little.

I realize I've stopped to gawk. I look down at my feet. My shabby shearling boots. Realize I'm wearing leggings and a too-big coat and get a little lost in the inlaid marble sun medallion as I try to control my instant feeling of inadequacy.

"Yes," I say, looking back up at the expectant faces of Sofia and Hayes. "Sorry." I laugh. "I'm just... wow, this place is a palace, Sofia."

"Wait till you get upstairs." Hayes chuckles, urging me forward again.

We stand in front of the bank of brass-fronted elevators. The art deco design continues here. Something that looks like an upside-down waterfall engraved into the gold facade parts in the middle as a door opens and we get in.

There's a bench in there. And an attendant. "Good afternoon, Miss Astor," the woman says. "How are you today?"

"Oh"—Sofia laughs softly, placing a hand on her heart as she looks at Hayes and me—"I'm having the best time."

"So happy to hear that," the attendant replies.

I wonder, as we ascend to the heights above New York, what it would be like to interact with so many people in the course of one day. And for it not to be a special occasion, like it is for me, but an everyday occurrence.

I don't know if I'd like it. Intimacy isn't my thing. I prefer to write about it. I prefer to live it in my head and put it down on paper.

The doors open directly into Sofia's apartment and the first thing I see is New York. And the park down below covered in white.

"Wow," I say.

"Jesus," Hayes says. "You have never been this impressed with my place."

"No, well…" I laugh and stutter. "Your place is super impressive, Hayes. But I've been there before. And it's like a museum. I can relate to a museum. I just can't relate to this at all."

"You hate it," Sofia says, pouting.

"No." I chuckle. "I love it." Then I take a deep breath and look around. Everything is decorated in black and gold, just like downstairs. So Sofia. Long drapes hang at the edges of floor-to-ceiling windows. The floor up here is classic black and white tiles laid in a diagonal pattern. And they have glittering flecks of gold where the grout lines should be. Something you'd see in a pre-war penthouse, for sure.

There's a staircase leading up to a second floor and a grand living room beyond the foyer. My whole body turns to take it all in. To picture her here, all these years, writing.

"Where's your office?" I ask.

"Down that way." She points, then squeaks out a surprise as Hayes leans down to kiss her. "Be back soon," he says, and gets back in the elevator. "I'm gonna go find Connor and Bennett. Kiera, don't forget. You need something to wear this weekend."

Right. The party at Louise's house.

I've never been there. I wonder if it looks more like Hayes' museum? Or Sofia's penthouse?

Then I start thinking about how different Hayes is from when I first met him at school in senior year. Back then he was wild. A party guy. Always drinking, and smoking pot, and driving fast and doing shit rich-boys with no fucks to give do.

But over the years he's mellowed a lot. Turned back into the boy his parents raised instead of the one who rebelled.

I like all his parts. The bad ones, the good ones, the wild ones, the mellow ones. And I like the fact that I know him—have known him—all the ways I know him. Because even though everyone else ghosted on me—or maybe I ghosted on them? Not quite sure about that—he was always there.

At first it was kind of like dating. Except we didn't kiss, or fuck, or anything like that. We just met up, or went out to lunch, or went to dinner, or a movie, or a gallery opening.

Mostly it was in Burlington not New York.

I realize that Hayes Fitzgerald has been the only constant thing in my life for the past ten years.

Well, that and writing.

Sofia and Camille were there online, but that's different. It's much less personal. I didn't get to smell their perfume, or see their home décor change over the years, or help them decide if a guy hitting on them at a party or a bar was worth their effort.

And now all that is gonna change. I know Connor didn't say we're gonna be together, and Sofia and Hayes didn't say we're gonna be best friends, but we are. I know it.

Once Hayes leaves Sofia and I stare at each other in the large foyer.

We will be best friends, right? We already have so much in common.

"So..." Sofia says.

Oh, God. Please. Do not let this turn into one of those awkward we-have-nothing-in-common moments.

"Wanna see the office?" Sofia offers.

"Yes," I breathe. Relief flooding through my body.

Because my fear is stupid. We have a ton of things in common. Writing, for one. Books, offices where we write books... Connor. Hayes. Sex. Books. Writing. Camille and Bennett. School. Books. Writing. Sex...

I don't know about this. The whole idea seems crazy now that we're alone at her place. Like an unobtainable dream.

"It's down here." She leads me through the large living room, past the gleaming stainless steel chef's kitchen, to a hallway that goes both directions once we reach it. We turn right and head towards the side of the building that faces the park.

I know before we even step inside that she has that same view. And she does.

The New York skyline sweeps out before me. Her walls on either side are lined with navy blue painted built-in shelves with a splash of gold peeking out from behind the books. They climb all the way up to the vaulted ceiling. An elegant writing desk, painted to match the built-ins, sits in the middle of the space. It's very art deco with an oval top and skinny brass legs that taper to a point on the floor. Laptop closed up on top and a gold velvet armchair tilted to one side, like she just got up to take a break, but will return to work soon. It's a corner room, and the other window faces a side street, not Fifth Avenue. There's a large sectional couch the same gold velvet as the chair pushed up against the window on that side. Almost a perfect square.

Sofia notices me looking at the couch and says, "Camille lives right across the street in that building there." She points and I look out at the terrace just a short distance away. "Sometimes we write together. Well, not together. I sit here on my couch and she sits there on her couch and we write."

"Wow," I say, unable to stop the awe in my voice. "I write on my couch too, laptop propped up on a pillow, wearing leggings. But it's nothing like this. I bet you even get dressed every day, don't you."

"You're stupid." She laughs. "But no. I mean, yes. I do get dressed everyday. But I don't always write in here. Sometimes I write in bed. Especially when… you know. *Those scenes* come up."

I raise my eyebrows at her. "You get off on your own sex scenes?"

"Don't you?"

I laugh. Loud. Shake my head. "No."

"Never?"

"Well, sometimes. But I don't like… stop writing to masturbate."

"Oh." She fans herself. "Lucky you. I turn myself on so hard sometimes I lose a whole afternoon."

"You do not." I giggle.

"I swear to God. Sometimes Camille has to come over here and shake me out of it."

"Sicko," I say.

She shrugs. "You should try it." Then she blushes unexpectedly and says, "I'm really glad we all got back together yesterday."

"Yesterday, Jesus. How has it only been one day?"

"Feels like you never left," she says, closing the small space that separates us to wrap her hand around my arm. "And I really hope you stay, Kiera. I mean that. This… whatever it is we're doing. I love it already. I want things to be like this for a while. Maybe even a long while. And I'm excited to see Louise. Aren't you?"

"I dunno," I say, slipping out of her grip to walk forward to the windows. I press my forehead to the cold glass and look down at the street below. Maybe this is too much change for me? Things seem to be moving forward pretty fast and I've always thought of myself as a girl stuck in the past. That's why I live where I do. That's why I don't have to go to the library or the coffee shop down the road for internet, that's why I don't mind not having cell coverage or even a TV. That's why I listen to old records like Bennett.

Hmmm. I get lost in that realization for a second. Bennett and his Victrola and all those old records. Did I steal that from him?

"Shit."

"What?" I ask, not turning to look at her. Because I'm second-guessing everything and I hate it. Why do I always do that? I always withdraw when things go fast. Why?

"We forgot the book. I wanted to read it today."

"We don't need to read it, Sofia. We know what it says."

"Do we?"

I turn to look at her. "Of course. We know how it ends, at least. With us breaking up and going our separate ways."

She shrugs. "Maybe whoever wrote it gave us a HEA?"

"I don't see how," I say, a little bit of annoyance leaking out in my tone. "It was one of us and we're not HEA kind of people."

"Speak for yourself," she says. And now she seems annoyed. "HEA is my job. It's yours too."

"Yeah, but you write the kind of story that leads to an HEA. Mine are dark. And most of the time I just want to kill them at the end."

"What?" She giggles. Like this was a joke.

"For real. I hate writing happy endings. Hate it."

"Why? That's the best part."

I shrug. "Not for me. I like the crisis myself. I like that moment when everything is so hopeless and I know my readers are getting pissed off."

"Hmmm," she mumbles. "You're kinda weird, you know that, Kiera?"

I nod. "I know."

We're quiet for a little while after that. I turn back to the window and press my head on the cold glass. Watching the little people down below. Thinking up stories about them.

"You see that lady?" I say, breaking the silence. Sofia is close, but not right up against the window like me. "That one with the red knee-high boots?"

Sofia takes two steps and looks down. "Yeah."

"Who wears boots like that in the fucking snow? I bet they're like four-inch heels."

She huffs. I think it's a laugh but I'm not a hundred percent sure. "New Yorkers. They're probably leather too," she adds.

"Yeah, and by the time she gets to the first-date dinner she's all dressed up for they'll be ruined."

"But her date… he's super rich. Like Hayes."

"And weird," I add.

"Super weird. But in a kinky way. And he insists on buying her a new pair. Like immediately. Before they even have dinner."

"Because he's a controlling asshole and needs her to be perfect if they're gonna dine together in the Corinthian restaurant."

"No." She laughs. "Because he's worried that her feet are wet and cold."

I snort.

She grips my arm again. Leans into me. Rests her head on me. Sighs. "We're gonna be OK."

I turn my head. Slowly. Look at her. See those amber circles in her eyes. "You sure about that?"

She nods.

"Because I don't think we are. I think we're a bunch of very fucked-up people and it's all downhill from here."

"It's not," she says.

But she's wrong.

Everything is wrong. Connor showing up with that book. Letting him stay the night and fucking him. Hayes appearing in a helicopter and taking us back to that crazy mansion. Emily. Just the fact that she was there. That whole hide-and-seek game she played was just the cherry on top.

And then last night, of course. And today.

"It's all wrong," I say. "Every bit of this is wrong."

"Stop it," she whispers. "It's not wrong."

"Not us," I say, turning to face her. "This."

She squints her eyes at me, like I'm talking about her apartment. Or New York. But her furrowed brow relaxes. She takes a deep breath. "Just don't think so hard. That's how I get through it."

And I want to say… *Get through what? What are we getting through?*

But I can't. I can't make myself ask those questions.

Because deep down inside I know all the answers. And deep down inside I know that's where they need to stay.

Buried.

CHAPTER TWENTY-ONE

I'm surprised to find Camille in my office. She's with Bennett, but he's supposed to be there. She's not.

"Hey," I say, walking in and dropping my briefcase on the floor next to my desk.

It's a large office. My dad's offices, actually. I just have one corner on the east side of the building. Thank God he's all the way on the other side because that means I can sneak in without seeing him.

But everyone else saw me. So the reprieve will be short-lived.

"What the fuck was last night?" Bennett asks, picking up a pen from my desk, then clicks it incessantly as he leans back into the chair next to Camille.

I raise one eyebrow at him. "I'm not sure I understand the question, Counsellor."

"The fucking… fucked-up… fuckery!" Camille spits.

"Well, thanks for that, Camille," I say, sitting down in front of my desk. "It's all clear now."

"The book, Emily, the game of Clue, the dinner," Bennett says, listing all the fuckery.

"Did you guys ever find the crazy bitch?" Camille asks.

I just stare at her, thinking back on what happened earlier. Did I make that up? I mean, I thought it was real, but Hayes… would Hayes lie to me?

"Connor?" Bennett says, losing patience fast. Which is unlike him most days. Most days he's pretty laid back. "Answer us."

"I mean, what do you want me to say?"

"Did they find her?"

"Yes," I say. Because no matter if I saw her or not, she was found by someone.

"Is she back in the hospital?" Camille asks.

"I… don't know. I mean, yes. Yes. She's back in the hospital."

"You don't sound sure," Bennett says, still clicking that pen.

"I'm sure," I say, wholly unsure. "Now… is there a reason you're in my office right now?"

"Yeah," Bennett says, clicking that stupid pen again. I stare at his thumb as it presses and releases whatever that little sticking-up clicky thing is called on the end of a pen. "Your father called me in to look over your statement of candidacy and make sure all the committees are set up with the people we talked about." He juts his head to a folder sitting in front of me on my desk.

"These?"

"Yeah. It's all filled out except for your signature. You just never mentioned anything about the announcement last night so I was sorta surprised."

"What?" I say.

"You're announcing on Saturday night?"

I shake my head. "No, I'm not. I'm not even gonna run. Things have changed."

I look over at Camille and wait for her typical sardonic insult that will simultaneously cut me down and blow me up in the same breath. But she says nothing. Just looks at me with lots of questions in her eyes.

"What?" I ask her.

She shakes her head but speaks at the same time. "You ever get that feeling that you've been here before?"

I know what she's talking about. The word for it escapes me, but that's not what she's talking about. Something else…

"So anyway," Bennett says. "I guess I understand the announcement on Saturday night, but Louise? Why the hell?"

I want to say, *What are you talking about?* But I've used up my quota of dumbass questions for the day. Even I'm getting sick of my clueless repetition. So I take a deep breath and reply, "Louise is hosting my announcement party?"

They both nod at me, frowning. Like this makes them unhappy in a sad way. Which is weird. Then Camille says, "I'm not going." She shakes her head. "I'm not going. I'm not going anywhere anymore. I'm staying home in my apartment and…" She lets out a long breath of air. "I'm just not going."

"OK," I say. Cautiously. "But"—I put my hands up, palms out—"and I'm not trying to be a dick here, but you weren't invited. No one expects you to show up for my party. Hell, I'm not even gonna show up for my party."

"Connor," Bennett says. "Hayes called a little while ago and said we had to go. All six of us."

"Why?"

"I don't know."

"It's that book," Camille says. "That stupid book. Everything was fine until that book showed up and now everything is not. I'm not going to the party, you guys. I'm not going."

"It's fine, Camille," Bennett says. "You don't have to go."

"You can't go either. I need to stay with a buddy."

She looks at me like I'm the one making Bennett go to the party. "He doesn't have to go."

"Tell Hayes that," she snaps. "He's insisting that we all be there."

"Knock, knock."

For fuck's sake. My father chooses this moment to show up at my office?

"Camille. Bennett. Will you excuse us for a minute?"

Camille rudely turns her back on my father just as Bennett mumbles out, "Yeah, I'm done here. We gotta get going."

He grabs Camille's hand, leading her towards the door, but my father doesn't move. He's a big guy. Taller than me even and I'm over six foot. So he literally blocks their exit.

"Everything OK, Camille?" my father asks.

She refuses to look at him. Just keeps her head down and says, "Can we go?"

But my father doesn't move. "Dad, get out of the way."

He shoots me a stern look, then backs off. Camille slips by, dragging Bennett behind her by the hand.

"What the fuck was that?" I ask my father.

He steps into my office and closes the door. "I'm gonna assume you saw the paperwork? Go ahead and sign it so we can make everything official tomorrow morning and make the announcement Saturday night."

"Yeah, we need to talk," I say. "I'm not running."

"Like hell, you're not. Now sign the statement of candidacy and let's get this going."

"Dad, I'm not running."

"You are running, Connor. This is what you've been planning—"

"No, this is what you've been planning. I don't even want to be in politics."

"No one wants to be in politics, son. It's just something that needs to be done."

"Look," I say, sighing deeply and running my fingers through my hair. "I've made my decision. I'm not—"

But my phone dings a text in my pocket, cutting me off. I stare at my father for a few seconds. We say nothing. Then another text comes in. I break the standoff and pull my phone out, reading the messages.

Hayes: *Don't confront your father today. We are going to Louise's house for that party this weekend.*

Hayes: *Just trust me.*

Just trust him.

"You're running for Senate," my father says. "So sign the paper and let me handle everything else. Just go home and have a drink."

I feel like I'm living someone else's life right now. Or I'm in some kind of alternate reality. Everything is a little bit off. This is my father, but I feel like I don't know him. This is my office, but I feel like I have no purpose here.

"Connor," my father snaps. "Everything has been filled out for you. Just sign the fucking paper."

My phone dings again.

Hayes: *Are you getting these messages? Don't tell your father you're not running yet. I'm on my way over to your office now. Just tell him what he wants to hear and meet me downstairs in five minutes.*

I pick up a pen, open the folder, glance down at the papers. Just two sheets. So simple to run for Senate. Just one signature.

I sign, close the folder, and hold it out for my father. "Here. Done."

He forces a smile as he walks forward and takes the folder from my outstretched hand. "What's going on with you?"

"Nothing. I'm just not sure this is what I want to do."

"Well, that's not nothing. That's a complete one-eighty to what we've been planning and discussing for the last five years."

I want to say so much here. Things like, *I haven't been planning anything. You're the one who made all the plans. I just went along.*

But I don't have the energy. And besides, it feels like a losing battle. A battle I'm not prepared to fight.

"The party on Saturday is important, Connor."

"I realize this," I say.

"Your speechwriters are hard at work and we'll have that for you in the morning. I don't know what's going on with you and your… friends. But it needs to stop."

"What are you talking about?"

"I know where you've been. Bennett told me you were up in Vermont visiting… that woman?"

"You mean Kiera?"

"Don't get involved with her again. You know how hard I worked to extract you from that whole mess back in school. She was the reason that whole year happened."

I think about that for a moment. Because it's so obviously not true. I mean… I can't put my finger on why everything happened the way it did in senior year, and my father certainly doesn't know the whole truth because I never said a word to him, but it definitely wasn't Kiera's fault.

"Sure, Dad," I say. "Whatever."

He stares at me for a moment. It's a stern, don't-fuck-with-me stare that I haven't seen him wear for a long time. I actually lean back in my chair, a little off balance. Then his face softens, like he's making a conscious effort, and he says, "Good. We're on our way now, Con. In three years you'll be on your way to DC and that's when your life really starts."

"Can't wait," I say, forcing a smile. But it's just like the lie he told about Kiera. So obviously not true.

If he picks up on that, he holds it in. Because he's wearing his public persona smile right now. I learned to recognize it early. Fake.

"I'll get this over to Steven and he'll be your handler from here."

And then he walks out.

I don't like that word. Handler. I've known Steven my entire life. But he's my father's friend, not mine.

My phone dings again. A quick look lets me know that Hayes is downstairs waiting.

I didn't even get to take my coat off, but it's already evening. And I don't want to be here. So I pick up my briefcase and make my way down to Hayes' waiting car pulled up alongside the curb in front of the building.

I get in. "Jesus Christ. I don't think I realized it before today, but I don't like my father."

Hayes just offers me a glass with Scotch over ice. "You signed the papers?"

"How'd you know?"

"I saw Bennett and Camille come out. He told me. Did you sign?"

"I signed."

"Good."

"How is that good? I told you, I don't want to run for office. And he's already up in my shit about Kiera."

"Did you tell him about the book?"

I shake my head. "No."

"Good. Forget about him until Saturday. I have a plan."

"What plan?" I ask, taking a long, much-needed sip of my drink.

"Tomorrow," he says. "We'll go over it tomorrow. Tonight we're going home and forgetting about all this bullshit."

"Home?"

"Sofia's place. Kiera's there. And that's where we're gonna stay. At least this weekend."

I relax a little. Sink down into the soft leather seats of the car. Think about last night. Not the weird parts. And by weird I don't mean the fucking foursome we had. I mean… Emily. The book. That kinda weird stuff.

"Sounds nice," I say.

Hayes nods, looking absently out the window. "Yeah, it really kinda does."

I picture how we'll spend the evening. Dinner? Drinks? Sex? It all sounds great. But all this comes with so many questions. And this time none of them are about Emily and the book.

"What are we doing?" I ask.

Hayes glances at me, then returns to looking out the window. "We're living, Connor. That's all this is. For once in our lives, we're living."

I think about that all the way up to Sofia's Upper East Side apartment. Wonder if he's right. I haven't felt this… melancholy, for lack of a better word, in a very long time. Maybe never. But I don't feel like I wasn't living these past ten years. I did a lot of shit. Went to law school with Bennett. That's what I did first, though I never practiced. Just passed the bar and hung those accolades up on my office wall. But it was planned that way. It was just the required background for an eventual political career.

I dated some girls. One for a few years.

What was her name?

I huff out a laugh. Embarrassed, ashamed? For not remembering.

"What's so funny?"

"Did you know I dated a woman for almost three years and right now I can't even remember her name?"

He looks at me like, *And that's funny why*?

"It's funny because you said… we're gonna live now, you know. And I was thinking, hey, I've lived. I've done plenty. Got that law degree on my wall to prove it. But I swear to God, I can see this girl's face and I can't even remember her name."

"It's like you blocked her out." Hayes sighs.

"Lisa," I say. "No, Liza. Yeah. Fucking Liza. She was a…"

But I don't have the word ready so I need a second to think.

"She was a what?" Hayes says.

"A wife, ya know? That type of girl."

"Let me guess, your father loved her?"

Did he? "Yeah, he kinda did."

"So why'd you break it off?"

I shrug. "It just felt so fake, ya know? She was boring."

"Stepford Wives often are," he deadpans.

And I laugh. Because he's right. And those are the words I was looking for. "Yeah, that chick was no Kiera. She's never gonna write an erotic story."

Hayes is quiet as we slowly make our way through rush-hour traffic. Then he says, "Did you ever read Sofia's erotica?"

"No. I didn't even know she wrote that stuff until Kiera told me. I thought she was sitting up in her princess tower penning literature all these years."

"Did you ever read Kiera's stuff?"

"No." I shake my head. "Why have you?"

He nods. "Yeah. It's pretty dark shit. You know, Stockholm syndrome kinda shit."

"Wait, this is Kiera? Or both of them?"

"Both."

"Huh," I say.

"Why?"

"It's just… Kiera's kinda dark like that so I get it. But Sofia." I shake my head. "Never pictured her writing anything other than boring tales of boring women."

"You know what's really funny?" Hayes asks me.

"What?"

"Camille writes uplifting shit."

I laugh. Kinda loud. "Get the fuck out of here."

"No, really."

"You read all of them?"

He nods. "Yeah, she writes funny stuff with positive messages."

"Gross," I say.

We both laugh.

Then he says, "I've missed you, Con."

I grin and look at him. "Yeah, ditto. Feels good to be with you guys again. I've had Bennett in my life for what seems like forever. But it's not the same. I'm not glad that book was written, but if it had to be written then I'm glad it brought us all back together." Then I think about it a little more thoroughly and add, "Well, except for Emily."

"Why not Emily?" he asks.

I just laugh at his joke.

"No, really. Why not Emily?"

"Because she fucking shot Kiera, Hayes. She could've killed her."

"But if all that shit in the tower is true—"

"What do you mean *if* it's true?"

"—then it wasn't her fault."

"What the fuck are you talking about?" But even as the words are coming out of my mouth I'm picturing Emily this morning. *I didn't do it.*

"I'm just saying that she did what she had to, that's all. It was an impossible situation. I think we all agree on that. Some nameless, faceless stranger controlling us without our consent. Making us perform sexual acts and shit. It's so fucked up. You can't really blame her."

"Well, yeah, I can. Because she did that the very first night. Nothing even happened at that point. We didn't know what that year was gonna turn into. She just… got an order and followed it. Which is fucked up. So yeah, I blame her. She split us up from the beginning. Maybe if we had a chance to talk shit over before—"

"Talk what over?" Hayes asks.

"Whatever." I laugh. "The tower."

"Have you ever been back there?"

"Why the fuck would I go back?"

Hayes shrugs. "I dunno. Just to see if you could get back in. Take a fresh look at things from a ten-years-later perspective?"

"No, thanks," I say, kinda feeling sick just thinking about it.

"You never showed for any of the alumni dinners."

"No. Why did you?"

"Not at first," he says, looking me dead in the eyes. "But the past few, yeah."

"Huh," I say, trying to picture that. "Did anyone else go?"

He nods.

"Who?"

"Louise."

"Hmmm," I say. "Weird. She's so fucking weird."

"Do you know what she does?"

"No," I say. "Never saw her again. Never heard anything about her again."

"She's a doctor."

I nod. "I guess I can see that."

Hayes holds my gaze. Too long, so it becomes uncomfortable. I'm just about to ask him why he's looking at me that way when he says, "Yeah. I'll be interested to see your reaction to her on Saturday."

"Speaking of Saturday," I say. "How did you know my father was going to throw a party at her house? Bennett said you mentioned it earlier."

"Just a really good guess."

Which is a really strange response that deserves all the follow-up questions, but the car stops in front of a building that must be Sofia's, and Hayes opens his door to get out.

He looks over his shoulder, one foot already exiting, and says, "Forget about all this shit for a night. The girls are waiting upstairs."

And then the rest of him is out on the street and the door closes, leaving me alone.

Sofia's apartment is like a smaller copy of her building lobby twelve floors down below. Black marble floors with glittering gold lines separating each tile. Long sheer black curtains flanking each of the floor to ceiling windows, crushed-velvet yellow couches placed facing each other, and armchairs in deep navy blue on either end creating a seating area that reminds me of Hayes' third-floor library.

She and Kiera are busy in the gleaming stainless steel chef's kitchen when Hayes and I enter the main living area, their backs to us.

"Hey!" Sofia calls out, putting a tray of bread into the oven. "I hope you two are hungry."

Kiera looks over her shoulder, washing her hands at the sink, and smiles as she turns and wipes them dry on an apron.

I stop where I'm at and just stare at her. Fresh now, like me. She's wearing an outfit similar to the ones I've seen her in all week. Beige leggings, long brown sweater with a low-hanging neckline, and those shearling boots that make her look like a model in a brochure for mountain cabin rentals. Her unruly blonde hair is pulled up in a ponytail, but it's not a neat one—like how Sofia has her hair today—but messy and wild. Just like her.

I smile back. Let myself get lost in her for a moment.

"Let me help," Hayes says, hanging his coat on a hook that holds an assortment of aprons. I stop and wait, wondering if he's gonna put on one, but he doesn't. Just unbuttons his shirt cuffs and starts rolling up his sleeves as he leans in to give Sofia a kiss on the cheek.

My eyes dart to Kiera, watching her as she watches them, and then she lets him kiss her cheek too.

"What can I do?" Hayes asks.

"The meatballs," Sofia says, pointing to the lower of her double ovens.

"On it," Hayes says, grabbing some oven mitts.

Kiera is walking towards me now, so I reach for her and pull her into me, unable to stop myself from leaning into her neck to smell the fresh scent of her hair. "Hey," she says. "I think I missed you."

I laugh a little, kissing her neck. "I think I missed you too."

I glance at Hayes and Sofia, wondering what they're thinking about. Wondering if they've noticed the way I have that we've paired up. That foursome we had last night is feeling very far away now. Like a dream or something.

But they're not even looking at us. Way too busy with dinner. Having some conversation that I can't really make out, but acting like this is a normal Thursday night for them.

Acting like this is familiar.

"Jesus," Kiera says. "You guys look like a freaking power couple in there getting ready to throw a dinner party."

Sofia chuckles, looking over at us as she stirs a pot of what I assume is pasta on the stove. "We've been throwing *Game of Thrones* watch parties for a few years now. I've got him well trained."

I pull away from Kiera so I can see her face. We laugh.

"Get the fuck out of here," I say.

"Seriously," Hayes says. "When did we start doing that, Sof?"

She stops her stirring and ponders this. "Season three? Four?"

Hayes points to her. "Red Wedding season. When was that?"

"Season three," she confirms. "God, where did the years go? It seems like yesterday."

"Five years?" Kiera asks. "How come you never told me about this? I would've loved to come to those."

Hayes shrugs. "I didn't think you were into it."

"You had those parties here?" I ask, looking around at Sofia's apartment. The large flat-screen over her fireplace. Picturing how she'd arrange the seating to accommodate a horde of *Game of Thrones* fans. Imagining the conversation about dragons and dwarfs. Unable to reconcile this image of Hayes.

"Yup," Sofia says. "It's kind of a big deal. Sometimes we have like twenty people. Camille always came, Kiera. Bennett didn't come to all of them, but he made a few each season. We have other parties too, if you're not into the fantasy stuff. I'll add you to our Facebook group."

Facebook group? Hayes and Sofia have a Facebook group to coordinate their parties?

"Hmmm," Kiera says. "You should've invited me, Hayes. I've been having lunch with you at least once a month this whole time and you never said a word about watch parties with Sofia and Camille."

Yeah, that's weird too. How is it that I got through these ten years barely talking to any of them and Hayes had a secret relationship with all of them but me? And is it weird that Bennett never mentioned this? I mean, I've seen him like almost every day since we graduated from Essex.

"I'm starting to take this personally, Hayes."

He laughs, busy with the fucking meatballs.

"Seriously, why didn't you reach out to me?"

His laugh falls away and he's silent for a few moments.

"Hayes? Did I like… offend you or something?"

"No." He laughs again. But it doesn't feel real. It feels a lot like a… a reaction. "No," he reiterates. "I just figured you were busy with your father's plans for you, that's all."

Well, that's not weird. I mean, I get what he's saying. I've kinda been on this whole you're-gonna-be-a-senator ten-year plan for the last ten years.

But it *is* weird. Because it's the way he says it that bothers me.

"Who wants to set the table?" Sofia asks.

"I will," Kiera says. "But I'm warning you, I have no idea where the forks and spoons go."

"No one cares," Hayes says, winking at her.

"Hey, where's Camille and Bennett?" I ask.

"They're skipping dinner," Sofia says. "Busy, I guess."

Hayes frowns, staring at Sofia for a long moment, then goes back to what he's doing without comment. But he's clearly worried about that development.

I take a deep breath and let it out as I watch Sofia tell Kiera where the tableware is kept. Then I walk over to the bar area in the living room. "Anyone want a drink?"

"Wine," Sofia says, pointing to a wine fridge under the counter I'm standing in front of. "Any of them are fine."

"I keep a bottle of '64 Glenlivet in the cabinet with the key in it, Con," Hayes says. "Help yourself as well."

I just shake my head for two reasons. One, the bottle I find in the cabinet with the key is a rare one worth as much as a new mid-size car. And two, he keeps one here. Like he's got spares in keyed cabinets all over Manhattan.

"Kiera?" I ask, getting glasses and choosing a bottle of wine.

"Whatever Sofia is drinking," she says, busy with the table setting. I stop what I'm doing to watch her for a moment. Because she looks so damn cute as she second-guesses herself with the position of knife versus spoon. Picking them both up, placing them back down, then switching them around one more time before blowing a stray piece of hair out of her eyes and mumbling, "Fuck it," as she moves on to the next place setting.

And even though I'm smiling and pretty happy in this moment, I also feel a little sad that these people—these friends—haven't been in my life all these years.

I've missed them. And I wish Camille and Bennett were here too. As weird as last night was, it was nice. And not just the kinky foursome sex part either. All of it. I've missed Camille's filthy mouth and dark sense of humor. I want to know more about her books. Ask her questions about them like, *So how do you reconcile these two sides of yourself in your writing?*

I've missed Hayes' weirdness and control. I've missed the soft quietness of Sofia and the way Kiera can rock a pair of leggings and suede boots and still make my heart beat fast when she looks at me. Even Bennett felt different in the presence of the group. And knowing that he's been a part of this and I haven't makes me wonder what else I've missed out on in his life.

Why didn't anyone tell me they were still friends?

And it's not the same for Kiera. She was up there in Vermont, distant like me. But Hayes brought her into his world regularly. He included her.

It's hard for me to believe that I wasn't deliberately excluded.

But why?

By the time I'm finished making all the drinks Sofia and Hayes are placing steaming bowls of food on the table and Kiera is standing in their way, oblivious with hands on hips, admiring her place-setting accomplishment.

Who cares? I tell myself. Who cares how we all got here tonight? The only thing that matters is that we're here.

We all sit down and there's a long pause where no one speaks and I have this rapid, heart-beating fear that we aren't special. That maybe they have fun without me, but with me it's nothing but awkward silence…

But Sofia lifts her glass, smiles at each of us individually, and says, "I've missed you," as we meet her gaze and raise our glasses. "It's been too long and I hope this is a new beginning. I hope that we will come together more often."

"To the friends we left behind," Hayes says, looking at me. "And the circumstances that brought us back together."

I nod. "Cheers to us."

"The Dirty Ones," Kiera says.

We look at her. Another awkward moment of silence as we picture all the things, all the nights, all the years that come with those three words.

But she just shrugs. "Might as well own it. We're not doing much to dispel the rumors."

Hayes laughs first. "To the Dirty Ones. Long may we reign."

And then we drink, and we eat, and we talk. And it's better than it ever was in the past. Because we're different people now. Grown up, doing our thing, being who we are…

And this time around it feels like a decision and not a reaction.

Later, after dinner is over and we're paired up on the two couches—Kiera's head in my lap as I play with her wild mane of hair, Hayes with his arm around Sofia as she talks in her soft, quiet voice about the new story she's working on, mostly to Kiera, who asks her questions and adds commentary—Hayes and I look at each other. Read each other's minds.

There is no foursome in our future and that's OK. It's a part of us and we're not ashamed of it. But this new thing we are comes in twos.

Eventually Hayes gets up, pulling Sofia to her feet, and says, "See you both in the morning."

Kiera and I stay on the couch for a few silent minutes and then she says, "Are you staying? Sofia gave me her best guest room. And I'm telling you right now, it's got a view to die for."

I smile, still twirling her long strands of hair in my fingertips. Loving the night so hard and daydreaming about all the nights we'll spend like this in the future. Not wanting to move, but anticipating what comes next at the same time. "I'm not going anywhere. I'll never leave you again, Kiera. I'll never lie to you, I'll never cheat on you and if you fall, I'm still gonna be there. Because it's my job to catch you."

She sucks in a deep breath of air, holds it as she turns her head, eyes on mine, and lets it out. "That sounds a lot like a vow."

I nod. "It is. I could kill myself for not being in your life all this time. I don't know what I was thinking."

She sits up, swings her legs over the edge of the couch, and stands up, pulling me with her by the hand. "Come with me," she says. "I've got more to show you than the view."

CHAPTER TWENTY-TWO

I'm nervous, excited, afraid, and turned on as I lead Connor down the hallway towards the bottom-floor guest room.

Nervous because I'm not sure what we are yet. The excitement I still feel coming off the heated sex of last night has many question marks attached. It felt so good, how connected we all were. No jealousy or insecurities. So I'm afraid that maybe what Connor and I have together isn't true love. Maybe it's just true lust? Maybe we are the Dirty Ones and that's all we'll ever be?

But I'll never know the difference between these two things if I don't open myself up.

I want him forever. Connor Arlington has always felt like the man I was meant for. And even though I didn't feel his absence all these years, it's caught up with me now.

I feel it now and he's holding my hand. I ache for the moments we've missed. I yearn for all the things I could've had and didn't get. I long for him to be in my life, to grow old with me, and love me the way I love him.

The room is dark. Lit up only by the city lights outside. But it's so beautiful. I've always loved my quiet life in Vermont but if there's one thing that could drag me away from the country and the lake, it's this. The twinkling lights of one of the world's greatest cities.

"Come here," Connor says, turning me towards him and sliding his hands around my waist. I slip mine up his arms. He took his suit coat off hours ago, so it's just the soft cotton under my fingertips and the hard muscles of his arms that I feel as I gaze up at him.

"Hi," I say, smiling, picturing what we'd look like to someone standing in the open doorway or someone outside, looking through some other wall of glass, seeing us in our moment.

Two people in a romantic embrace. In a romantic moment.

I wonder if they're writing our story in their head the way I write those of strangers I see from afar? I wonder if we come from a tragic past filled with mystery and secrets? Or if we've lived the charmed life of a prince and princess? I wonder if they'll be writing our happily ever after right now? Or if that dark, black moment is still out in front, calling us forward into the story?

I guess I lied earlier. I guess I do like the HEA and could do without the crisis.

"Hi," Connor says. "I've missed you."

"Today?"

"Not just today. All the days that came before today, Kiera." He tucks a stray strand of hair behind my ear and leans in. My heart thumps wildly in the moment I wait. Thumping like crazy when his lips touch mine.

It's a new kind of kiss for us. A claiming kiss. One that says, *You're mine. And I'm yours.* One that speaks lifetimes of moments in this moment. A kiss that starts a new beginning and ends an old, well-buried past.

I'm writing our story in my head, I realize.

"Come with me," Connor whispers. "I want to see you better."

He doesn't leave me. Doesn't pull away and take my hand and lead me closer to the twinkling lights. He turns me a little, hides my face in the shadows as he backs me up against the window and pressed my shoulders into the glass.

I keep my eyes closed, still writing the story. Still picking and choosing just the right words to describe us. Our night. How later, when we're done, I'll get out my notebook and put it all down on paper so I'll never forget how this feels.

I will capture all of it. Never forget a single moment of this night.

His fingertips slide under my long sweater and find their way to the bare skin hiding underneath. I suck in a breath of air at his cold hands, but a moment later the chill is gone and we're warm together.

Just as I get used to that he lifts my sweater up and over my head, reminding me that it's December. But just as quick as I think that thought, his hands are back, playing with my breasts as he continues to kiss my mouth.

It's the most perfect kiss, I decide. So gentle. Silent, but saying everything at the same time. I wouldn't have written it any other way.

He reaches around my back, unclasping my bra, making it loose. He slides it down my arms, taking his kisses to my neck now. I don't know if I want to fall into him and lose myself in the feeling of baring myself to him or just start ripping his clothes off, but he takes that decision away when he drops my bra to the floor and takes a step back. Unknots his tie and pulls it through his collar while I watch.

I lean back into the window, experiencing the cold glass, but not caring. Because his fingertips are pulling his shirt out of his pants. Unbuttoning each button slowly. Carefully. His gaze locked on mine when I look up.

He takes a breath. Breathes it out. Then takes off his shirt.

I will never get tired of looking at his body.

I reach for him. Splay my fingers wide across the right side of his chest, feeling his heart beating fast. He grabs my breast again. Lifts up from the bottom so he's cupping me with his hand.

His mouth becomes a small crooked smile and I know he's feeling my heart beating fast too.

There is one moment now. Just one where we are still. Connected by these hearts. Just one person.

Then he's pushing me against the glass again, his mouth seeking another kiss. It's urgent this time. I reach down for his belt and unbuckle it quickly, lost in the soft jingling it makes. Like fairies in the woods calling us home.

The button is popped, the zipper dragged down… and then I take him in my hand and squeeze.

"Kiera," he whispers. "Don't ever stop," he says, pulling my leggings down. Reaching under my knees to lift me up. Balancing me against the window as he presses himself into me. Connects us, skin to skin.

His cock is between my legs, hard and ready. I grip his shoulders tight with one hand and reach between my legs to place him at my entrance.

"No foreplay?" he asks, smiling.

"This whole night was foreplay. I don't get any more ready than this," I reply, just as he thrusts forward, filling me up, hard and fast, until I gasp and he relents, satisfied that he's inside me as deep as he can get.

Our bodies still for a moment as we kiss again. I imagine him thrusting hard. Fucking my brains out in front of this window. I imagine how dirty it looks. My leggings stretched tight at my knees, which are pressed up against my breasts. The wild look of lust and longing in his eyes as he pulls out, just a little, just enough, and then slowly pushes himself back in deep.

And then he does that again. And again. And again. Connor loves me in a way I've never experienced before. Never even dreamed of before. It's agonizingly slow. It's painfully soft. It's excruciatingly perfect.

But I want more. I am greedy, I know this. I am selfish to need him so much. My desire so ravenous. My lust so voracious. My longing so… so… *so* insatiable.

And he reads me. He sees my feelings like I see his. He turns them all into words and writes his own story about me. About us.

He says, "Yes."

And that's all he needs to say. Just one word is all we need.

So I say it back.

"Yes."

It's a signal to begin again. To start a new chapter or maybe a new book.

He goes faster. Pulling and pushing. In and out of me. I grip him every way I know how. With my knees against the hard muscles of his arms. With my fingers, digging into his shoulders, unable and unwilling to let him go. With my pussy as I clench around his cock and let him know that yes, he is all I need to be satisfied.

With my kiss, as our tongues tell the whole story.

We are as physically close as two people can be to each other when one is being held sexually captive, fucked hard up against a window. But our feelings… the love. It's possible to get closer in love, so I reach for him the only other way I know how.

I reach for him with my soul.

And he's got a net, or a web, or maybe a trap—ready to catch me.

I don't know how long I spend in that trap. I don't care. The world stops, and time stops, and we hold each other captive as we come.

Him moaning. And me, moaning.

And I think, as he leans into me, head on my shoulder, breath coming out in long, winded gasps… I think… *I know him now.*

I know him.

Eventually the world turns again. Time starts back up. He releases my soul and I release his soul, and he carries me over to the bed and gently puts me down on top of the covers.

He stands there in his unbuckled pants, his chest bare, looking down at me.

And then he takes off my boots. He drags the leggings down and discards them on the floor. He toes off his shoes, and takes off his pants, and gets on the bed next to me.

We're both cold, my nipples tight, pulling the skin of my breasts taut. But then he covers me with himself. His cold skin touches my cold skin and together we become warm.

We don't get under the covers. Not yet. We lie there, wrapped up in each other. Holding each other. Thinking, just thinking.

Writing the end of the story.

I don't know when I fall asleep, but sleep is always like that. I just know it's late when I wake up. Or early, depends how you look at things like time.

Gently, so I don't wake him, I untangle myself from his embrace, pull my sweater back on, and go looking for my notebook.

It's a beautiful notebook. I don't need any more light than the twinkling ones outside to see it because I made it with my own hands from a beautiful old book with a gilded cover of yellow flowers inlaid over navy blue leather. It was falling apart, sitting on a shelf in a thrift store in Burlington, and I rescued it. Turned it into something new. I made the papers inside. Sewing the binding up with my own thread and fingers. And I've been saving it for a special occasion. A special story. One that deserves to be written in such a beautiful book.

This is the story this book deserves.

Connor loves Kiera and Kiera loves Connor. All the black moments are behind them. At least for now. At least for the rest of this night. And it's time to be happy.

I sneak out of the bedroom and walk the long hallway to the other side of Sofia's lower floor and slip into the office.

I consider writing at the desk because it faces Central Park and you can see the Upper West Side on the other side, peeking out from the carpet of treetops like the future coming up with the sun.

But Sofia's window couch that faces Camille's apartment beckons me with an invitation on the other wall of windows.

Come, it says. *Come here and see what I've got to show you.*

It's just a side street view. Except for Camille's building, there's mostly old townhouses on this street. Partly hidden by the bare branches of trees. But Sofia pointed out Camille's apartment earlier, so I crawl across the large sectional couch, just like Sofia described herself when she told me about her writing routine, and prop my back up with pillows. Press my warm feet against the cold glass and imagine the two of them. Writing with each other, separated only by panes of glass and forty feet of air.

I wish I was part of that.

I will be part of that.

Maybe I can sell my cottage and move to the Upper East Side? Be a real trio like we pretend we are online?

Yes. I'd like that.

It's only then that I notice a book on the couch next to me. I pick it up, and lean forward, catching some light outside so I can read the spine.

The Great Gatsby.

It's a first printing, I know that immediately. Bound in navy blue leather with F. Scott Fitzgerald's name embossed in gold gilt over blue on the front-side of the cover, I'd recognize it anywhere because I've wanted one for years but could never justify the expenditure for an item that was nothing but pure sentimental indulgence.

God, how the three of us loved that story in school. We read it incessantly that year.

Why did we do that?

Oh, God! How did I forget? This was the book Connor used to read to us. It wasn't just the dictionary and grocery lists, was it? So stupid that I forgot.

Jesus, how I used to love hearing him read this story. His voice was perfect. So magic.

I would just get lost in that time. The art deco, the giant mansions, the opulent parties… all of it.

But I put it aside because I didn't come in here to read someone else's story. I came in to capture my own.

So I grab my pen, half-hidden in a pocket attached to the inside cover of my notebook, and begin to write.

CHAPTER TWENTY-THREE

I realize I've had this dream before. Kiera is there. All of us are there. Me, and Hayes, and Camille, and Sofia, and Bennett.

But the thing that's different this time around is that Louise is there.

She *was* there. But for some reason she feels like an interloper in this dream. Like she's so out of place in this dream, I dream myself up some annoyance. Try to follow her. Tell her to leave. But the dream does that dream thing and morphs into a party, and for some reason I'm really short in this dream so I'm like waist-high to everyone. And no one sees me as I push my way through the crowd, and duck under the serving trays of waiters, and try not to notice that I don't recognize a single person anymore.

Everyone's a stranger.

But I see Louise through a parting of the crowd. She's wearing a very flashy gold dress, the kind made up of little pieces of metal that look like scales and reflect everything back at you, only it's blurry and dark. Like shadows dancing across her gold body.

And she ducks into a hallway that becomes the twisted passageways of Hayes' mansion. And then Louise is gone and Emily is there, putting a single finger up to her lips and whispering, "Shhhhhhh."

So I stop and open my mouth to ask her where Louise went, but I don't think I have a mouth anymore. Because I can't talk.

Before I can freak out about this dream turning into a nightmare, Emily says, "I didn't do it. You know I didn't do it."

And then Louise is there in her dancing-shadows gold dress, saying, "She did do it, Connor. And you need to believe that or bad things will start happening."

I wake up to a phone buzzing. Sweaty. So hot. And tangled up in the covers. Wondering where the fuck I am when I look outside and see the wrong view though the glass.

The phone buzzes again.

I sit up, remembering. "Kiera?" I whisper. Because the other side of the bed is empty and last night is coming back to me now. I glance at the phone and see Camille's name and a short message. *I need to talk to you. Now.*

I'm at Sofia's. I'm in bed with Kiera and she's gone.

I don't feel panic at this, more curious about where she went.

The bathroom, I decide. But the bathroom door is open and she's clearly not in there. So I get up, pull on my pants, and go out into the hallway.

I can still smell the faint scent of dinner as I walk down the hallway and stop, peering into the living room.

I'm about to go check that way when I hear the tell-tale sound of a page being turned coming from the office at the other end of this hallway.

I find her there, belly-down on a couch facing a large window, notebook positioned in a beam of light coming in from the twinkling city outside, writing furiously.

"Hey," I say, walking into the room.

She looks over her shoulder, then gets up on her knees, and turns to me. "Sorry. I just wanted to write some things down about the last few days so I don't forget. Did I wake you up?"

"No, I had a weird fucking dream."

"Want a piece of paper so you can write it down?"

This makes me happy. Kiera, late-night journaler. Always ready to take on the world with her pen.

She always had a notebook in her hand back in school. I can remember seeing her around campus in the years that came before that year, sitting under a tree writing furiously, like she is now.

Other people did that too. Camille and Sofia did. But they did it in a group. There was always a posse around them. Kiera was a loner before we became friends in senior year.

And she always had weird journals too. Handmade ones from old book covers. The one I remember most vividly was *The Great Gatsby*. She left it unattended once and I picked it up, so interested in what she felt the need to scribble down so furiously. Like she was gonna forget some detail that makes all the difference.

Like she was doing just before I interrupted her.

"Can I see it?" I ask, walking over to the couch. She scoots over, making room for me, so I crawl onto the large square sectional and join her in the middle.

"You mean, can you read it?"

"No. I mean, sure. I'd be thrilled to read it. But I just want to look at that book. You make these, right?"

She looks down at the notebook in her hand, then back up at me. "Yeah. You like it?"

"They're beautiful. I remember you always had these handmade notebooks in school. I've always wanted to just… sit down with one and study it."

"My words?"

"Those too," I say, feeling like I just said this. She laughs. "But the books, Kiera. You make really beautiful books."

She looks at the journal again, trying to see my perspective, I think. Then she shrugs. "My mom was always making these. We have this library—well, we had." And then she looks up, like she's thinking. "I don't even know if it's still there."

I have a lot of things to say about what's happening with her mother's estate and that house, but this is not the time.

"But anyway," she continues, "I've been making these notebooks my whole life. You can look at it."

She hands it to me and I hold it. Reverently. The hardback cover has been altered. Hell, everything has been altered. But the cover is some old edition of some romance book, I think. There's a flowery woman on the front in muted, faded colors, which is original. But the title is clearly a small piece of printed paper glued above it. "*Things I Thought I Saw*," I say.

"Yeah, it's not a story. It's just… you know. A diary, I guess. Just scraps of days. Things I might want to remember later."

I open it up, with no intention of reading her private thoughts, just interested in how she put this all together. None of the pages match. Some are made up of thin parchment. Some are old, yellowed accounting ledgers. Some are even worn, yellow envelopes that you use for inter-office mail. "It's really nice."

"Sofia loves them too. I'm gonna go home on Sunday and grab a few extras I have to give to her and Camille for Christmas."

"You're going home?" I ask, closing the book and setting it aside. But it bumps into another book. "What's this?" I ask, picking up the other book.

"Can you believe Sofia has a first fucking edition of *The Great Gatsby* and she *reads* it?" She laughs. Shakes her head. "I mean, what the fuck is wrong with her?"

"This?" I ask, turning the book in my hand. "How do you know it's a first?"

"I know," Kiera says. "I'm obsessed with this book. Like I have about sixteen different copies at my cottage. But not this one." She laughs again.

"Hmmm," I say. "I think I knew that."

"Yeah?"

I nod. "Yeah, because you had one of these journals back in school. You wrote in it all the time. And the cover was a lot like this."

"No," Kiera says. "No. No, no, no. No way. I never made a journal of *The Great Gatsby*. My writer's heart would shrivel and die if I tore up a copy of that book to make a journal. And I certainly never owned this edition."

I shrug. "It must've been a later edition. But it definitely had this," I say, pointing to F. Scott Fitzgerald's name in gilded gold on the front.

"That's impossible," Kiera says. "I just… I didn't own a copy. And they don't make them like this. There is no other edition like this. And anyway, like I said, I'd never cut up a *Gatsby* book."

I just stare at her for a few seconds. Because how is it possible we have two totally different memories? I know for sure. For. Sure. That book I picked up back in school had this cover. It most definitely said *The Great Gatsby* on it.

But she's telling me I'm wrong.

"You're mixing it all up, Con. That's all. You used to read *Gatsby* out loud to us that year, remember?"

"What?" I shake my head. "No. I never read this book. I almost failed my American Lit class in freshman year because I read the CliffsNotes version before the final exam. I barely even remember what it's about."

Kiera laughs. "You're stupid. You read this to us all the time. You probably just never looked at the cover."

"I don't know," I say, so confused. "You'd think I'd remember a guy called Gatsby."

We stare at each other for a few moments. And I don't know what she's thinking… but I'm wondering, *What the fuck? How did this whole Gatsby thing get so turned around?*

"Can I read this one?" I ask, not sure why I'm asking since it's not her book. But very sure why I want to read it. I need to see if I remember anything. "I swear, I never read this book. Out loud or otherwise."

She sucks in a breath of air. Thinks about this for a few moments. Then says, "If you're very careful you can read the first page. But no more than that."

I can't help myself, I laugh.

"I'm serious. I don't think you understand what this book is."

"I'll be careful," I say. "Promise."

"OK," she says. "Then read it out loud." She stretches her body out, long legs bumping into me, cold bare feet tucking themselves under my knee, as she positions her forehead right up against the window and looks out at the building across the street. "But just one page."

So I begin…

"'In my younger and more vulnerable years…'"

Kiera sighs, but I keep going, logging her reactions as I narrate the story for her. She sighs a lot, curls her body up—I miss her cold feet when she does that—slides both hands under one cheek, and closes her eyes as I continue. Already one hundred percent certain that this was not the book I used to read to them back in school.

She doesn't stop me when I turn the first page. Or the second, or the fifteenth. In fact, we're almost on chapter two when she sits up and places both her hands on the window, looking out into the night.

"Do you see that?" she says.

I stop reading and look out the window. "That light?"

"Yeah. Did you know that's Camille's apartment? What time is it? I wonder what she's doing up?"

I look around the office and spy a digital clock. "Three forty-seven." Then I see a figure walking around. I put down the book and crawl across the sectional so I'm right up next to the window with Kiera. "Is that Bennett?"

Kiera huffs out some air. "I bet they'd be pissed if they knew we were spying on them."

"Holy shit, I kinda knew that Sofia and Camille lived this close, but I never imagined they could see each other from across the street. It's weird. And sorta kinky too."

"Shut up." She laughs, turning her head to look at me. But she goes back to the spying pretty much immediately. "Oooo, there's Camille. Wait. Are they fighting?"

"It kinda looks like it," I say.

They are. It only takes a few more seconds to realize that. Camille is walking around the room, pulling open drawers and closing them again. That room must be her office because there's lots of drawers. And bookshelves. She starts pulling books out, throwing them down on the floor.

"What the hell?" Kiera asks.

"Shit," I say.

"What?"

"Camille texted your phone. That's why I woke up. She said she needed to talk to you."

Kiera bounces up and off the couch. "Be right back."

I listen to the sound of her padding footsteps as she goes down the hall, but things are getting heated across the street now. Bennett has Camille by the wrists, leaning down into her face, like he's yelling at her.

Kiera comes running back in. "Call her," I say. "Right now. Something is happening over there and whatever it is, it's not good."

Ringing. Loud, as she puts her phone on speaker.

Across the street we watch them stop their argument to look at something. The phone, I think. But they ignore it and go back to the fight.

Voicemail. "You've got me," Camille's voice purrs on the recording. "Now what are you gonna do?" *Beep.*

Kiera hangs up and tries again, but now Camille is throwing open her terrace door and walking out in to the freezing snow.

"What the fuck is happening over there?" Kiera asks, tossing her phone on the couch. "Come on, Sofia has a terrace too. We should stop them. Make them come over here and tell us what's going on."

Before I can say anything she's throwing open the door to the terrace. Biting, cold December wind whooshes through the office, blowing papers off the desk.

"Camille!" Kiera yells. "Pick up your phone!"

Camille stops. Looks at her from across the street. I want to get up and go outside. I'm halfway into the process of doing this, when I see what she's holding in her hand.

A gun.

Oh. Fuck.

I'm up. I'm outside. Ignoring the freezing snow as my bare feet cross the terrace and I stand in front of the thick spindles of concrete that act as a railing.

"Camille!" Kiera yells again. "What the fuck are you doing? Put that down!"

Camille is distracted and Bennett makes his move. He wrestles the gun away from her, but she takes it back. There's a fight and Camille ends up on her bare knees in the deep snow. Bennett ends up with the gun.

"Go back inside," Bennett calls. "I'm taking care of it!"

"Taking care of what?" I yell.

"Shut the fuck up!" someone yells from a window down below.

"Camille!" Kiera screams again. Because now Camille is standing again. Not only standing, but climbing up onto the ledge of her balcony, her short, white nightie flapping in the wind. "Camille! Get off the fucking ledge!"

"I can't do it!" Camille yells. "I can't do it!"

"Of course you can't!" Kiera screams. "You're gonna go back inside! Right now!"

The terrace door above us opens and then I hear Sofia scream. "Camille! What are you doing?"

"Camille," Hayes' deep, commanding voice calls. "Get your ass off that ledge or I swear to God, I will—"

But he stops. Mid-sentence.

Because she jumps.

Kiera and Sofia scream.

I yell, "Fuck!"

And Hayes is just quiet.

I want to say I didn't hear the sound of a body crashing into the street down below, but I did.

And that's when the gun goes off and we realize…

Bennett just shot himself in the head.

CHAPTER TWENTY-FOUR

It's a living nightmare. One I can't wake up from. One in which Camille's body is destroyed by a twelve-story fall to the concrete below and Bennett's brains are splattered on the side of her apartment. One where I cry, incessantly. Sofia too. We hold each other as the police arrive and begin the questions.

They take my phone. They go knocking on doors, trying to find anyone who can give another point of view. They ask us things like, "Why would they do this?" And we have no answers.

They start prodding us about our history and make assumptions that are true, but that they have no right to know about.

Connor looks lost. Reporters start talking about it on the news. "Early this morning Camille DuPont, great-granddaughter to the late matriarch, Helene DuPont, took her own life by jumping from her twelfth-floor penthouse in the Upper East Side. Her friend, lawyer Bennett Winthrop, shot himself in the head in the minutes following. Connor Arlington, rumored to be announcing his candidacy for the US Senate tomorrow evening at an event hosted by Dr. Louise Livingston, was present at the scene when it happened…"

And so forth.

His phone is taken, but it rings incessantly in the pile of phones over on Sofia's kitchen counter. His father shows up, demands to be seen at Sofia's front door, but he's turned away.

Connor seems relieved at that, but I don't know. We could use a powerful man like Mr. Arlington right now.

Because the questions are becoming hard to answer.

"What is your history with the deceased?"

"We were friends," Hayes says. "Long-time friends."

"When was the last time you saw them?"

"At my office," Connor answers. "Just a few hours earlier."

"Why was Camille DuPont there?"

"I don't know," Connor admits.

But the ones they ask me are the really suspicious ones. At least my *answers* are. I can tell by the way the two detectives shoot sidelong glances at each other as I speak.

They separate Sofia and me, just like they did Connor and Hayes. But instead of letting us answer questions in the living room, they take us to separate parts of the apartment.

Sofia is taken upstairs and I'm taken to the guest room where there's evidence of the sex Connor and I had. My underwear, haphazardly strewn about on the floor. His shirt and belt.

"How long have you and Mr. Arlington been dating?'

I don't know how to answer that. I tell them, "I don't really know if we're dating. We just… reconnected after ten years." But that just gets me more intimate questions like, "Did you have sex with him?" And "Did Miss DuPont ever have sex with him?"

See what I mean? How do I answer that?

Uh, yeah. We've all fucked each other before. Sometime all in the same bed. At the same time.

No, I can't say that, can I?

"How did you meet the deceased?" This detective is a woman. I guess I figured she'd be more… sensitive? As a fellow female?

That's not the case.

"We went to school together."

"So you were friends all during school?"

"No. Mostly just senior year. I really don't run in the same circle as they do."

"And how did that come about?"

"What?"

"How did you become friends with them? Were you in the same club? The same dorm? If you didn't meet any of them until senior year, then what prompted that meeting?"

"Is this really important?"

"We need to know why the six of you were yelling across a street, twelve stories up, in the middle of the night. Because the end result of that argument is two dead people, Miss Bonnaire."

"Obviously, I know that. I was there. I saw the whole thing."

"Was there a disagreement?"

"Not between us," I say. "I already told you that. Camille and Bennett were arguing across the street in her apartment."

"And you and Mr. Arlington were in the office, reading a book at three AM?"

"Correct!" I say, getting frustrated.

"Why were you up?"

"Wh-what?"

"Why did you wake up in the middle of the night and go read a book in the library? Mr. Arlington said you fell asleep and when he woke up, you were gone."

"I was writing," I say. "I'm a writer."

"So you were working on a book."

Shit. I see where this is going. "Not exactly."

"Then exactly what were you doing?"

"Just writing down my thoughts."

"About?"

"About Connor. And me. And… it's just a diary," I say.

"Where is this diary?"

"In the office," I say. "On the couch, I think."

The detective turns to her partner and says, "Can you get that for me?"

He nods and turns away.

"You can't read my diary."

"I'm afraid it's evidence. We're going to catalogue it, Miss Bonnaire."

"It's private," I snap.

"Nothing's private in a…" But she stops. I swear to God, she was gonna say murder investigation. "In a double suicide that has no logical explanation."

"I don't know why they were fighting. I was trying to tell her to call me. She called me—"

"I thought you said she texted you?"

"She did. That's what I meant. I didn't see it until after they started yelling when Connor told me that's what woke him up."

"So he"—she makes air quotes with her fingers—"'forgot' to tell you she sent a text stating…" She looks down at her notepad. "'I need to talk to you. Now.'"

"You have my phone," I say. "You can see that I didn't call her. I didn't talk to her until I started yelling! Why are you asking me all this?"

"Because, Miss Bonnaire, Camille DuPont called her lawyer earlier this evening and left him a message too."

"She did?" I say.

"Yes. And that message mentioned your name."

"My name?"

"And Connor Arlington's. And Sofia Astor's. And Hayes Fitzgerald's."

"All of us? Why would she be talking to her lawyer about us? Especially when Bennett *is* a lawyer."

"Was," she corrects me.

I want to throat-punch this woman.

"He wanted to talk with his lawyer as well. So I understand the six of you had a dinner the night before last?"

"Yes, that's right. At Hayes' house on Long Island."

"And there was an incident whereby"—she glances down at her notepad again—"Emily Medici—" She stops to laugh here. "Wow. You really do have an interesting circle of friends. Anyway, the reports I've seen say that Emily Medici escaped."

"They found her the next morning. I think."

"They did not, Miss Bonnaire. Emily Medici is still at large."

"What? But I thought—"

"Do you know who"—she looks down at her pad again—"the Associates are?"

"W-what?"

"She got a text from a number that came up as 'The Associates' in her phone."

"What did it say?" I ask, my voice barely a whisper.

"It said, 'Time to start a new book.' Do you know what that means, Miss Bonnaire?"

I have enough sense to shut up then. And two more unanswered questions later I'm saying, "I think I need a lawyer."

There were a few tense minutes when I thought they were going to arrest me or force me to go down to the station. Which is such a cliché thing to say, but whatever. They said that.

Then Hayes stepped in—he was never in danger of being arrested. Neither was Sofia or Connor. They only seemed to be interested in me.

But Hayes stepped in and started talking legal bullshit and a lawyer actually did show up, and then the interrogation was over, and they left, and now it's almost dinner time.

"No one mentioned the book?" Connor asks.

We're in Hayes' limo on our way to Connor's apartment on the other side of the park, Sofia and I on one bench and Connor and him across from us.

"I didn't," I say.

"Me either," Sofia confirms.

"Good," Hayes says, texting furiously on his phone. "We don't want to mix these two things up."

I squint my eyes at him, not really understanding. But I guess I get what he means. The new book. The old book. Camille and Bennett.

My eyes are so tired from crying. Why did this happen? Why did they do this? I will never come to terms with this day. Ever. I don't care how many stories I write, there is no fictional plot that can make me feel better about the reality.

I want to ask Hayes about Emily but I can't. I can't deal with any more mysteries tonight.

"So listen," Hayes says, his tone all business. "We can't stay at your house, Con. Your father is there."

"How do you know?"

"I have people watching it. He went there about three hours ago. But you need to go inside and put him at ease. Tell him the party is on, you're gonna give the speech, and—"

"Are you fucking kidding me?" Connor says. "Camille and Bennett killed themselves last night!"

"I know that," Hayes replies in an overly soft tone. "But you need to convince him you're still on board with this Senate run."

"Why?"

"We'll get to that. Probably not tonight, but tomorrow at the party for sure."

"I'm going with you," I tell Connor.

"No, you're not," Hayes says. "The three of us are going up to your cottage, Kiera. Connor, get your father out of your house by seven and get to the heliport. We have things to… see."

"See?" Sofia says.

Hayes looks at her. I can tell he wants to shut her down with a curt, *Later, Sofia.* But he stops himself. Says,

"I'll explain everything when Connor gets there. Just get rid of your father, Con. And the easiest way to do that is to tell him everything he wants to hear. Got it?"

Connor draws in a deep breath, lets it out, and then nods. "Fine."

"Will we get in trouble for leaving New York?" I ask.

"Fuck them. We didn't do this. But we know who did. And we're gonna prove it."

Before I can say anything else, the car stops in front of Connor's building and a slew of security people surround him as he steps out. He tries to wave to me and say, "See ya later," but the mob of tall men in black coats whisk him away before that happens.

The three of us spend the entire ride to the helipad on top of a building a few blocks away in silence. And that continues when we get in the chopper. No one even puts their headsets on to talk.

Hayes texts on a satellite phone the entire time, but I have no clue who he's messaging. I'm too tired. Too worn out from losing two of my friends. Too afraid of what's coming. All I can do is lean into Sofia for comfort and close my eyes.

Pretend I'm somewhere else. Like I always do. Imagine myself in some other story. Some other person playing some other part.

Live the dream and make it real.

CHAPTER TWENTY-FIVE

The security detail isn't quite out of the ordinary, but at the same time… it's excessive. "Why are you guys here?" I ask, riding up with them in the elevator to my two-bedroom apartment. I don't like to call this place home. It's just an apartment. I didn't even choose it, my father did. None of the furniture is mine and I have never looked forward to coming here after a long, stressful day.

The security ignores me, but I don't even have time to get annoyed about this because the doors open onto my… not penthouse… and we walk down the hallway to my front door, which is already open.

Another member of my father's security detail ushers me inside to find my father pacing back and forth in front of the living room window.

It's only then that I realize if I had binoculars—or maybe a small telescope—I could probably see into Sofia's apartment across the park.

Weird. That I never knew that. Also weird, and kinda creepy, thinking about my father being here last night peeking at Kiera and me while we fucked in front of the window.

I don't know why I think about this, especially when, as soon as my father sees me, he whispers, "He's here. I'll call you back," like that whisper is enough stealth to hide the fact he was talking about me with someone. "Good God, Connor. What the hell was that?"

"Camille and—"

"Not that," he barks. "The police! Why were you talking to the police?"

"I mean… it was a pretty clear-cut thing, Dad. Camille and—"

"You never talk to the police, understand? Not without a lawyer. Do you have any idea the kind of damage control I've been doing today?" He pauses, exhales loudly, then says, "We're leaving. Let's go."

"Go where?"

"To the Hamptons. Dr. Livingston is putting you up for the night at her place. That way we have all day tomorrow to prep for the announcement."

My first instinct is to fight him on this, but then I hear Hayes' words in my head. "Just make him think you're on board."

So fine. I do that. When I try to pack a bag, my father snaps, "Never mind any of that. We've got everything you need at the Livingston estate."

Has he always been such a dick? Or is this something new I'm just noticing?

I really don't think I've ever seen him this on edge.

"I need to stop somewhere and get a phone. The cops took mine." It's a lie. Well, a half a lie. They did take our phones, but they gave them back. Hayes refused to unlock his, which pissed them off. But they were really only interested in Kiera's phone, which she unlocked voluntarily. I only tell this lie so I can go into the tech store half a block down before we leave as an excuse to call Hayes and let him know what's happening. I get the feeling my father isn't going to like that phone call one bit, and since Hayes hinted that we're in stealth buddy system mode, I'm trying my best to be stealthy.

It was the absolute wrong thing to say. My father's face actually goes red.

"What?" I say. "What was I supposed to do? There's nothing incriminating on there, for fuck's sake. I just wanted to cooperate so they can figure out why Camille and—"

"Just... shut up, Connor. I'm at the end of my rope tonight."

Which is a pretty dickish thing to say since, you know, two of my oldest friends just fucking killed themselves last night. So I say, "You know what? I'm not going to the Hamptons. I'm meeting Kiera up at her place in Vermont. There's a helicopter waiting for me downtown and—"

But that's the last word I get out.

Because someone hits me over the head and I drop to the floor.

"For fuck's sake, Steven!"

"Here," someone says. Some familiar voice I know I recognize, but can't place.

And then there's a hot, burning sensation traveling up the vein in my arm and...

And everything goes dark.

I wake up in a room. Tied to a bed. Head pounding. People yelling beyond the door underneath which a glowing line of light leaks through.

I try to yell, but my voice won't work.

I squirm and thrash and the only thing I get for my trouble is a nurse appearing with a needle. This time it doesn't go into my arm, it goes into an IV.

Then the darkness is back.

I dream again. That same dream, I think. I'm short and looking for my friends among all the strangers. I can hear Louise, but then I wonder… maybe that's the real Louise. Because this is her house, I'm sure of it.

Then Emily is there again. She says, "Shhhhhhh. Don't let them know you know."

"What do I know?" I whisper back.

And she says, "Everything, Connor. You know everything. They just made you forget."

CHAPTER TWENTY-SIX

"He's not answering," I say. "Why isn't he answering?"

I look at Hayes and Sofia sitting close together in my small cottage couch. Hayes is trying to play this cool but I can tell he's worried.

Connor didn't meet the helicopter and we can't get a hold of him.

"Just..." Hayes sighs. Like he's more than tired. More than frustrated. That sigh says something else. I don't know why I think it sounds like giving up, but it does. "Just," he repeats, "relax, OK? We'll figure it out."

"We're so stupid," Sofia says. "We forgot the first fucking Dirty Ones rule. Buddy system. Why did we let Connor go home alone?"

"Because he needed to talk to his father and make him think all those fucking plans he has are still on track."

"I think he failed," I whisper. "I don't know what you're doing, Hayes, but it didn't work. He's in trouble. We need to go back to the city and find out where he is and what's happening."

"No," Hayes breathes out. And yup. That's defeat in his voice. It scares me because Hayes isn't the kind of guy who gets defeated. "We can't go back now. We're here." He looks at me from across the sitting area. I'm in a chair, legs tucked up to my chest. "We need to just… do this without him."

"Do what?" Sofia asks. "Why are you being so cagey? Just tell us why we're out here in the middle of buttfuck Vermont when we need to be in the city tomorrow."

Hayes stands, buttons his suit coat, and extends his hand to her. She takes it without comment and lets him pull her up.

They make a beautiful couple. Hayes and his dark, mysterious good looks. Sofia in her equally dark, mysterious beauty. And I wonder why they haven't gotten together like this before now?

He smiles at her. Trying to make everything OK, I think. But she only gives him half a smile back. I just sit in my chair frowning, unable to force even a quarter smile.

Hayes turns to me. "Come on, Kiera. We gotta go see something."

"See what?" I ask. He extends his hand for me too and I take it, reluctantly getting to my feet.

"You'll see."

"Why can't you just tell us?" Sofia asks.

We've both been asking this question the entire evening but Hayes just says, "You need to see it. Dress warm, we gotta go into the woods."

"We're going to the tower, aren't we?" Sofia asks. "I don't want to go."

"Me either," I say. "I've lived across the lake from it for ten years and never had an urge to go see it again."

"We have to," Hayes says. "I have to show you something."

"Hayes—" Sofia starts.

But he cuts her off. "Believe me. You want to see this. It's not a bad thing, I promise."

Both of us sigh with frustration and defeat.

"Go put on something warm. Kiera, do you have extra boots for Sofia? And a pair of pants she can wear? Because we have to walk through the snow."

"Sure," I say. "One sec."

I go into my bedroom and start looking for some warmer clothes for Sofia to change into. But the whole time I'm picturing the tower. That walk into the woods. The gate, the thick underbrush we'll have to fight our way through.

It's probably worse now. A decade of new growth is a lot of wild brambles to deal with.

I find some warm clothes for Sofia and go back into the living room, then feel awkward because they're in the middle of an embrace. "Um," I say. "Here you go."

Sofia breaks away from Hayes, focuses her sad eyes on my handful of clothes, then takes a deep breath and nods. Disappears down the hall to change.

Hayes puts on his coat, then holds mine out to me. Helps me into it.

I want to ask him all the questions but we've tried. This whole time we've been waiting for Connor Sofia and I have been on repeat and Hayes just finds a new way to say, "You'll see."

So I don't say anything. I just put on my gloves and scarf and stand in front of the door, sweating like crazy until Sofia appears.

We leave the house and get into the car Hayes had waiting for us at the local airstrip when we landed. It takes almost an hour to get across the lake and the only thing interesting that happens is Hayes produces a pair of boots and a thick winter coat from the trunk and puts all that on. We're the only ones on the ferry. And how Hayes managed to get a late evening crossing is something I don't even bother thinking about. His kind of money can buy almost everything.

When we reach New York on the other side we drive south to the Essex College campus. Which is quiet and mostly dark because almost everyone is on winter break. You're not allowed to stay in the dorms over break so all those buildings look lifeless. Only the theater building has any lights on tonight. Probably a Christmas play. They do those every year for the local townspeople.

But our car takes us past the theatre building to the very south edge of campus. I get a sick, sick feeling in my stomach as we grow closer to the woods and when we stop in an empty, snow-covered parking lot it's all I can do to stop myself from hurling.

Hayes presses a button to make the divider window go down. "Stay here and wait for us," he tells the driver. "Keep the heat on high back here. We're gonna be freezing when we get back."

Sofia and I share a worried look.

"Come on," Hayes says, getting out and pulling Sofia along with him. I scoot over, take his hand and let him pull me out as well. We walk in silence to a slight break in the trees where the path to the tower is and hands me a flashlight.

He has one too, but Sofia doesn't. We talked this over earlier. We will hold hands the entire time. Hayes will have a light. I will have a light. And Sofia will not let go of us.

I turn on my light and look at him.

He doesn't give us a chance to turn back, just pushes aside the bare branches with one hand, making creepy shadows with his flashlight, and drags Sofia into the woods with him. I have her hand, so she drags me along behind her.

"What the fuck are we doing?" Sofia whispers into the silence.

"Just relax," Hayes says. "I told you, it's not bad."

"I don't like this," I say. "It's so fucking creepy. I feel like I'm in a horror movie where the stupid teenagers do everything wrong. We're gonna get killed tonight."

Hayes stops so abruptly Sofia bumps into him and I bump into her. "Stop it, Kiera. We're fine. There's nothing out here but us. I promise you."

"He's the creepy outsider who lures the stupid girls into his diabolical plan," Sofia says.

"Yeah. He's got like… a lair out here. Some shabby cabin filled with doll heads and shit."

Sofia laughs. "And he wants to dress us up like dolls."

"Jesus Christ," Hayes says. "Stop writing a story. Nothing's gonna happen, but this is serious."

Sofia shoots me a look over her shoulder, but then trips over something and goes back to paying attention.

"Where's the fucking gate?" I huff a few seconds later. "It should be here already, right?"

"There is no gate," Hayes says. "At least not out here."

"Hmmm," Sofia says. "They took it down?"

"Just come on."

We keep going. My feet are freezing because my knee-high shearling boots are really more for looks and not made for winter trekking, so they're soaking wet now. The snow is very deep in some places and by the time Hayes pulls us through the last of the trees into a clearing, my pants are covered in those annoying ice balls.

"Where are we?" Sofia asks.

"Yeah," I say. "None of this looks right. Things sure have changed in ten years."

Hayes turns to us and I flash my light at his chest, trying to see his face, but not wanting to blind him in the eyes. "I just want you to look around, OK?"

"What are we looking for?" I pan my light around and realize exactly where we are.

"Oh, my God," Sofia says. "We're in a cemetery?"

"When did they put this in?" I ask. So weird.

"It's always been here," Hayes says. "Look." He pans his light onto a nearby headstone. "The date."

"Eighteen seventy-nine?" Sofia asks. "What the hell?" She looks around. I look around. "Where's the tower?"

"There is no tower, Sofia. There never was a tower."

"What are you talking about?" I ask, thoroughly confused. "We came here all the time. Hell, I came here every fucking week all of senior year. Of course there's a tower. It's where we… did that stuff and I… wrote the book."

Hayes swallows hard, looking at me intently. "You did write a book that year, Kiera. But not the one you think. And it didn't happen in a tower. It happened in the top floor of the theatre."

"What?" Sofia says, letting go of our hands and spinning around. She grabs my flashlight and begins walking away.

"Sofia!" I say. "Where are you going?" I run through the deep snow to catch up. Hayes right behind me.

"There's no tower, Sofia," he says.

"It's here. Or we're in the wrong place. It's got to be here. I remember it."

"Sofia," he says, his long legs taking him past me so he can grab her wrist and make her stop. "It's not here. It was a fucking lie, OK? The whole thing was a fucking cover-up."

"A cover-up for what?" I ask.

"Think hard, Kiera," Hayes says, staring into my eyes. "Think very hard about what really happened that night. You were here, remember? In the cemetery. We were all here. Bennett and I were here with Emily. You were here with Camille and Sofia. And Connor… Connor was here with his father."

"What the hell are you talking about?" Sofia asks. Loudly now. "No. That's not how it happened. We were…" But she stops and looks at me. "We were…"

"We were all here," Hayes says. "But not for the reasons we thought. There is no tower, you guys. There never was a fucking tower. That's not what happened that night."

"But the book," I say. "My notebook."

Hayes has a pained, sad look on his face.

"I have a scar, Hayes. Emily shot me in the fucking shoulder. I was in the hospital for a week. No one made that up."

"You did get shot that night, Kiera. But it wasn't Emily who shot you. It was Mr. Arlington."

Memory is an unreliable thing.

My mother said that to me when I was lying in the hospital after I was shot.

"That's not what happened," she said. "You don't understand what you saw."

And I was on a lot of drugs, but not enough drugs to erase that memory of her and what she said. Certainly not enough to erase what I witnessed at the Legacy Alumni Party that night I moved into the dorms at Essex senior year.

She was there that night. She had been baking for days. Something she did only once a year for this party.

She is an alumna and I was her legacy, so every year I was at Essex we attended the party together. She wore a long, gold gown with several layers of cream chiffon in her skirt so the gold was more of a pale yellow to the eye. Her lips were the most beautiful shade of pink and her long, blonde hair was pinned up, but little bits and wisps escaped in flowing tendrils in all the right places. She was very soft and sexy. Looked every bit the erotica author part, if you knew who she really was.

And I did. So she did.

I was in black. I wanted to be different than her. I wanted my stories to be different, I wanted my life to be different, I wanted to be the opposite of Antoinette Bonnaire in every way imaginable.

So I wore black and my dress was short and tight. My eyes were lined, my lashes were fake and thick, and my lips were red. I was dark and hard. A creature of the night.

I think that's why they noticed me that night.

Connor Arlington and Hayes Fitzgerald.

Sofia Astor and Camille DuPont.

It was the dress, but not the dress. It was me, but not me.

So I caught their eye while I was watching my mother flirt with Christopher Arlington at her pastry table.

I saw Connor and Hayes watching me watch her from across the room as I leaned against a doorjamb, firm scowl on my face. And then I was approached. Not by Connor and Hayes, but Sofia and Camille.

Sofia, always in a red dress at these kind of things, was wearing something professional and appropriate for a job interview at Victoria's Secret. Meaning extremely sexy and seductive, but in a way that said, "I have power, don't fuck with me." Which caught my eye and I remember thinking, *So. She wants to be different tonight too.* Because it was a skirt suit with a tight, cropped jacket that accentuated her pushed-up breasts. She wore diamonds around her throat and four-inch heels on her feet.

Camille was in blue. A column silhouette dress embellished with glittery things and a tulle overskirt to soften up her tall, thin frame. This was Camille as I'd seen her the past three years. Not that we spent much time together, but we were in the same classes and fashion was something Camille took seriously. She brought her Fifth Avenue life to upstate New York with her.

It was hard to look away and be aloof, so I failed at that. I watched them carefully as they approached me, smiling like she-wolves with an agenda.

"You look lovely tonight, Kiera," Sofia said.

"Thank you. You two as well."

"Where's your book?" Camille asked. "You don't go anywhere without a book."

She didn't mean a book for reading. She meant my notebooks. Of which I have many. But the one I had tonight was small, a little bigger than my palm, and I had it clutched in my hand behind my back.

"This book?" I said, revealing my secret.

Sofia looked at it with longing. The cover was real. Some hundred-year-old erotica book with gold-gilded lettering I found on my mother's shelves this past summer. But all the pages had been ripped out so I could make new pages and sew them in. It felt good to do that. Rip apart a story and remake it into something new. Something mine. "What do you write in there?" Sofia asked.

"Everything."

"What's that mean?" Camille asked.

I shrugged. "What I see."

"So you write about us?"

"I leave out the names. Only use initials. It's mostly just a character study."

"Can I read it?" Sofia asked.

"No," I said.

She pouted a little. And even though I already had an opinion about who Sofia Astor was, I put it on hold. Because I knew she was a writer, like me. Like Camille. We've been taking classes together for the past three years. And she intrigued me with the few stories she shared in class. Camille as well. Though for different reasons. Sofia had an impressive grasp of the English language. Her words were poetic and rhythmic and I enjoyed them. She was going to be published soon. I knew that. Was a little jealous of it, to be honest. Because she had New York connections and really, that's all that matters when you're an aspiring author.

"No," I said again. "But if you want, we could write something together." It was a loaded offer. I was going to use her and I knew that the moment the words came out of my mouth.

She took in a deep breath, tried to hide a smile and failed. "When?"

"I don't care."

"Now?" Camille asked.

I hadn't included her in the invitation. Camille's words were sharp and her sentences short. They were nice. Very readable. But very different than Sofia.

I considered this as my gaze wandered back to my mother and Christopher Arlington.

Camille caught that and said, "Your mother is very…"

"Flirty?" I finished for her.

Sofia laughed. "He does that every year. Not just with her, either."

I nodded. "I know. I've written about him a lot."

"Oooooo," came out both their mouths.

Then Camille laughed. "Well, if you want to know what happens next, we can show you."

"What do you mean?" I asked. Too sharply.

Sofia leaned in, cupping a hand to her mouth, and whispered, "We know where he takes them."

"Where?"

"Come with us and find out."

So I did. We went to the south edge of campus, which was not too far from the theatre building where the party was, and stopped just before entering the woods.

"We gotta take off our shoes," Camille explained. "They'll just get ruined."

"You've done this before?" I asked.

"Every year." Sofia laughs. "We write about him too."

"He's fodder." Camille giggled. "Dirty, erotic fodder for sexy stories we sell online."

"Really?" I asked. And this time it was me who couldn't hide her smile. "I think I'd like to know more."

So we slipped off our shoes, hid them in a bush, and padded along the well-worn path leading into the woods with bare feet.

CHAPTER TWENTY-SEVEN

I'm sitting in a chair holding a drink.

Everyone is here for the party. The butterflies have clear wings and the balloons are lavender. My parents' party, I realize. I'm at my parents' anniversary party.

I look around for everyone else. Sofia is dancing with Hayes in the middle of the room.

Bennett is on his phone. Having a furious text conversation with someone. Camille is drunk, spinning in circles, arms outstretched, reaching for butterflies.

And Kiera… God, she looks beautiful in her long black gown. The skirt is made up of layers upon layers of sheer fabric and she's twirling near Camille. Delicate fingertips lifting her dress so she doesn't trip, smiling up at the balloons and butterflies like Camille.

"Kiera?" I say.

And even though there's hundreds of people here and the hum of conversation drowns out my words, she hears me. Because she stops spinning and wobbles, dizzy, trying to find my face.

"Are you drunk?" I ask.

"We're all drunk, Con," she says, stumbling forward, hand out, reaching for me. "Come on, let's dance! It's a party!"

I'm confused by this. Sofia and Hayes. That makes sense. Bennett ignoring a party for his phone. Total sense. Camille, drunk and giddy. Check.

But… "Kiera," I say, getting up. Wondering for a second how my drink mysteriously disappeared from my hand, but not really caring. "What are you doing?" I ask, approaching her. She's spinning again. Just like Camille.

"I like it now," she says.

"Like what now?'

"The dizzy. If I give in, it'll go away."

"What will?"

She stops abruptly and grabs my shoulders, looking me in the eyes. "The bad people, Connor. If I just… let myself be dizzy and… and believe," she says, whispering that last word. "If I just believe… Oh, I know!" she says, spinning again. "I'll write it down. I'll write it down and make it real."

"Kiera," I say, grabbing her hand to make her stop. "What are you talking about?"

"Shhhhhh," she says. But when she does that, she turns into Emily. "Don't say it too loud, Connor. They're listening."

My eyes are closed and when I open them the first thing I hear is my father's laughter. Others join in as I blink away the fogginess inside my head.

"What do you think of that, Connor?" my father says.

I have to blink several more times to make him come into focus. But even then, everything and everyone around him is blurry. Like he's the most important man in the room in a spotlight of clarity and everyone else is just… murky, amorphous figures.

"Here's your speech, Connor," a man says, thrusting a paper at me.

I look up at the man, recognize him as Steven, and take the papers automatically.

"All you have to do is read it," Steven says.

"It's almost time," another voice says. I look up, searching for it, but never manage to find who said the words.

"Louise?" my father says. "Is he OK?"

A woman bends down in front of me wearing a low-cut gold and black dress. Flashing a small penlight at my eyes.

I blink and push her hand away. "What the hell is going on?"

"Connor," the woman says, "Do you know who I am?"

I look at her, my fucking head pounding like I was in a bar fight. "No," I say. "Who are you?"

She straightens up, her attention already on my father. "He's fine. He'll be fine."

"What's wrong with me?" I ask.

"You got drunk yesterday," my father says, squeezing my shoulder. "Camille and Bennett gave you quite a shock. But you're sober now, son." He squeezes again. "You'll be fine. Just read the speech Steven prepared and you'll be fine."

Somehow… I don't think that's true.

"Are you sure he doesn't need another dose?" my father asks the gold-and-black-dress woman.

"Another dose of what?" I ask, pressing my fingertips into my forehead.

"I think he's good. One more dose and we might..."

But she doesn't finish.

I glance up and find her and my father sharing a look.

"Honestly, Christopher. Another dose is pushing it. He's fine." I'm sure her voice is familiar. I'm sure I know who she is. "After the speech we can dose him again and—"

"Dose me with what?" I say, some clarity coming back now. "What the fuck is happening?"

"You're at my house, Connor. I'm Dr. Livingston," she says. "Remember? I've been your psychiatrist for years."

I study her face again. Because I can see Louise in those features. And that is Louise's voice, I decide. But this woman... "You can't be Louise. You're *old*."

"Connor," my father says. "That's enough. Now get up and let's go. You have an announcement to make."

Someone grabs me by the shoulder and urges me to stand. But there's a moment when I wobble a little. Like I'm the one who's drunk and not Camille and Kiera.

Wait.

I shake my head.

That was a dream.

Wasn't it?

Was it? Emily's whisper in my head asks.

It was Kiera Bonnaire who caught my attention that night of the Legacy Alumni Party. I'd been watching her since freshman year. Her and her aloof nature. Her wild, long, blonde hair. Her Vermont attitude and woods-y clothes. Her notebook and pen.

What did she write in those notebooks?

Sometimes I'd catch her watching me from across the lunch pavilion. Then she'd look away and furiously scribble for several minutes. Like a mad woman with an obsession for *me*.

I'd wanted her for years. Not just the way most guys want girls they can't have. I wanted to know her. Keep her. Make her mine.

I watched that night. Watched her watching my father with her mother. Wondering if she saw what I saw. Wondering if she was gonna write it down in the small notebook she was hiding in her clutched fist.

So when Sofia and Camille joined her—started whispering things, led her away—we followed.

Hayes was just there, that's all. Drunk already. High too. Making rude jokes about my father and her mother. Rude, but true.

I took the flask he offered, drew a long gulp of some smooth whiskey, and we followed them. Found their shoes sticking out of a bush leading into the woods.

I knew what we'd find at the end of the path. This wasn't the first time I followed my father into the woods with a woman, but it was the first time I'd get there before him.

Bennett was there too. Kissing Emily Medici up against a tree, his hands wandering under her dress, her head back with neck exposed as he whispered dirty things in her ear to keep her attention.

The late summer night was warm and they were both flushed and sweaty.

They pulled away from each other as we approached, Emily fixing her hair, Bennett tucking in his shirt, playing it off. Weird Emily Medici wasn't anyone's first choice for a romp in the woods, but whatever. Hayes and I were busy following the girl with the notebook.

Bennett joined up, Emily trailing behind him because he had her hand. He wanted to know what we were up to, but he wanted sex too.

The whole fucking thing was an accident.

We found the girls standing in front of the Arlington family mausoleum, trying to get in. It was locked, but guess who was here? An official member of the family with the combination.

The whole fucking thing was fate.

We entered, all seven of us. Laughing, whispering, shushing each other. Bennett was grabbing Camille, trying to make her scream. Apparently he'd forgotten all about Emily. Hayes was leaning into Sofia, trying out some rude one-liners. She slapped him once or twice, but he took it as a challenge. I was next to Kiera, leading the way.

"Over here," I said, low and hushed. I took her hand, found the one with the notebook, so I took that too.

"Hey," she protested.

"I'm not gonna steal it," I said. "I just want to hold your hand."

She let me.

Hayes made a joke about that, but we ignored him. I took her past the raised tomb that held my great-great-grandfather and around another corner where the rest of the family was buried. We sat down, all of us except Emily, who was pacing and clearly pissed about being tossed aside by Bennett in favor of Camille, and started passing Hayes' flask around.

"What are we waiting for?" Bennett asked.

But that's when we heard the electronic lock on the mausoleum door disengage and everyone went silent. Listening as the door creaked open.

Kiera snatched her notebook back and crawled away from me, trying to get a better look. I followed her and we slumped against the wall, just close enough to the cover and hidden in a shadow so we could see their shadows as they entered.

There was no talking. It was hands, and lips, and heavy breathing.

My father's indiscretions were no secret in the family. My mother would've divorced him years ago if she could.

But she couldn't. She was as weak as he was, just in a different way.

I remember thinking how humiliating this was for her. To be at the same party and know he was out here doing this.

Emily was still standing. Her leg right next to my head. Trying to get a glimpse, like us.

Bennett, Camille, Sofia, and Hayes were still pressed back against the far end of the short hallway, hands over mouths covering smiles and stifling snickers. Eyes wide with, *What the fuck is happening?*

Oh, nothing to see here, friends. It's just Connor's father cheating on his mother. With Kiera's mother. Kiera, whom I'm infatuated with and want to know better in ways that are a lot like my father's intentions with her mother right now. That's all.

"Oh, my God," Emily whispered, catching on.

The shuffling hands and kissing lips paused and we all held our breath.

"Is someone in here?" Antoinette Bonnaire asked.

And then footsteps approaching.

But just before they came into view, the electronic lock on the door beeped again.

A twist in the story, readers. A very unfortunate twist.

Because after the door creaked open one more time I heard, "Hello, Christopher. I thought I'd find you here."

And it was my mother.

"Who the fuck is that?" my father asked.

"Uh… uh…" some dumbstruck dumb fuck stuttered. A man, that's all I knew then. My mother had brought my father a little surprise. A little game of tit-for-tat. A little payback. A little taste-of-your-own-medicine.

"What the hell are you doing?" My father again.

"Getting rid of this year's trollop."

Meaning Antoinette.

I don't know exactly what happened in what order then. I only know Emily screamed, Kiera was on her feet, and I was pulling her back while she was pulling me forward, and my mother had a gun. Shots were fired. There was more screaming, and shuffling, and yelling, and moaning. And two more shots.

And in the end the dumbstruck dumb fuck was dead and Kiera was shot in the shoulder.

"Connor," my father snaps. "Get your shit together. There are three hundred people and a slew of networks here tonight. In five minutes you're going to be announcing your candidacy for the Senate."

My head hurts like fuck.

What just happened? Was that a dream? Was it a memory?

I don't know. I can't tell. My vision is blurry, and my mind is foggy, and…

What I do know, what I do see… are two books on a table just off to my right.

Two books. The first is a notebook. One of Kiera's. Old. Aged. Worn and tattered *The Great Gatsby* cover, just like the one Sofia had in her office. Pages that weren't meant to be inside, inside and half sticking out. Made by her hands. Written in with her pen.

There are dozens of Post-It flags hanging off those pages. Six different colors to keep the six different characters in the story straight.

Our book.

And next to it, looking shiny and new with only a few Post-Its flagging important story elements, is *The Dirty Ones.*

"What the fuck are those?" I ask, pointing to the books.

"Later, Connor."

"Fuck later. I'm not going out there until—" And that's when I see that Louise woman coming at me with a syringe.

"This will help," she says, pointing the needle at me.

"Fuck you," I say, backing off.

But many hands have me by the shoulders. Preventing my escape.

"Louise," my father says. "Are you sure he'll be able to talk? He needs to make this speech tonight. The plan is in motion, we cannot stop now."

"Connor," the Louise person says. That isn't Louise. How did she get so old? "It's up to you. Either pull yourself together, go out there, and read the speech, or I'll have to give you something to calm you down."

Just go along, Connor. You must convince your father that you're still on board.

But where is Hayes?

Where is Kiera? Where's Sofia?

That wasn't a dream I had. It was a memory. Everything we thought we knew about what happened to us that year is a lie.

My father is a filthy, cheating bastard and my mother finally had enough and tried to kill him for it. Someone else died instead. How, I'm not sure. I think only Emily has that answer. I think only Emily saw that whole scene play out.

But what I do remember is that my father had the gun when Kiera stepped out of the shadows. My father is the one who pointed it at her. My father is the one who pulled that trigger and shot her that night.

"We could make an excuse," Steven says. "Have Connor just announce, then leave with no speech. I'll swoop in and say he's still recovering from the death of his friends."

My father blows air out through his nose. He's glaring at me.

You need to make the announcement. Hayes again. In my head. *The media will be there.*

He knew.

He knew Louise was a doctor. He knew she used drugs on us to make us forget. He knew Emily saw the whole thing. He knew that book was written by Kiera and he knew that it was the truth.

I'm making one promise with this book.
Just one.
It's the truth.
We are the Dirty Ones and this is our story.

That's why he wanted us to read it together. That's why he said, "It's not fair, Connor. To keep her as a mistress. She deserves better after all she's been through. Either love her whole or set her free."

"No," I say, forcing myself to stand up, ignoring the pounding heartbeat in my head, and make myself walk straight as I hold out my hand. "No. I'm fine. Give me the speech and let's do this."

CHAPTER TWENTY-EIGHT

We are dressed in some mighty fine clothes for Connor's candidacy announcement party. Sofia, always in red. Me, in winter white. Hayes in a tuxedo. We don't have invitations, but we don't need them. Because we come in with Hayes' parents. There's some discussion about turning us away when we exit the limo, but Mr. Fitzgerald handles it like the old society pro he is.

Inside I look for Connor. We don't split up. Never again. Buddy system all the way tonight. So we all look for him, but he's not here.

"They have him in a room somewhere," Hayes says, reading my mind. "Don't worry. He's here. He's the only reason this party is happening, Kiera."

I know it's true, but all I can think about is what they've been doing to him since he was taken on Thursday night.

They killed Camille and Bennett. We're still not sure how. Hell, we don't even know who they all are. But we know they did it.

And they shot me once already.

I don't remember all of it. We need to have a very long discussion about what happened that year. But I remember some of it. After we left the cemetery we got back in the car and drove to the theater building. Went up to the top floor. Hayes pointed things out to jog our memory, and I'm sure he's right, it was just very hard to picture what he was telling us.

Mr. Arlington, Connor's father, shot me that night.

But I was lucky. Because I lived. Someone else did not.

"It's starting," Sofia says, pointing to a group of people coming through a wide set of double doors. I lean up on my tiptoes, one hand on Sofia's shoulder, one hand on Hayes', desperate to get a look at Connor.

"There he is," Hayes says.

My heart stops when I see him. Because he looks horrible. They have make-up on him and yes, he's in a suit every bit as nice as the tux Hayes is wearing, but… "Oh, God," I say. "What did they do to him?"

Sofia reaches for my hand. Squeezes it. "He's OK," she says. "He's alive. He's fine, don't worry."

Everyone starts to make that whisper sound that happens when something is about to start, and then the whole crowd presses forward as Connor approaches the platform set up at a stage at the head of the ballroom.

Connor's father stands at the microphone. He's wearing a tux, like everyone else but Connor. I imagine the conversation that went along with that choice. ("Can't be in a tux when you announce your candidacy for office. Looks too pretentious. Very one percent. And that's something we need to avoid, son.")

He taps the microphone. "Is this thing on?" he jokes.

That man shot me. Shot. Me. Because I saw something I shouldn't have. And if Sofia and Camille weren't there with me, if I wasn't with them at the time, if Bennett and Emily and Hayes didn't see it too, he'd have killed me.

You fucked up that night. You fucked up and instead of owning up to what you did, you ruined us. Turned that whole year into a lie. But you can't kill all of us, can you, Mr. Arlington?

Not true. He could still kill all of us if we don't do this right. Even Connor. Especially Connor.

"I want to say thank you for coming to celebrate what is probably the happiest day of my life." Mr. Arlington turns to look at his son. Connor is pale. Hands clasped in front of him. Flanked on either side by that campaign guy, Steven, and…

"Holy shit," Sofia whispers. "Louise did not age well."

"That can't be Louise," I say. "She's so… old."

"She was always old, you guys," Hayes says. "We just saw her wrong because of the drugs. She wasn't a student with us, she's a crazy fucking psychiatrist sent in to reprogram us."

I don't like that word. *Reprogram.* Especially when I'm looking at Connor and it's so clear. So very crystal clear that they've given him drugs tonight.

What if he doesn't remember me? What if he still believes what they made us think?

Or worse. What if he knows? What if he knows the truth and doesn't choose me?

"I need him to see me," I say, moving forward, but Hayes pulls me back.

"Not yet," he whispers. "Stay still, Kiera. He needs to make a decision. For once in his life, Connor Arlington needs to be the one to decide his own fate."

"My son," the Arlington patriarch continues, "has an announcement to make tonight. Something I've been hoping for. Something we've both been working towards for the better part of the last decade. So let's give it up for the man of the hour!"

People clap and cheer. It's a political event so there's red, white, and blue banners with the Arlington name on them that get waves. Looking up, I see a net filled with balloons. Not lavender—was that even real? Was any of it real?—but also red, white, and blue. Ready to be released after he makes his candidacy official.

"Good evening," Connor says into the microphone. More cheering from his father's loyal supporters. The whole thing is ridiculous. Everything has been planned and plotted. Set up for who knows how long. More than a decade, I'm sure. For whatever reason, Connor was the chosen one in this family and this night is just the first of many if he goes through with this. "Thank you," he says. "Thank you all for coming."

He's holding some papers. His speech, I realize. He's gonna do it. He's gonna read that speech. One he didn't write, I know that for sure. He's gonna say those words, and make this real, and—

But then he puts them aside.

I look at his father, pursing his lips. He leans in and whispers something but Connor puts up a hand.

The crowd begins to murmur things. Things I'm thinking too. "What's he doing?" "What was that?" "What's going on?"

Connor searches the crowd and people start looking around. His father finds me first and just as he opens his mouth—most likely to call for security—Connor says, "There you are, Kiera."

He's slurring his words a little and I feel sick all of a sudden. Sick that he's going to say something wrong. Something that will rip his life apart and take me out at the same time.

"Come up here," he says.

And then the crowd parts, and the whispers are louder now. "Who's that?" "Who's she?" "What's happening?" There's a direct lane of empty space between me and the podium where Connor stands.

Hayes leans into me, pulling the book out of my purse and placing it in my hands. "You know what to do," he says.

I do.

No matter what Connor's choice is. No matter who he chooses. I have a mission here. A mission to expose them.

"Come on," Connor says, motioning to me with his fingers in a way that conveys power. A way that let's everyone know he's in control. A way that makes me nervous.

How much does he know?

But there's no more time because my feet are moving forward and soon I'm at the podium, looking up at him.

"I have a choice to make tonight. You see… I love this woman."

Gasps from the crowd.

"Connor," his father says sharply. And even though he's whispering, I'm close enough to hear him now. "Stop it right—"

"Her name is Kiera Bonnaire. And she writes erotica."

I suck in a deep, deep breath. A few people laugh loudly. Several close to me snicker.

"Come here," Connor whispers, holding out his hand. "Come up and stand beside me."

I search for the stairs that will take me up to him, but several men are blocking my way. Telling me in no uncertain terms that this is not gonna happen.

Connor turns to his father and says, right into the microphone, "She wrote a book called *The Dirty Ones*. It's sitting on the *New York Times* bestseller list right now at number three."

Loud gasps. No one is bothering to whisper anymore.

"And she made a promise when she wrote that book. Just one. She promised that the story was true."

"Connor," his father says, loud now. "Stop. Right now. You have no idea—"

"I know exactly what I'm doing," Connor says, looking me straight in the eyes. "And you can stop her from joining me if you want, but this announcement will be made."

"What is it?" someone calls. "What's the announcement? Are you running for Senate?"

It's someone from the media, I realize.

"No," Connor says. "No, I'm not running for Senate. Because I've been told by my father since I was a child that to be in politics you have be a role model. Which is absurd, when you think about it. So a life with an erotica author isn't something I could have. Wasn't something I could keep. Was something I'd have to give up. Or at least," Connor says, looking at his father again, "keep it a secret, right, Dad?"

His father goes pale.

He knows.

Connor knows, and Christopher knows, and I know and now the whole world is gonna know too.

"The way my father kept his affairs secret."

It's almost impossible to hear him now. The room has erupted in a cacophony of talking. The media are yelling questions.

"But one of my dear friends told me something the other day. He said, 'She deserves better than that.' And he's right. She does. So I'm telling you now, I'm in love with this woman. She writes dirty, filthy, dark erotica. And she's damn good at it too."

I can't help it. I smile.

"Because she wrote that book right there and every word is true. And not everyone can take a true story and weave it into a tale."

"That book can't be true," someone calls out from the crowd. "That book says—"

"That book says," Connor interrupts, "that my father had an affair, got caught by a group of college kids and his wife, then killed a man, shot Kiera Bonnaire in the shoulder, and hired psychiatrist Dr. Louise Livingston to drug us all up, week after week, month after month, and feed us a fake story to cover it up. She bullied us. She made us perform sexual acts with each other. She pumped us with drugs, and fake stories, and then—to make it feel as real as it possibly could—she made Kiera write it down." He stops to point to the book in my hand. "That was not this book. That book is in the room behind me. This book," he says, "is the true story of us. The Dirty Ones."

"Lies," Christopher Arlington sneers. "That's all lies!"

"No!"

Every head turns to see Emily coming up behind Connor. Holding my book. The other book. The one with the *Great Gatsby* cover I didn't think was real.

"I was there! I'm a Dirty One and none of this is lies. This is the book Kiera wrote ten years ago after he blamed me for shooting her and had me locked up in a mental hospital for attempted murder."

"Ridiculous!" Christopher barks. "Cut the cameras! This press conference is over!"

No one cuts off a camera.

"I was there too," Sofia says in her soft, gentle Sofia voice as she steps forward. "I'm a Dirty One. My initials are in that book. SA. Sofia Astor. He did this to me as well."

"I'm a Dirty One too," Hayes says. "HF. Hayes Fitzgerald. He fucked me over pretty good as well."

"But," Connor continues, still speaking into the mic even though it was turned off. Doesn't matter. He projects his voice through the whole room. "There's more. CD is Camille DuPont and BW is Bennett Winthrop. You might recognize their names from the news yesterday after they"—Connor makes air quotes—"'killed themselves.'" He shakes his head. "They didn't kill themselves. I don't know what happened to them, but I suspect you'll find drugs were involved and they will trace back to—"

"How dare you!" Louise spits. "How dare you say these things in my home!"

"How dare you," Connor spits back. "How dare you fuck with the minds of innocent kids. How dare you erase me and my friends. How dare you lock up Emily Medici in a mental hospital because she refused to believe your lies! How dare you, Dr. Louise Livingston," he seethes. "How dare you rewrite our story."

CHAPTER TWENTY-NINE

You are not allowed to steal words from people.

You're not even allowed to borrow them without permission.

What they did to Kiera—what my father did, what Louise did… it makes me sick.

And I was the reader. They made her write those words and made me tell the story. Week after week. Month after month. That dark, sick, twisted tale of sexual perversion was woven into our minds with equal parts masterful manipulation and mind-altering drugs.

For what?

To save himself from a second-degree murder trial? That he would probably just buy his way out of?

They fucked with *our heads.* Made us believe things we never did. I don't even know which parts are real and which parts are fiction. Did they have an anniversary party with balloons and butterflies? Did we meet up in person as a whole group? Or in pairs? Was Kiera really at every single session?

"My friends are dead," I tell the crowd, not done yet. So not done yet. "My friends are dead, Emily was locked up in a hospital, and every one of us had our words stolen. But they also stole an *entire year* of our lives. They ripped our reality apart and replaced it with something ugly, and disgusting, and sick."

I stop and look out at the silent, stunned crowd.

"You came here for an announcement? There it is. The truth."

"Why should we believe you?" a reporter asks.

"You don't have to believe me," I say. "I didn't make this little speech for you. I made it for them." I point to Kiera, and Sofia, and Hayes. Emily is close to me now, so I grab her hand and hold it up. "I made it for us. What happens next doesn't matter. I did this for us. We are the Dirty Ones and this is our story."

I walk around the podium, jump down from the stage, and extend my hand to Emily. I grab her by the waist and lift her to the floor, keeping her hand, so she knows who I am in this moment—her friend—and walk towards Kiera. I take her hand, she takes Sofia's hand, Sofia takes Hayes' hand.

And we leave. Together.

Minus two.

Because we came back from this sick, grand delusion one day too late.

And we just gotta learn to live with that.

CHAPTER THIRTY

Louise Livingston was arrested the day of Camille's funeral. Bennett had been put to rest the day before, and when Connor, Hayes, Sofia and I walked back through the door of Sofia's apartment we thought we'd run out of tears for Camille. That's how hard we cried.

It's funny how these two were so much a part of me, then they weren't, then they were again. Funny how I can feel so empty for one man I hadn't talked to for ten years less than a week ago.

Even Hayes cried for Bennett. It was a silent cry. No sobbing or hysterics. Just… overwhelming sadness.

Connor really did lose his best friend. Bennett was the only kid he'd grown up with since he was small. The only kid he shared all the success and failures with.

I'm not sure if I cried harder for Bennett dying or that little piece of Connor's heart that went dim that day because it was empty.

I just know I cried so hard I couldn't open my eyes when we got home.

The guys got drunk. Sofia and I crawled into her bed and held each other all night. And when we woke in the morning, just when we thought we'd get to start a new day, we did the whole thing all over again.

Only this time it was Sofia falling apart. This time it was Sofia saying goodbye to her best friend.

And guess what?

It turns out you can't run out of tears.

But Connor saved us that night. He opened up one of Camille's stupid erotic comedies and read it out loud.

The entire book. Cover to cover. Every single page, even the note at the end. We streamed it live for her fans and they watched by the millions.

So hard.

They loved her so hard.

We cried with them until we laughed. And then we cried some more when her characters got their HEA.

Because we were one day too late.

One day.

And Camille DuPont would never, ever get another chance at happily ever after.

It took another seven days for Steven what's-his-face to be arrested as an accomplice. There was a whole slew of charges. Too many for me to list now. Then every day after that for almost a week, there was another arrest. More people. Even Connor's mother.

Hell, if my mother was alive, she'd have been arrested too.

But it took another three full weeks before Christopher Arlington was finally led out of the front door to his North Shore estate in handcuffs and put in the back seat of a police car. Helicopters circled overhead, catching it on film.

For Connor, it was another funeral. Another loss.

None of us cheered.

It's taken months for me to unravel the long process of how this book came to be written in my voice. By my hands.

It was me. But not just me.

Because it was Hayes Fitzgerald who started unraveling this tightly wound secret.

Several years ago he got in his helicopter with a drunken directive for the pilot to take him to Essex College for the annual legacy dinner. He says now he can't explain how it all came apart in his head. Maybe it was the alcohol or the drugs that allowed the memories to come pouring out of the broken dam. Or maybe the brainwashing was just wearing off.

All he knew at the time was that he was broken. Shattered into millions of pieces. That he spent all those years that came after graduation in a drug- and alcohol-induced stupor.

Not because he was an addict, but because he was afraid. Scared to death of the secrets locked inside his head. Terrified that one day they'd come spilling out of that cobbled-together dam and he'd go insane, just like Emily.

But as is the case with most fears, once you face them they lose power. They make you stronger.

He came to me next. Under the pretense of meeting for lunch with an old friend, he took me out and we met up with his therapist. A nobody psychiatrist working out of an office in the worst part of Burlington who mostly took pro bono cases but had an online website offering hypnotic therapy for recovering lost memories. She had teased most of what really happened that night out of Hayes before he brought me in, but he needed me to get the whole story.

Or so he thought.

There was no tower. Almost everything we thought was true was just lies.

I wasn't taken to the hospital after I was shot, I was taken to the Essex College Student Health Center that night. Stitched up, good as new, and then all seven of us were locked in a room on the second floor of the theatre building to "get our story straight."

Emily was combative and Hayes, like the knight in shining armor who grew up in a castle of a mansion, came to her defense. Hayes Fitzgerald is just not a guy who goes along. He's a fighter. So they blamed my gunshot wound on Emily to get rid of her. This weird girl who everyone already thought was crazy, just went crazy. And they used her to threaten the rest of us.

See what happens when you don't go along, children? You get the Emily treatment.

Louise Livingston was there to help us. With drugs. With her own twisted version of hypnotic therapy. Though she wasn't in the business of recovering them, she was in the business of planting them.

And plant them she did.

She has never explained it. What I know of what happened is just a whole bunch of mis-matched memories. But it's all there in the new book and I've read it over and over again, trying to make the pieces fit together the best way I know how.

The most tragic thing about this whole nightmare might be that if we had just read a little further that night Hayes locked us in the third-floor library we'd have gotten to the truth before morning. The beginning of the book was what we thought happened. But the truth—the real events of that night—came in the next chapter. If Connor had just read that part about me getting shot the whole truth would've unfolded. We'd have figured out it was all lies and Bennett and Camille would've never have left.

Bennett and Camille would still be alive.

Hayes blames himself for not being more forthcoming.

But it's not his fault. No one should feel guilt and shame for trying to be careful with the people they love.

He was just trying to unravel our memories in a thoughtful way. Afraid that untangling things in the wrong way would lead to a total breakdown.

We don't know what triggered their suicides. Maybe they started remembering on their own that night? Maybe Connor's father got to them first and made threats? Hell, maybe Louise showed up with her drugs and started planting new memories?

Yes, we got answers. But we still have questions. And these mysteries will never be solved because the only two people who know what really happened are dead.

I think Connor's father wanted to kill me that night we witnessed the shooting. I think I was the wild card. Just some nobody. Some expendable nobody. Someone who didn't belong in their world. Someone who couldn't be kept quiet out of family obligations.

But my mother was there. I think she stopped them. And if I'm being honest, I think it was her elaborate writer's imagination that came up with this plan. But of course I'll never understand that part. It's just something I'll have to live with and I keep my own imagination in check because I know how easy it is to believe the story we write in our heads.

As far as The Dirty Ones go… I think Camille, and Sofia, and Bennett, and Hayes, and Connor—who were not my friends at that point in time—saw my death that night. Saw that they could save me with these lies.

But I think giving us this story gave us power too.

They wanted to divide us that night. Make us hate each other.

But that's not what happened. We fell in love. As a group, I guess. We grew closer. We became friends. These special people who were raised in privilege took my side and saved my life.

That's my story, anyway. That's the happy ending I need to write.

I have no memory of my visits to the therapist with Hayes. He deliberately told her to erase the revelations after each session because once he told me that he was looking for the truth I shut down and refused to see him again for months.

It was a slow process. Once a month he'd take me to lunch and we'd meet up with the hypnotist. In these secret sessions they put a pen in my hand and told me to write it all down. Easy, for someone like me. Someone who was born to write stories like a person possessed.

But it wasn't easy. It was slow. Only a sentence or two each month for almost a year.

But after my mother died I spiraled into a deep depression and the words came easier. Poured out of me like they were spilling out of the same dam. Like I knew I was free. Which makes me sick to think about, but still, it's the truth. And it must be faced.

And at the end of all that I wrote a book.

Hayes is the one who took it to an agent. Set up a shell corporation and they shopped it, made a deal and eighteen months later it debuted at number three on the *New York Times.*

He lied to me. Manipulated me.

And I love him for it now. Because without Hayes we'd still think that nightmare was real.

The truth must be faced eventually. It always finds a way.

Hayes thought he could publish my new book and draw them out without involving the rest of us. Make them see that we held the power. But Connor stumbled onto the book at the airport and his plan came apart.

It's humbled him. It's made Hayes cautious for the first time in his life. Allowed him to see that he is also fallible. That he is also human. But even though I don't blame Hayes for Camille and Bennett—and neither do Sofia and Connor—I think it's a good change for him.

It's good to know your weaknesses. It's important to understand how one decision can cause events to spiral into something you no longer control. Especially for people like Hayes, who carry the weight of unimaginable riches and power on their shoulders.

We have drifted apart these last few months, but in a good way. Paired up into something normal and safe. Sofia and Hayes. Connor and me.

We left The Dirty Ones behind and maybe I don't really know who we are now, but I know who we aren't.

And that's enough.

Someone, probably Connor's father, actually had the gall to submit his candidacy paperwork. The entire state of New York still thinks he's running for US Senator. He's got a huge lead in the polls and it hurts Connor, I can tell. To see that happen. Because he knows his father is out on bail waiting for trial, just watching those numbers climb, smug with the realization that all his plotting and planning paid off.

Connor pretends it's not happening. We've been in Vermont since the day of his father's arrest. He found the will in my attic and has hired a lawyer to sort it out.

The house will be mine. Essex College was implicated in the deceit—that's what they're calling it in public. Deceit. As if that guy Connor's mother was with ten years ago didn't get killed. As if I didn't take a bullet in my shoulder. As if Emily wasn't locked up in a mental institution for an entire decade. The dean was arrested and is also awaiting trial.

The college is not fighting the lawsuit Connor filed.

Oh, yeah. I think people forgot Connor was a lawyer.

Well, everyone remembers now.

The delusional notebook I wrote back in senior year is evidence, but I have been assured that it will be returned to me.

What a fantastic work of fiction that will be.

I can't wait to burn it.

Meanwhile, *The Dirty Ones* has been on the *New York Times* bestseller list for almost six months. It's got my name on the cover now. And Connor's. And Hayes'. And Sofia's. And Bennett's. And Emily's. And Camille's.

Because we are the Dirty Ones and this is no story.

It's the truth.

EPILOGUE

FIVE YEARS LATER

***The long** plowed* driveway leading up to the cottage is lined with cars. I have no idea how they're all gonna get out after this thing is over, but eh. Not really my problem. They're the dumb fucks who wanted to come to Vermont in the middle of January for a five-minute press conference.

I'm not even there. I'm looking out the attic window of the big house working on a project for Kiera. Her birthday is coming up next week and I have something special planned.

We got married the month after my father was found guilty of second-degree murder. He's serving a thirty-year sentence in a federal prison because it turns out he was implicated in a whole slew of election fraud charges as well.

Louise was killed in a freak car accident three days before her trial began so she never served any time.

I don't even care. Can't make myself care. Even if it was my father's doing.

Steven turned state's evidence against my father and got out a couple months ago. We haven't stayed in touch. My mother went to prison for eighteen months, but she's been out for a while now. Boarded up tight in the family estate. Estranged from her children.

Am I surprised that my brothers and sisters took my side?

Yes.

Pleasantly.

I see them often, appreciate them more than ever, and do my best to be a good brother.

I opened a law practice in Charlotte after I was admitted to the Vermont Bar. Kiera and I have lived here happily for almost five years. And even though I can see Essex College from my attic window, I don't look for the tower that was never there. I see a steeple, and the various buildings, and sometimes I even watch the rowers from the back porch.

It can't hurt me anymore.

I don't give it that kind of power.

"It's starting!" Kiera calls up from the first floor. "Come down here!"

"One sec!" I call back.

I miss Bennett every day. So much. He wasn't the kid who was ever gonna do great things, but he was a guy with a big heart. Someone who took care of Camille and did his best. He always did his best.

They never proved their suicides were murder and I live with that regret in my heart. The regret that we didn't save him and Camille. I even miss Camille. I read her book out loud to Kiera and stream it live for the fans every year on the anniversary of their deaths.

It's called *A Bunny In The Oven.* I didn't even know there was such a thing as cuddle-kink—I laugh every time I say that word. But there is. It's a crazy-stupid, crazy-funny, crazy-sexy Camille version of a middle-aged New York City transplant who now owns a rabbitry—another thing I didn't know existed—and solves weird erotic mysteries in this little country town.

Fuckin' thing has sold like ten million copies in the last five years since Camille died. Super crazy.

And also super cool.

It makes me feel good. Because Camille was loved and they won't let her die, even when she's dead. They remember her. They keep her words alive. They send us cards, and flowers, which we put out on the back porch of the cottage, and if the lake isn't frozen near the shore there's a boat parade. If it is, people set up ice-fishing huts and dress up like… middle-age New York transplants who now own a rabbitry.

Fucking shit is weird.

I love it.

"Connor!" Kiera yells. "Come down now! It's starting!"

"Coming," I say, picking up the present I've been up here wrapping. It's not her birthday yet, but I'm gonna give it to her tonight anyway. Because it's a special day. That's why we called the news conference.

I walk down the two flights of stairs to the living room and find her sitting on the couch wearing leggings and a too-big sweater. Her shearling boots are really slippers, but I won't tell.

"Oh, my God. Hayes is looking so smug. You gotta see—" She stops when she sees the present. "What's that?"

I hold up a finger. "Wait," I say. "Just let me look at you for a moment. Write a little story in my head about this day."

She giggles.

She's so beautiful when she giggles. Her long hair is messy. She didn't bother brushing it today, just swept it up into a hair tie with no fucks to give. No makeup. Not a single thing about her that isn't original, and natural, and perfect, and true.

"I'm Hayes Fitzgerald, representing Connor and Kiera Arlington, and I have two important announcements today." Hayes' voice comes from the large flat screen above the fireplace. He's standing out on the shoveled front porch, red, white, and blue streamers hanging all over the place. There's people in the yard holding signs that say, *Run, Connor, Run*!

He and Sofia married right after we did. They already have two kids who don't have nannies and share a bedroom with a bunk bed they got at Sears when they're at our house. They live at the cottage house in the summer and her New York penthouse in the winter.

Hayes turned his family estate into an actual museum. People have weddings there and shit. Parties and corporate events. One year a group of Girl Scouts camped there for a week. Two kids actually got lost for a day but they eventually found them in the bowling alley having the time of their life, half dazed from a sugar-high and sick to their stomachs after raiding the fully-stocked snack bar.

Fuckin' Fitzgerald monstrosity.

Sofia still writes, but she and Kiera write together now and Sofia uses her real name. They have a long-running erotic mystery series about two female bounty hunters trying to round up a half dozen sexy assassins for the CIA. It's called *The Broken Ones* and it's pretty good too.

And pretty hot. Sometimes Kiera reads them out loud to me before bed but she never gets far. I usually throw the book at the wall and just tackle her under the sheets.

But it's all her fault. I can't help that my wife is a damn good erotica writer.

Emily got her life back. She comes to stay with us a couple times a year. Got a boyfriend and shop on Esty making some artsy shit she learned how to do in the hospital. She even had her own gallery show in New York last year. Sells a buttload of… whatever it is she calls that stuff. Sculpture? Maybe? With a side of weird?

She was always weird but now she's just New York artist eccentric weird. i.e. All the right kinds of weird.

"First," Hayes says. "And most importantly, Connor Arlington would like to announce—"

People begin cheering. They have no clue.

"—that Kiera Arlington is pregnant and they're expecting their first child in April."

Everyone stops cheering. There's the usual whispers. "What did he just say?"

"Oh, and second. He won't be running for the Senate. He humbly asks that you please do not write his name in on the ballot. Thank you for coming."

Hayes turns and walks back into the cottage and closes the door.

The camera pans around the disappointed crowd. The reporter begins to talk to her news station anchors with a confused look on her face.

"I love it!" Kiera yells. "That was the best."

They keep thinking I'm gonna run.

But I'm not. Ever.

I would never give up this simple, perfect life for a job that would suck my soul dry and leave me dead inside like my father.

I made a decision that day back at Dr. Louise Livingston's mansion. A vow, of sorts. To the truth.

And that vow is at odds with what these people want from me, so I'm just gonna have to continue to disappoint them.

"Now tell me," Kiera says. "What's that?"

I look down at the gift, perfectly wrapped in navy blue ribbon and gold paper. "Open it and see."

She squeals and runs over to me, taking the present from my hand.

She has no use for ribbons and paper, so she tears them off and opens the box. Holds up the book.

A hardcover version I had specially made just for this. Because Kiera's writer heart would be broken if I ever gutted this book to make her the notebook she holds now.

"Oh, my God. I love you."

"I know," I say, pulling her in for a hug.

"A *Bunny in the Oven* notebook with handmade pages. Did you—"

"I did," I say. "For you both." I rub her swollen stomach under her too-big sweater.

Because I have learned two important things since the truth came out five years ago.

One. I know how to make a decision. I can commit. I have committed to Kiera in every way imaginable but I'm constantly challenging myself to think up new ways.

And two... our dream world is gone. The parties we thought we went to, the good times we thought we had, the illusion we thought we lived... all fake.

But it doesn't matter anymore.

Because our reality is so much better.

Kiera might not think she likes the happily ever after, but she does.

And we're gonna write it together.

Welcome to the End of Book Shit. This is where I get to say whatever I want about the story and you get to listen. Or not. You can skip if you want. These are never edited so please excuse my typos. I usually have a few of those.

So I just wrote an EOBS about how I was sick of standalones and then I go and write a standalone. Figures. Someone who thought they knew me once said I change my mind a lot. I think it was an insult but I didn't take it that way. Because who cares? Right? Who gives a fuck if you change your mind? And anyway, I was thinking more along the lines of standalone series. This book here is 100% standalone.

So The Dirty Ones. I've been holding on to this title for over a year. I wanted to write the book that whole time but I didn't have a story that would live up to it. I knew I wanted it to be something very twisted and very mysterious, and I'm always up for a good conspiracy theory. But I didn't want this one to be "Company". I started one of those with Johnathan McClain (The

Triangle). That's the only thing I knew for sure (Not Company) until… one day… I'm watching the last episode of the final season of Gossip Girl (yes, you heard me right, Gossip Girl) and I loved that ending. The whole Upper East Side thing. The whole too rich thing. The whole outsider writes a book about being an insider. And it had a Gatsby feel to it.

And right then is when this story came to me. Someone wrote a tell-all book and sold it as fiction, but it was a true story.

How the hell I got from that to… THIS? lol I'm still trying to figure that out. It's just that dark, twisted daemon inside me, I guess. Begging to be let out.

But I literally got up, went into my office, and made this cover. And from then on the muse just dictated. Oh, there were bumps along the way. Any time you let the daemon take over your art it's gonna be messy as fuck. So I had to step in a few times and say, "Whoa there, asshole. Let's make sure all the puzzle pieces fit, K?"

He was cool with that. (My muse is a guy. I know most muses are beautiful women, but fuck it. Mine's a sweaty, shirtless hot dude in hell.)

The most important thing to me in this story was the world. Which is not common for a romance, but fuck it. I don't care for common. And when I sent the first draft to Johnathan to read he said something to me about how he can tell I love world building. (I think he actually said I like describing places and it showed.)

Some places, some things, some people… are just PRETTY. And this book is one of those things.

I loved the imagery in this book most of all but Kiera came in a close second. Kiera and her notebooks. Kiera and her writing. Kiera and her cottage and her slipper-boots and the way she doesn't brush her wild hair. Kiera with the no-color eyes. Kiera and her butterflies. Kiera, the secret to the whole mystery.

Camille was actually the surprise hit for me. I sorta fell in love with her obnoxious attitude, and so even though I sacrificed her in the end I gave her a sweet send off.

I was also really digging on Hayes. He's a little bit "Ford", isn't he? I tossed around the idea of dragging this shit out for at least one more book and giving Hayes a story, but nah. Let's let the guy be happy, shall we?

Sofia was soft in my mind. Soft, and girly, and overflowing with "potential". Like Blair on Gossip Girl, only less of a bitch. (I love Blair, BTW. She's my favorite GG character. She and Chuck made the perfect template for Sofia and Hayes)

Connor was just… a normal dude, I think. Not the Alpha, like Hayes. Not the logical one, like Bennett. Just a guy who was born "this man" and was trying to deal with all the unexpected ambivalence and disappointment he felt, even though he had no right to feel that way.

I, for one, think everyone is allowed to feel what they feel, regardless of what station in life they were born into. So the guy had everything and wasn't happy? Anyone who can't relate to inner turmoil can go fuck themselves. Don't ever let anyone tell you you're not allowed to be disappointed in what you have. That's what makes people strive to do more. Telling someone to feel satisfied is just a recipe for "average" if you ask me.

Grateful, thankful—these two things have nothing to do with satisfaction. Sure, I'm grateful for a lot of things. But if I was "satisfied" I'd never have started writing. If I was "satisfied" I'd quit while I was ahead. I sure as fuck wouldn't be taking risks with Johnathan McClain by trying to sell a TV series right before I hit my fiftieth year on this earth.

But this book is also about the illusion inside us. It's about how memory is an unreliable thing. How events shape you and cling to you, long after they're over. It's about facing your demons, standing your ground, and then pushing forward.

What part of the story was real and what part was fantasy? Did they really have all that sex?

I dunno. If you think they did, then they did.

Because in the end it doesn't really matter. Illusion, or delusion, or reality… what difference does it make? When you read a story, and the story is good, you buy into it. You believe it. You live it with me, and my characters, and my sweaty hot-hell-dude daemon.

We went to all these places together. We got stuck in that blizzard, we flew in that helicopter, we landed on that lawn, we fucked in the third-floor library bedroom, we ate dinner at that ridiculous table, and we got lost in that mansion.

The mansion was my favorite scene. Specifically the one where Connor gets lost. I just can't relate to a house that is so big you can get lost. But some people live like this, ya know? And isn't it cool that you and I got to live it a little too?

This is why I love writing. My crazy mind comes up with all these fantasies—things you and I both know aren't true—and we disappear into these worlds, and become friends with these characters, and live their lives for a little bit.

So which part is real?

When you figure that out, let me know. Because in my mind they're all real. Ask any of my Rook & Ronin superfans why they love that series and they're gonna say "Ford!" or "Veronica!" or "Spencer!" Or whoever. They become them. Well, I bring them to life first, then you become them, and then… the most miraculous thing happens…

In our heads we're part of the same world. We live the same lives. We experience the same emotions, fight the same fights, lose and win together. And in my books, we also—somehow, against all odds—fall in love by the time it's over.

It's fucking ridiculous and spectacular at the same time. That stories pull us together like this. Isn't it?

I am more Kiera than I'd like to admit. I too look at people on the street and make up stories about them. I can whip up an entire history for a person as I stand in line at the grocery store. I've been doing this for as long as I remember. And even though I say I never wanted to be a writer—I have always been a writer. I just wrote those stories in my brain instead of putting them down on paper.

I remember writing three things as a child.

One, a short story about a horse named Ruby who get separated from her mother and chained to a stall in a barn. Lol. Even at age eight I was writing dark shit, right!? haha It was called The Fastest Horse. I illustrated it too. Because I wasn't a writer, I was an illustrator. I only wrote the story to match my pictures.

The second thing I wrote in 6th grade. It was some dark, twisted horror story that ended up being like five pages. Which is a lot for a sixth grader. And I remember my teacher, Mrs. Sowards, taking me aside and telling me, "Julie, that is some story. Where did you get that idea?"

I said something like, "I dunno. It just came out." And that was the end of that conversation.

The third thing I wrote was an opening paragraph in seventh grade. Just an opening paragraph. That was the assignment so that's all I did because by this time I was one of the "cool kids". I did homework to get the grade, but I gave no shits about it.

So anyway, I wrote this opening paragraph and when my English teacher, Mrs. Ledale, handed them all back, I didn't get mine. I was just about to raise my hand and ask for my shit back when she started reading it out loud. She finished, walked over to my desk (I had to sit in back at one of the "idiot desks" honest to God, that's what she called them. I actually had an idiot table because she ran out of extra desks. Three of us had idiot desks and I was one of them.) So she puts it down on my table, looks at me, and tells the whole class, "Now that is how you start a story." She asked me if I was gonna finish it, but I said, "Nah. I'm not into writing."

Those are the three pieces of fiction I wrote before I woke up one day and decided to write books when I was 42 years old. I wrote lots of non-fiction though. Hell, I pulled a Master's thesis out of my ass over a long weekend. :) 49 citations, bitches. I don't even remember what I titled it. Something about microbial forensics and in it I accused the FBI of covering up the infamous anthrax scare after 911. Good enough to graduate, so hey. Whatever. I sit at the idiot table, remember?

But my point is… stories. Everyone has them. Every time I scroll through my Facebook timeline I stop on those America's Got Talent or Britain's Got Talent posts to watch. Not because I want to hear these nobodies sing, but because I want to hear their story. Simon and I both want to know how the hell a pediatric nurse with six foster kids got to be up on this stage with a voice that earns him the golden buzzer.

And you know how they did it? Because they weren't satisfied. Sure, they were grateful and they were thankful. But it's another thing entirely to be satisfied.

Well, that's it for this story. I have two more books I "could" write that go with it. Not a series and not quite a spin-off. Something I don't really have a name for yet. But I'm gonna wait until that hot, shirtless hell-dude comes back to tell me what to write. So you might have to hang out for those a while. The guy is kind of an asshole.

But in the mean time I got a book up on pre-order for February called **In To Her**. Take a look where ever you buy books, and if you like what you see, go ahead and click that pre-order button.

Thank you for reading, thank you for reviewing, and I'll see you in the next book.

Julie

JA Huss never wanted to be a writer and she still dreams of that elusive career as an astronaut. She originally went to school to become an equine veterinarian but soon figured out they keep horrible hours and decided to go to grad school instead. That Ph.D. wasn't all it was cracked up to be (and she really sucked at the whole scientist thing), so she dropped out and got a M.S. in forensic toxicology just to get the whole thing over with as soon as possible.

After graduation she got a job with the state of Colorado as their one and only hog farm inspector and spent her days wandering the Eastern Plains shooting the shit with farmers.

After a few years of that, she got bored. And since she was a homeschool mom and actually does love science, she decided to write science textbooks and make online classes for other homeschool moms.

She wrote more than two hundred of those workbooks and was the number one publisher at the online homeschool store many times, but eventually she covered every science topic she could think of and ran out of shit to say.

So in 2012 she decided to write fiction instead. That year she released her first three books and started a career that would make her a New York Times bestseller and land her on the USA Today Bestseller's List twenty-one times in the next four years.

Her books have sold millions of copies all over the world, the audio version of her semi-autobiographical book, Eighteen, was nominated for an Audie award in 2016, her audiobook, Mr. Perfect, was nominated for a Voice Arts Award in 2017, and her audiobook, Taking Turns, was nominated for an Audie Award and a Voice Arts Award in 2018.

In May 2018 MGM Television optioned five of her books to be made into a TV series.

Johnathan McClain is her first (and only) writing partner and even though they are worlds apart in just about every way imaginable, it works.

She lives on a ranch in Central Colorado with her family.

If you'd like to learn more about JA Huss and you can visit her on her website at www.JAHuss.com

You can also join her fan group, Shrike Bikes, on Facebook at www.facebook.com/groups/shrikebikes and you can follow her on Twitter at @JAHuss

Printed in March 2019
by Rotomail Italia S.p.A., Vignate (MI) - Italy